VICTORIAN GOTHIC

Tales

VICTORIAN GOTHIC

Tales

D R MILLER

Visit the author's website at: www.drmillerauthor.co.uk

Book design by Publishing Push

ISBN: 978-1-80541-500-8 (paperback)
978-1-80541-506-0 (hardcover)
978-1-80541-501-5 (eBook)

Published by PublishingPush.com

Instagram: @drmillerauthor
Facebook: Victoriangothicauthor

Contents

A Spurned Woman

I

On her knees in sticky black mud, she tucked a long strand of matted white hair back under her hood and out of the way. She could see the trap had triggered but knew she should not get too hopeful. That often happened in the rain.

She allowed herself a weary sigh.

As always, she would check it anyway. Just in case.

Cold rain dripped relentlessly from her hood as she leaned a little further over the trap to shelter it from the inclement weather. She winced at the shot of pain in her misshapen knuckles as she raised the trap on end and peered in.

As she expected. Nothing.

She allowed herself a growl of frustration and glumly hung her head. As though answering her cry, her stomach growled back at her. She shrugged off the disappointment with another sigh, then went about the fiddly task of resetting the little trap. She knew the rain would probably set it off again, but beggars can't be choosers. She had to try. Sooner or later it would catch something; a rat, a squirrel, a young rabbit if she were lucky. The trap was not big enough to catch anything larger than that. In fact, she was not even certain it was strong enough to hold any creature that was hellbent on escape.

She carefully balanced the gate of the trap to its open position and had almost managed it when:

Heck, heck, heck.

The coughing fit overcame her suddenly and violently. A gnarled finger inadvertently caught the trap causing its little gate of sticks to swing shut once again.

She cursed under her breath, spat phlegm, and waited for the inevitable second bout of coughing before trying again.

Heck, heck, heck, heckkkkk.

She wearily raised her head and looked around the forest while absently swilling a second glob of phlegm around her gums. Sooner or later, one of these sicknesses would take her, she knew. To her, it was as inevitable as this evening's sunset. This illness had been particularly bad. It had settled on her chest and left her wheezing and whooping for breath like a braying mule. She had taken to her bed during the late snows and, other than to collect snow, ice and rainwater to drink, had only ventured outside again after exhausting most of her winter supplies a few days past. She rubbed at her chest, hoping it would somehow ease the tightness that clutched at it.

When she was not coughing, the patter of rain upon rotting wood and young spring leaves was the only sound in the forest. Even the birds seemed too miserable to sing. The forest floor was still sparse from winter, but green shoots were already beginning to show. Soon there would be ferns, bluebells, snowdrops, daffodils, wild garlic, chickweed and most importantly, dandelions, mint, and nettles which she would use in her remedies to finally help rid her of this damned affliction.

It took two more attempts to set the trap before sheltering it from the elements as best she could with a frayed mat made of twined hazel. Taking hold of the thick, knotted staff which lay beside her, she planted one end firmly in the ground, then leaned heavily upon it with both hands in order to drag herself to one knee and finally, with a grunt of effort, onto her feet. She could swear that she heard her hip creak with the effort.

Quicker the warm weather comes the better, she thought, finally spitting her mouthful of phlegm onto a mossy piece of wood.

She leaned down to retrieve the dead rat she had found earlier. Holding it up by the tail, she studied her prize diligently. It was a black rat; thin with part of its face pecked away and a round hole in its abdomen through which blue entrails bulged. Its legs splayed out at angles to its body and its tongue dangled from its open mouth.

She smiled a toothless, satisfied smile. Finding such a prize was the one good thing which had happened today and despite the rat's condition, it would see off her hunger until tomorrow.

Her stomach grumbled at her again, a long, low mewling noise like a complaining cat.

It was time to head back. Although it was not yet noon, she had been out long enough and was already tired as well as hungry. The rest of the traps would just have to wait until tomorrow. With a yawn, she began the slow trek towards home.

Crouched over as she was, she made for a strange sight as she trudged through the forest. At first glance, an onlooker would have been forgiven if they mistook her shambling form for a bear. On the rare occasions that her muddied skirts revealed a glimpse of her legs, they were so caked in mud that it was impossible to distinguish flesh from boots. Although she had only a slight build, she wore several layers of wool under a hooded cloak patched together from various hides; deer, rat, badger, mink, squirrel, rabbit, even a fox, complete with tail. Above all else she wore a huge, heavy sheepskin, the wool of which was yellow and hung in filthy, long mudded strands almost to the floor. It was her favourite and most precious item, the only thing she had left from the old days and it had always served her well.

She puffed hard as she slowly clambered over broken branches and through mazes of treacherous animal holes. Before the illness, she could check all sixteen traps before mid-morning. Now, here she was struggling for air and only able to manage seven before blowing like an old mule. She would need to rebuild her stamina over the next few months if she were to be fit enough to survive another winter. That thought did not enthuse her. In fact, she was unsure in herself which part she dreaded more: the painful effort of regaining her energy or the hardship of surviving another three or four months of winter at the end of it. Maybe it was time to just let go. Let nature take its course and allow the forest to swallow her remains. It was not the first time she had considered that. In fact, it would be impossible to count the times over all her many years, but only twice had she ever seriously considered it. The first time was after she was attacked by a bear. The injuries had caused her so much agony that it would have been the easiest thing to allow herself to succumb to a warm, numbing draught, except there it was again; that little voice in her head that refused to just lay down and die. The second time had been much more recently, after the last time she was cast out. Her despair had very nearly gotten the better of her, but her anger at the injustice had kindled a fighting spirit within her that wanted to show them all that she would not be beaten down. And she had most certainly shown them.

Back at the fallen tree at last, she decided to sit for a short break before continuing. Her breathing was ragged and rattled deep in her chest. She sniffed hard and used her fingers to wipe her nose and flick the snot away.

The rain was beginning to ease a little. She unstrapped a battered waterskin from her belt, pulled the stopper at the second attempt and held it steady with both hands while she took a long draught of cool refreshing water.

She should stop by the stream and refill it. If she did not, she would only need to do it later.

The Devil take it!

She just wanted to get home and warm up in front of the fire. Muttering a foul curse, she fumbled the stopper into place and strapped the waterskin back onto her belt. She stood up with a grunt of effort and wearily waddled down the hill towards the stream.

The ground was soft and spongy along the bank of the stream at the best of times, but with the deluge of rain over recent days, the water was high and fast and the banks slick and treacherous. Although the water was not anywhere near deep enough or fast enough to carry a person away, it was icy cold and the last thing she needed was for the cold and damp to get beneath her layers. She had only ever slipped in once, but it had taken several attempts to clamber out and back up the slippery banks and she was not as young or as mobile now as she had been then.

The accident had opened her eyes to the reality that she was not young anymore. She had found a suitable point at a bend in the stream where the water ran slower and piled stones there to make a firm jetty. She constructed a low railing by driving two stakes into the ground either side of the jetty and lashing a crossbeam between them at waist height. This had made collecting water much easier. Her only concern was if anyone should happen to pass by and notice the little construction. She was always very careful not to leave traces of her presence in the forest. Oh, she was well aware her footprints were unconcealable from a skilled hunter, but she had cleverly taken steps to make sure that nobody would venture into the forest to see those footprints in the first place. Countless years of solitude had given her time to become adept at woodcrafts. It was a simple thing to craft seasonal hexes and figures from sticks, twigs, leaves, berries, feathers, even animal skulls and bones. She hung these as a warning around her self-imposed boundaries where she did not want any would-be trespasser to cross. Over the years, she had hung hundreds of them, replacing old with new every few months to show anyone who happened upon them that these were not just old relics, but something to be feared here and now. The ploy had worked well throughout the years; only once had she ever found someone in her part of the forest. . . It was just a shame that her swollen knuckles and cramped fingers did not allow her to make as many replacements nowadays. So, after much consideration, it was because of this safety net she had built around her that she had taken the decision to build the jetty. After all, it had slowly but surely become a necessity rather than a luxury.

She used her trusty staff to carefully control her descent down the slope towards the bank of the stream and gingerly stepped onto the little jetty of stones. She winced as she forced her knee to bend, then removed the stopper from the waterskin and, wrapping the strap around her wrist, held it in the stream with one hand whilst holding onto the wooden rail beside her head with the other.

She peered out from under her hood to take in her surroundings. It had become a habit of sorts whenever she stopped anywhere, but here, it was the best way to avoid catching her reflection in the water.

The rain had finally stopped, but the pitter-patter of water continued to echo loudly throughout the forest and would do so for hours to come. She did not mind that. She found it restful and knew it helped hide the sound of her own passing.

When the waterskin was filled, she hauled it out of the chilly water, stoppered it and replaced it back on her belt. Pulling herself to her feet with a grunt of effort, she looked up at the pathway before her. She would have to tether a rope here sooner or later to aid her ascent. She was too old and – for the time being – too frail for this. She had considered carrying more water each time to reduce how many trips she needed to make, but she could no longer cope with the extra weight. Maybe in a few months; when the weather had warmed and she no longer had need of the heavy sheepskin.

Heck, heck, heck, heck.

Better to get it out of her system now than halfway up that slope.

Heck, heckkkk, heck.

Spitting phlegm on the jetty, she slowly began to climb back up the bank. By the time she reached level ground, she was wheezing and fighting for breath, but she could not rest now. Her knees ached, her hip ached, her back. . . Her chest was a furnace of pain, but she needed to rest in the warm, not out here.

With a resolve built on so many years of living in the wilderness, she pushed on. Her breathing was shallow and rattled in her chest; her left leg began to drag from tiredness and her steps became more a shuffle than a walk, but eventually she reached the most ancient part of the forest. Here, the trees grew taller, thicker and grander than elsewhere in the forest. Mostly oak elm and beech, they were centuries old; gnarled and wizened with misshapen trunks and thick, twisting branches which bore the scars of their old age. These were the trees she loved the most. These were the ones with a story to tell, the ones she felt akin to.

At last, she arrived at the two ancient fallen oaks. The dead trees lay in a V shape. At the base of the V, thick roots intertwined and towered above her like a giant black maw. The rotting trunks, although laying on their side, were her height and half again and the branches that remained created a natural defence against the larger forest creatures.

She wearily shuffled round the nearest trunk to the top of the V, where thick brambles intertwined dead branches to form a huge tangled carpet of impassable thorns.

Impassable for most, but not her.

Pushing the end of her staff into the bramble, she used a curved knot near its tip to catch hold of something within and, with a sharp tug, part of the bramble pulled away. A roughly made wooden door opened to reveal a black space beyond.

She ignored the reek which accompanied the open door; rot, earth, smoke, sweat, ashes, faeces; all smearing together with countless less potent scents to form an almighty stench.

She stepped through the doorway into the darkness beyond, pausing briefly to let her eyes adjust to the darkness beyond the pillar of light above the hearth. She called it a hearth, but in truth it was no more than an ash-filled fire pit made up of a ring of half-buried, blackened stones. Above the hearth was a ragged hole cut into the layers of wooden beams, sods of earth and moss which formed a crude ceiling and roof. From the remains of a grey log nestled amongst the ashes, wispy tendrils of smoke rose to caress a beaten iron pot which hung from a wooden frame. The contents of the pot could not be seen in the dim light, but the foul smell certainly announced its presence.

Other than a pile of logs beside the hearth, dried ferns and animal pelts littered much of the rest of the floor. The only furniture was a crudely made bed of larger logs lashed together and topped by a haphazard multitude of old sheepskins. Some of these had been stitched together but all were filthy and full of insects.

The ceiling and walls were a stark contrast to the uncluttered floor, however. Something hung from every wooden beam; rodents, fish and other pieces of meat curing, herbs drying, bundles of rushes, root vegetables hanging in threadbare nets, hides, wooden bowls, an iron ladle, a flint axe, a wide-toothed and rusting wood saw, a bone-handled knife and many strange things which could not be discerned through the soiled glass of the old jars they were kept in.

She pulled the doorway closed behind her and searched the resulting gloom for a spare string hanging from the ceiling. She batted one, two, three aside before finding one with a small, rusted hook on the end. She skewered the dead rat she had been carrying onto the hook, then hung the waterskin from a knot of wood above the bed. She shrugged off the sodden sheepskin and left it in a heap on the floor before unfastening a tie at her neck and hanging the cloak over a piece of split wood near the entranceway.

She allowed herself a sigh of relief at shedding the weight, then reached behind her as far as she could in and attempted to rub some of the soreness out of the muscles of her back. The stretching only resulted in another coughing fit.

Heeeeeeckk, heck, heck, heck.

Damned cough! Damned chest! She thought, angry at her own feebleness.

Heck, heeeckk, heck.

Her breathing was ragged as she wiped the back of her hand across her nose, snorted, spat, then worked quickly to stoke the fire back into life. Before long, heat and light filled the little dwelling and the rancid stench of whatever festered in the bottom of the cooking pot began to overpower all other scents as the noisome mixture began to warm through yet again.

She busied herself by taking the knife and cutting chunks off an onion until half of it was in the pot. After that, she took down the rat she had just hung. She skinned it deftly, hanging the pelt back up to be tanned later. Holding the remains of the rat above the pot, she opened the torso with two firm strokes and emptied the offal into the mixture. She wiped the knife on her clothes and took up the axe. Then, on the ground and without any care of where the blade fell, she split the carcass into five pieces and scooped them all into the mixture before finally adding water.

She replaced the utensils and, with an almighty sigh, lowered herself heavily onto the bed to wait for the foul-smelling concoction to boil. Rat was not her favourite dish, but the meat was already on the turn. If she left it another day it would be inedible, even for her stomach.

Waste not, want not.

The first winter after she was ostracized, all those many years ago, she almost died from starvation. She had not known how to forage properly, how to cure meat; she did not have the little patches of onions, carrots, potatoes, beets and cabbages growing nearby that she had now. But she had learned quickly. She had to. And one of the first lessons had been that beggars could not choose what they ate. For a time, everything she swallowed seemed to shit out faster than she could eat it, but she soon came to recognise how to walk the line between maggot-ridden-but-edible and rancid. Her stomach had been used to the luxury of fresh bread, eggs, milk, vegetables, maybe even the occasional chicken or piece of mutton if the animal was old and needed slaughtering, but she slowly became accustomed to the change in diet. At first, she would always remove the entrails from her meat. Then, when food was short, she would add in all but the stomach, intestine and bile duct. After just a few years, if it was a small mammal or bird, it all just went in the pot.

Fortunately, she had always known which berries or mushrooms she could eat and she quickly became adept at catching fish. It was a simple diet, but it kept her alive for that first winter, although she had been nothing but skin and bone by spring. She was all too aware of the fine margins between life and death; a bad winter or an illness like the one she had suffered recently would have killed her that first year without a store of food or warm shelter.

Her expression remained blank as she reflected, staring into the flickering flames of the hearth fire. Her jaw moved, but the movement was not in her control. Snot dribbled into her mouth and her eyes became teary. Not teary due to self-pity at the memory of hard times past, but because of the smoke from the damp firewood. There had been far too many hard times to waste tears on. She licked the snot away, pulled herself onto her feet with her staff and shuffled out of the little dwelling.

The air was cool without the cloak and sheepskin but felt crisp and refreshing after the smoke. Although the rain still held off, she could still hear water trickling and falling throughout the vastness of the forest. Walking over to a nearby oak, she turned, lifted her layers of skirts, then squatted to piss with her back resting against the trunk.

As soon as the flow started, she winced and squeezed her muscles to stop it. A simple thing, pissing, but yet another thing which had been causing her pain lately.

Slowly, she released the flow again and emptied her bladder, her gums pressed together against the hurt.

A noise grabbed her attention and she cast her wary eyes through the unending maze of peeling tree trunks. Hopefully, something had been caught in one of her snares, but it would wait until morning.

As she stood up, she heard something else. Was it just the echo of a broken twig? She strained to hear for a moment, then grunted and headed back towards her little dwelling. Her hunger did not afford her the patience to listen to every other sound the forest made.

Then she heard it again. This time she stopped mid-step as an icy chill ran down her spine.

"Hello? Are you there?" It was a woman's voice.

II

"Hello? Please help me."

The voice was high and full of emotion; misery, desperation, fear, tiredness, resignation; all emotions to which she herself had become accustomed over the years.

Help.

Her lip curled with contempt. Who had helped *her* when she had needed it? Where had *her* help been?

She could hear the stranger's footsteps now. Whoever it was, they were unused to the broken ground, cracking and snapping the undergrowth beneath each tentative step. Panting breathlessness accompanied the steps, ragged and broken. They were scared.

Good.

And yet, they had still come out here, despite that fear. '*Are you there.*' She stood statue-still as she pondered the words she had heard. Whoever this stranger was, they knew who they were looking for. Knew of *her*. And still they had come.

She was desperate.

The thought intrigued her. Suddenly, she was curious; who was this woman who had walked miles into rugged, unknown forest to look for her? And after all these years?

Or had she? Maybe the stranger was simply lost and had glimpsed her through the trees. Yes, that might be it, spotted her with her staff then lost sight of her again. It was not beyond the realm of possibility. But to become so lost that she had wandered this far into the forest? Past the hexes and warning signs? That was unlikely. They would not all have fallen or been lost over the winter months.

The stranger was close now.

She was sure she could remain hidden if she wished, but that little spark of curiosity had grown large enough now to be weighed against her disdain for human contact.

The stranger was just the other side of the tree. The rational part of her screamed at her to remain still, to let the stranger pass, and yet something nagged at her, pulled at her instincts. It was a feeling she had felt before, but not for so many years. . . *Clotho*. . .

Then, with newfound surety, she pulled her scarf up over her lower face and stepped out into the path of a tall, willowy woman. The woman uttered something between a gasp and a shriek and fell backwards, landing heavily on her backside and dropping the wicker basket she carried. She wore a green dress with a square cut bodice and three-quarter length sleeves. Over the dress was a white pinafore apron, but it did little to hide the torn, mud-spattered material underneath. She clasped a brown woollen shawl about her shoulders and wore a simple white maid's bonnet which fitted close to her head.

The woman's face was familiar. Wisps of mousey brown hair had escaped the confines of the bonnet and she guessed by the size of the bun that it combed past the shoulders. The woman was not pretty, but not uncomely either. Heavy eyelids contrasted with thin lips on a round face to give quite a severe visage. Her cheeks were ruddy, no doubt due to the exertion of walking in the chill air, but the feature which stood out was a crooked nose. It had been broken at the bridge and gave the impression that the woman was looking away to her left rather than directly at her.

Something inside her memory began to stir.

The nearest village was at least a day's walk away and the last time she had entered it she had not needed the staff as a walking aid. Even then, the huddled group of houses had tripled in size since her previous visit some years prior. She had always assumed that the settlers would quickly give up and move on to fairer climes, so the development had surprised her, as had their persistence.

Most of the dwellings had been single-storey and made from rough-cut timber with thick thatches and low eaves. One house, set slightly apart from the others, had a steep roof which housed a second storey. The only other building of note was a stone chapel which had replaced an old mud-brick church which used to stand on the same site and had been the first building completed when the settlement had been in its infancy, years before. The chapel had a thick wooden cross atop the bell tower which cast its long shadow across a high wooden arch, the entrance to the village. Seared into the wooden arch, was the name of the village: Godstown.

Godstown. Had these people no imagination?

She recalled she had needed iron at the time – why? She could not remember all these years later, but she had been in luck. The blacksmith's daughter had sickened and was near death. The girl – *what was her name? Had she even asked?* – must have only seen seven or eight summers, but had been tiny, all skin and bone, like she was made of twigs. Bedridden and suffering with a fever that would not break, she would not have seen out the week.

The blacksmith had baulked at her offer to begin with, but changed his mind when she told him she could heal his daughter. His sorrow had turned to hope like the sun emerging from behind a cloud and he had offered all the iron she could carry if she were true to her word. And so, that is exactly what she had done.

But, as was usual in her experience, the price was quickly forgotten once the service had been given. When the girl recovered the villagers eyed her with suspicion and the blacksmith, unwilling to stand apart from them, had told her she best be on her way. It might have gone badly for her if it were not for the little girl. It was she who shamed her father into keeping his promise, 'made under the eyes of God, in Godstown, no less' she had said, pointing to the shadow of the cross which he had happened to be standing upon.

She had not been certain which emotion had been strongest in the blacksmith; shame or fear. Either way, despite his curses and threats, she had walked away with her basket full of raw iron. She had promised herself then never to go back. Not even if she were desperate.

They could rot. They could all rot.

Whether it led to Heaven or Hell, everyone rotted the same in the ground. They would get nothing more from her and she had learned to live without any need for them.

It was a painful memory and her eyes narrowed as she wondered why it would occur to her now.

Wait.

That little girl.

It suddenly dawned on her.

"You remember me, don't you?" The young woman asked.

She scowled; not because of the question, but because she was angry at letting herself be read so easily by the first person she had seen after all these years. She was not used to hiding her thoughts and feelings and the idea that someone might know what she was thinking disturbed her greatly.

The young woman climbed to her feet and wiped muddy hands on her dress.

She could not help but stare at the younger woman. Could it really be the same person? How old must she be now. . . Could she have seen twenty summers yet?

"My nose, remember? I broke it against the bed post at the height of my fever. My name is –"

Don't tell me, I'll remember!

"-Evin. The blacksmith's daughter?"

Evin. Evin.

No. The names shooting in and out of her head were not even close.

"I, I don't think you ever told us your name," Evin continued. Evin was creeping towards her now, sideways steps, slow and purposeful, as though approaching a timid sheep. That annoyed her. Did this woman expect her to run? Then a more ominous thought. Was someone else nearby ready to throw a noose over her head?

She began to back away and look around her, peering through the trees with growing alarm at the thought, but again, Evin read her mind.

"No, no! I'm alone, I promise you!" She said quickly as she held her hands out before her, "I only came because, well, I need your help. You're the only one I could think of who might be able to help. I brought things for you," she gestured at the basket laying on the floor, "But you're deeper in the forest than I realised and I, well, I'm afraid I had to eat what I had."

Evin gave her an apologetic smile.

She began to notice the doubt in the young woman's brown eyes, the trepidation, the fear. But not fear for herself. She suddenly realised that this woman, this girl she had helped so long ago was not fearful for herself at all. It made sense. Why would she walk past all the hexes and warning signs scattered around the forest if she were afraid for herself? No, she was afraid for another and the thought intrigued her.

Evin took her silence as an invitation to continue, albeit uncertainly.

"You see, I'm a mother now and it's my child that's sick. I believe she has the pestilence and I, well, I remembered that you're a survivor." As Evin pointed at her face, she instinctively turned away to hide herself.

Her thoughts were a turmoil. How dare this woman seek her out after all these years? After the way she had been treated! Not only that, but to have the gall to put her up as an example of why she should give her aid! Her breathing became short and fierce and her hands clenched into tight, white fists at the impertinence of it. Who was this girl to pull on *her* heartstrings to get what she wanted? Where had the girl been for *her* all these years? When had she come and checked on *her*? Helped with *her* hardships?

No!

She felt herself trembling with rage as she stalked away from the girl, only to stop dead in her tracks as a wail of heartbreak and emotion erupted behind her.

"Noooooooo. . .! Pleeeeease!"

She closed her eyes, knowing she had trapped herself. If she had kept walking, she might have been able to ignore it; used her anger to put it to the back of her mind. Instead, she had stopped. That small coal of humanity that still burned somewhere inside had undone her and brought her ire crashing down around her, allowing her to hear the forlorn sobs that accompanied the girl's pitiful cries.

She took a deep breath, then turned to see Evin on her knees, hugging herself as tears streaked her mudded cheeks.

"You have to help her!"

". . ." She went to speak, but nothing came out. When was the last time she had used her voice? Other than to cough or sneeze?

"I. I wi' do. Wha' I can." The voice was a stranger to her and the broken, ill-pronounced words barely more than the rasp of a woodsman's saw.

She knew it was probably too late anyway.

III

It took them less than two days to arrive at Godstown. First, she insisted on eating her meal before they left. Years of hardship had taught her to waste nothing and she was not about to start now, not when she was uncertain when her next meal would be. After that, she had to rummage amongst the hangings in her hovel to find the herbs and concoctions she might need for the child when they arrived before finally wrapping a dirty woollen scarf around her face and pulling her cloak and sheepskin over her shoulders. Despite this delay in embarking on their journey, she knew where to find the village and it was a simple thing for her to navigate a path through the forest without getting lost, as Evin had on her quest to find her.

They would have arrived sooner, but her pace was much slower than that of her young companion, a fact which stretched Evin's anxiety to its limits. The younger woman, so impatient with the snail-like pace in her eagerness to return home, often found herself striding ahead of her aged companion only to have to wait for her to catch up. By contrast, the old woman laboured at the relentless exercise and often had to sit for a few minutes to catch her breath or was forced to stop in her tracks when overcome by a coughing fit. These fits became more frequent as Evin endeavoured to hurry her along and the resulting delays only managed to add to her vexation.

At the outset of their journey Evin talked incessantly. She knew why; renewed hope and a companion she was desperate to befriend; to build a rapport with. For the first few hours she spoke according to her heart's whim. She spoke of her memories of those feverish days as a child; her anger at her father for weeks afterwards; her father's apprentice who became her husband; her father's death; the birth of her own daughter, Sibylle.

She did not reply, interrupt or attempt conversation even once. She quickly realised that she cared very little for the tale as it only managed to sharpen the bitterness of her own lonely years. Instead, she found herself drifting between listening to the words and simply listening to the tone. After so long alone she realised it was the novelty of a human voice which she enjoyed rather than the tale it told. She listened to the little nuances in pitch as it ranged from high to low and back, to the emotion it offered, the bird-like trill at times as the words tumbled over each other in narrative excitement. Best of all, although she considered Evin's voice far from calming, it had the strange effect of distracting her from her aching knees and hip and the relentless tightness in her chest.

As the first day wore on, Evin's desire to reach home became more acute as she tired. By late afternoon she spoke less frequently and what she did have to say was taut, clipped.

An underlying sense of fear had entered the young woman's tone, but it was no less fascinating to listen to.

They spent the night huddled together by a small fire. Sleep was hard to come by due to the damp air and the old woman's coughing and by morning even Evin was silent. They ate as best they could when they found berries, mushrooms and root vegetables on the trail. A dead blackbird became an extra morsel for the old woman. When she offered it to Evin, the young woman baulked and shook her head in disgust as her companion noisily sucked and chewed at the raw meat with bare gums.

By the time they broke through the trees to lay eyes on the wooden arch that led into Godstown, they were both exhausted. Accompanying the sight was a chilly breeze which they had not felt amongst the trees. Low, rolling clouds cast an ominous tone as they blew sluggishly over the village and the sun was nowhere to be seen.

She shuffled to a nearby stump and sat down wearily. She was wheezing terribly and tried to control her breath as she took in the village before her. She remembered the wooden arch, but back then it was new. Now, it was weather beaten and discoloured, the letters of Godstown almost invisible other than to those who knew they were there. To say that there was a road into the village would have been misleading. A mud track barely rutted by wagon wheels was testament to how little trade came here and how far away from true civilisation they still were.

The chapel was the same, but the buildings around it were not the rough wooden structures she remembered. These houses were still timber framed, but far more sturdy with brick walls and chimneys, thickly thatched roofs and shuttered windows. Smoke billowed from almost every chimney to give the village an air of homeliness, cosiness perhaps, which had not been there before. The village was too small for streets and roads, but there were open areas of mud and straw between the buildings where chickens roamed freely, greedily pecking at any morsel they could find. Alongside the clucking of chickens, she could hear muffled voices from somewhere and the bray of a donkey.

She suddenly felt self-conscious and her eyes darted towards Evin. Evin quickly turned her head, but she was certain the younger woman had been staring.

Looking for her reaction to being here once again, perhaps? Or wondering how likely she was to just turn around and walk back into the forest without helping her daughter. That was probably more like it.

Heck, hecccckkk, heck heck.

Cursed cough. It would be the death of her yet.

She sat on the stump and watched the village while Evin's impatience bubbled and boiled until it was almost beyond control. She knew it was vindictive; inimical even to the reason she had trekked all this way, but the feeling of control it gave her over another person, after all this time, was intoxicating.

She carefully waited until Evin was wringing her hands, frowning dramatically and pacing back and forth on the verge of voicing her concerns before finally, awkwardly, she stood up, pulled her hood low over her face, clutched her wooden staff and began walking towards Godstown.

Heckkk, heck, heck.

The inevitable second coughing fit took her by surprise and quickly dampened her enjoyment of the moment. The scarf slipped down her face and she quickly pulled it up again, covering everything beneath her eyes.

As she paused to catch her breath, she was surprised when Evin pushed her arm under her own ready to help her walk. She recoiled instinctively, but when Evin held firm, she knew she would not have the strength to pull away. Was this because she had sat on the stump? Was it a show for the other villagers? A demonstration of kindness perhaps? She had not offered any aid on the trek here, so why now? Whatever the reason, she was tired and hungry and it was not a disagreement she needed to have on the outskirts of a village she did not trust, so far from home.

Thick mud sucked at her boots. Her knees and hip throbbed so much that she realised she was pressing her gums together with the pain as she let Evin lead her along the track and under the arch. She was suddenly very nervous and self-conscious. Her eyes darted left and right, peering at darkened windows for the faces which she was certain were staring back at her from within.

How many years had it been?

Two days ago she would have laughed at anyone who suggested she might return to Godstown. Were any of those people still alive? Of course they were. It hadn't been *that* long. But did they know Evin was bringing her? Had she told anyone? And if so, had they even believed that she was still alive, let alone that she would agree to return?

All these doubts washed over her in moments, yet she realised they were all questions she should have asked before she had even set out on this ridiculous journey.

Her rising panic made her miss a step, but Evin held her firmly, almost pulling her along by the elbow.

And there it was. The smithy. Not quite as she remembered it, but recognisable all the same. She felt a chill go up her spine as she remembered the monotonous *clang, clang, clang* of the hammer. The furnace was not lit today, so she did not feel the waves of heat she remembered from before, but that just lent the building a cold and ominous feeling. The work area had been covered by a square, tiled roof with a steep pitch which led to an open centre to allow the smoke and heat to escape. The anvil stood beneath, dark and cold with a wooden trough beside it like a headsman's block and basket.

Evin led her inexorably towards the building; *like the accused to the scaffold*, she thought wryly. They were almost at the door when it burst open, making her jump in fright and her heart beat harder than it had for many a month. Her hand shook involuntarily and she gripped Evin's arm like a buzzard's talons in a vain bid to stop it.

A short man whom she presumed to be Evin's husband flew from the doorway and gave Evin a huge hug. It had been a long time since she had seen a young man and she quickly decided she was disappointed with this one. A thick shock of curly brown hair merged at his ears with a rough, ginger beard. His nose was wide and flat, his eyes small and his cheeks rosy red from his time in front of a furnace. Despite his lack of height, he was a powerful man with thick muscular shoulders and strong hands which were covered in burn scars from his work.

"I thought you were lost," he uttered as he held his wife tightly and kissed her cheek.

"I was, Jacin. Are we too late?"

She was not sure whether the strain in Evin's voice was anxiety for her daughter or something else. It had been a long time since she had been around people. Part of that was due to how they treated her, but if she were being honest with herself, it was also due to her own natural suspicion and there was something about Evin's husband, this Jacin, she took an instant dislike to. His name sparked a vague memory of her first husband, but there the similarity ended. It had been long ago in the dim past, a memory she would rather leave buried and forgotten.

"No. Come in, come in," Jacin said with a furtive look at his wife's aged companion.

As she entered the room, the first thing she noticed was the pungent smell of sweat and pestilence. It did not take long to take in her surroundings; in the corner to her left, under a window, lay a large bed covered in sheepskins and rough blankets. Beside that was a table with three stools, a hearth where a kettle hung above a small fire then a smaller bed in the opposite corner. It was here where their daughter, Sibylle, lay shivering in a restless ball clutching at her stomach. No more than eight or nine years old, her rough sleeveless dress was filthy black and soaked with sweat from her fever. Her thin arms glistened with clammy moisture. The girl's head was near the edge of the bed, her face hidden by damp, matted hair just above a wooden bowl half-filled with watery, bloody vomit which sat on the floor beneath her. In her pain and delirium, she had pushed her blankets into a crumpled heap on the floor at the foot of the straw mattress.

"Oh my darling –" Evin was half way to the bed before Jacin gripped her arm and pulled her back roughly.

"No, you must not go near her. I fear she is near death and I will not lose you both."

Jacin spoke with little emotion and his tone left no room for quarrel.

From under her hood, she could see Evin turn to her, trying to say the words which she knew were coming. She could have walked to the bed and studied the sick child, but instead she waited calmly for the request, the permission, to be voiced.

"Can you heal her?"

She did not answer, but instead pointed to one of the stools at the other end of the room. Evin instantly understood and twisted her arm free from her reluctant husband's grip to fetch the stool and place it beside the bed. Evin's hand hovered near Sibylle's head as though about to brush the hair from the girl's face, but a quick glance back at Jacin' scowl made the poor woman think better of it and she retreated instead.

She shuffled over to the stool and sank down upon it with a satisfied sigh, her back to Jacin and Evin. She rubbed her knee ponderously, before shrugging off her sheepskin and letting it drop unceremoniously to the floor. She pulled her hood back and let the cloak drop on top of the sheepskin, then tightened the scarf about her face and knotted it behind her head and the ribbons of her grey hair. She took a small bag from her waist and removed two small bundles before placing it on the floor in front of her. Taking one of the bundles, she unravelled a long piece of stained bandage which she painstakingly wrapped around her hand and fingers before tucking the end in to keep it tight. She did the same with the second bundle on her other hand. At last, when both hands were wrapped, she finally leaned forward to look at the sick child in front of her.

With a gentle touch which surprised even herself, she pushed the child onto her back and straightened out her legs. The girl was too weak to resist even her limited strength. *Not a good sign*, she thought. She examined the neck but found nothing untoward. Abruptly she pulled up the patient's dress to her hips.

"What in God's name are you doing?" There was anger in Jacin' voice and he covered the distance to her quickly. She was not sure whether a blow would come, but she hunched her shoulders and steeled herself for it anyway. An old habit.

To her relief, there was no blow, only a fearful silence as he looked at where her finger was pointing, towards his daughter's thigh. There, in her groin, were three white swellings, each the size of an egg. She had suspected it, but now it was clear. The girl was suffering from plague.

Jacin' reaction told her that he knew it too. Suddenly she realised that she was alone in the room with the child.

Good. Leave me to do my work, she thought with a sigh.

The swellings were large and white rather than inverted and black, so that was a good sign, but when she pushed the hair back from the girl's face, her hopes began to fade. The tip of the child's nose and half of the upper lip were black with rot. She leaned a little closer and pulled the scarf down just long enough to sniff the girl's face. The scent of putrefaction was pungent. It was a strong enough scent to make most people swoon or vomit or leave the room for fresh air, but she was hardened in her old age and had smelled plenty worse in her long, long years.

As she looked down at her patient, a tinge of pity speared her heart. The easy thing to do would be to give up; tell Evin and Jacin that their daughter was all but dead and the only kindness she could administer was to speed up her demise. But had she listened to that instinct inside her for nothing? Walked so far, just to give up? She herself could have given up at any time over the years, but she had not. She had fought death all the way, through hardship after hardship, sickness and injury and here she was; all those years of surviving had brought her here, sat at the bedside of this young girl who desperately needed her help. Desperately needed a miracle!

She laid a bandaged hand on the girl's forehead.

She thought grimly about what she would need to do to have any hope of saving the girl. The pain she would need to inflict. The anguish that would be with her for the rest of her life if she were to survive.

Then, as she stroked back the sodden hair, the girl opened her eyes. Big, blue eyes, glassy from fever but reflective of the nature of the soul within, nevertheless. Innocence, humility, kindness, forgiveness; she saw all these qualities within those eyes before they closed again with a smile.

She realised then that the decision was not hers to make. The Fates had brought her here. Plague had ravaged the girl's body for days and the chances of survival were small, but she was not here to simply let the girl die.

She reached into her bag and before long had an assortment of items in front of her; thread, a needle, scissors, two round pottery cups, a jar of roots, a jar of oil and a jar of leeches.

She leaned on her knees and stood up with a wince. The long walk had not been kind to her. She shuffled over to the hearth, threw a log on the fire and placed a pan of water in it to boil. She would need to work quickly if she had any chance of success.

IV

It took two days before she began to wonder if the girl might survive. She did not hope because hope meant she was becoming attached to the girl and in her experience, hope only led to disappointment.

Before she began to administer treatment, she had made the wise decision to jam the door shut. She had to cut away the putrefaction that was spreading across the girl's face and stitch the wounds, but the girl's screams and wailing had her parents hammering on the door and apparently attracted the attention of some of the other villagers. The banging at the door soon subsided to pitiful sobbing when the girl finally passed out. After this initial treatment, she had managed to move the girl to lay on her own sheepskin. She pulled the straw bedding from both beds, swept the room thoroughly and single-handedly marched it all outside to be burned. The dust triggered coughing fit after coughing fit which left her chest bruised and her breathing ugly and ragged.

Whilst she carried out this chore, Jacin' frustration threatened to boil over, whilst Evin was beside herself with grief. Evin had tried to enter, but Jacin along with several villagers had wisely held her back. Whether that was through fear of contracting plague or distrust of her, she did not know nor care at the time. She had stared warily at the village cleric however. He was a young man dressed in a black friar's robe with a stern outlook. It was clear that he had Jacin' ear and the pair returned her mistrustful looks with candour. Several times over the days that followed she would peer through the window to see the cleric solemnly chanting prayers and throwing his holy water around the smithy as though-As though what? As though it would keep the plague trapped inside? She had no trust for religion and quickly branded this particular practitioner an imbecile. She vowed to keep him safely at arm's length.

After the burning, the only times she opened the smithy door was to give errands to Evin. She sent her for fresh water, for blankets, for bread and to empty the slop bucket. Realising it was all she could do to help, Evin was always nearby and complied with her demands without argument, bringing her what she needed, while she nursed her patient as if she were her own. She had wrapped the girl in blankets saturated with cold water to control the fever; she had boiled down her own urine to control infection in the nose and lip; she had heated the pottery cups and applied them to the skin, sucking the lean flesh into them to stimulate blood flow; she had applied leeches to the buboes in her groin and two more she found in her left armpit. Throughout this time she refused Evin and Jacin entry to their own home or any sight of their daughter.

Just after noon on the second day, the fever broke. She stacked logs against a wall to build a makeshift support near the warmth of the hearth, covered them with her own, old yellow sheepskin and then sat the girl upon it. The sheepskin might be old and filthy, but the fleece was still thick and warm and it had always brought her comfort when she was sick. She had used it for a bed for the girl's mother all those years ago and she was sure it would bring similar comfort now. She found a frayed brown blanket which looked like a patchwork of stains to cover the girl with, tucking it neatly around the chest. It smelled musty, but no more so than her sheepskin. Late into that evening, the girl opened her eyes. For a few moments she saw a serenity in those eyes which made her old heart ache. She had not felt such tranquillity as the girl felt in that moment for many years and she suddenly yearned to feel something similar, even for just a moment. But with the blink of an eye it was gone again. The girl realised she was breathing through a bandage and no doubt felt the rawness of her face beneath it and the brief flash of peace was quickly replaced by anguish.

The girl tried to pull the bandage away but was still weak from sickness. She took the girl's hands and firmly held them to her sides, but this only made the child focus on her. The girl's anguish turned to panic upon seeing the visage of an old crone looming over her and was probably made worse when she tried to calm the girl by spitting *Shhhhhh* into her scarf. She suddenly realised it was the first time the girl had looked at her and understood immediately. How could she not understand? Before society shunned her, she had suffered the same reaction from adults and children alike.

"I. I heeeal y', I hea' yo, I hee yo," she tried to repeat the words over and over, to make the girl understand, but her frustration grew at her incompetence with the words. Then, suddenly, the girl stopped fighting her. Whether it was exhaustion or understanding or something else, she could not say, but when she let go of the girl's wrists and gently stroked her hair, the girl did not struggle.

"Yo 'een sick," she could feel the scarf getting heavy with drool as she spoke.

"'Lague. I heeeal yo, bu' yo. . . hace." She could not say the word, so used her gnarled hand to indicate her own face.

"Ma –" the girl began, then winced.

"Shh-shh-shoosh! Dun' skeak," she held a finger near the bandage where the girl's mouth was to indicate she should stay quiet.

Panic took hold of the girl's eyes and tears began to roll like raindrops down pale cheeks.

"I know, id 'urts. Yo are scarred, 'ut yo 'ont die. Yo 'ill li."

The girl did not understand.

She looked away for a few moments. She could only think of one other way to tell the girl about what she had needed to do, but she was reluctant to do it. There must be another way to say what she wanted to say. Surely? If there was, she could not think of it. Would it scare the girl too much? Was the girl strong enough? Or would she lose hope?

"Si. . . Si'ylle?" Sibylle looked at her, her eyes wide with fear.

"Si'ylle, I 'ad 'lague." She pressed a finger into her own chest, then held her thumb and forefinger a little way apart when she said " 'ittle o'der 'an yo. Yo are no' as 'ad as I." She shook her head slowly. She wanted to smile at Sibylle, to reassure her, but she knew she was incapable of that.

Her hand shook a little as she reached behind her neck and began to untie the scarf. When it was loose, she held it to her face with one hand while holding up a warning finger with the other.

"Yo no as ba' as I. Un's'and?"

Sibylle looked at her.

"Say id: Yo no as ba' as I. Un's'and?" She tried to emphasise each word to make sure she was being understood.

Sibylle nodded, her trepidation obvious.

"Say id!" She demanded.

"I am not as bad as you," the girl said in an obedient lisp.

At last, she was satisfied. She carefully held eye contact as she peeled the scarf away from her face.

It took a moment before Sibylle glanced down at the ruin of her lower face. Her eyes widened with horror and her eyes filled with tears before she clenched them closed and turned her face away, no doubt trying to forget what she had just seen.

"Yo no as ba' as I," she repeated.

When she saw Sibylle's shoulders wracked with sobs she became lost. She grunted at the shooting pain in her knee as she sat down beside the girl on the sheepskin and awkwardly patted her arm in a vain attempt to soothe her, but to no avail.

Suddenly a veil lifted in her memory. From a life long past, her mother's instinct came flooding back to her and she leaned over and hugged Sibylle as best she could. She began to stroke the mousey, matted hair. In a faded memory, she saw herself with her own daughter. She remembered how she used to sing a lullaby to soothe her to sleep; how did the tune go? She began to hum, staccato at first, each note separate from the last, but she soon began to recall the song and began to link the notes together into the haunting melody she remembered, a song she had not heard for. . . For how long? Images of her daughter flashed to mind; raven haired, wide smile, laughing playfully as they both performed cartwheels through an orchard of misshapen trees. She began to feel at peace as the old memories flooded through her, warming her heart and soothing her soul.

Heeeck, heck heck, heckkk.

The coughing fit came just as Sibylle had calmed.

She sat up and waited for the inevitable second bout. As she sat there, she searched her memory for another glimpse of the happiness she had forgotten for so long, but the coughing came too soon and the images were gone.

Heck, heck, Heckkk.

She left Sibylle to her grief while she prepared a paste of boiled down urine and Lady's Mantle to apply to the wounds. Eventually, seeing that Sibylle had exhausted herself with her self-pity, she turned the girl onto her back. She batted the girl's hand away twice before fixing her with a reproachful glare. When she was certain there would be no more insolence, she carefully unwrapped the bandage to reveal the lower half of Sibylle's face.

Although the wounds were still livid, they were already healing well and she offered a satisfied *hmph* more for herself than for her patient's benefit. She had only needed to cut away a small part of the side of the nose, opening up the right nostril a little. The rest had been more problematic though and she had been forced to slice away half the top lip on the same side in a triangle which left two teeth permanently exposed. With time and practice though, she was sure that Sibylle would be able to speak almost perfectly.

Sibylle stared at her as she applied the healing salve with rough fingers. She could see that the girl wanted to wrinkle up her nose; if not because of the lack of tenderness in her application, then perhaps because the sour stink of the boiled urine far outweighed the fresh scent of the herb it was mixed with. She could see that Sibylle's personality was strong for one so young. She liked that. She could see some of herself in those defiant eyes and if she were able to smile, she would have.

The strength of Sibylle's young personality did give her an idea, however. She clambered to her feet and beckoned to the girl to do the same. There was only a momentary pause before Sibylle shakily pushed herself up and stood beside her. They leaned on each other, the old and infirm and the young and weak, as they made their way over to the pan of water which sat upon the grate over the hearth.

"See yo'sel," She said, jabbing a crooked finger at the pan.

A flash of fear crossed Sibylle's eyes again, but she understood it perfectly. She had been here, in this very position. Oh, she had been far beyond Sibylle's years, it was true, but older meant less adaptable. Once Sibylle saw herself in the water, once she knew what the plague had done to her, she would judge herself as everyone else will judge her forever more. Her face would not be a figment of her imagination anymore, slipping from scarred to monstrous and back as her moods changed; seeing herself would force reality upon her and she was certain that Sibylle had a strong enough mind to accept disfigurement better than she ever had herself.

She jabbed her finger at the water again, hoping Sibylle did not notice how she shied away from it herself.

Slowly and with obvious doubt, Sibylle held her hair to one side and leaned over the pan. The poor girl let out a short gasp. A quivering hand found its way to her disfigured lip just as a falling tear rippled the water, breaking the reflection.

While the water settled, she leaned over and gently turned Sibylle's head a little way to the right. When the surface became a mirror once again, Sibylle saw only the left side of her face; still unblemished, as she always was.

As the tears came, Sibylle turned and hugged her, tiny arms squeezing her body as only a child would. The hug flustered her and she was unsure what to do. Momentarily, her arms were wide as her patient clung to her with a ferocity that surprised her after such a close dance with death. She was uncertain how to react to the intimacy of the moment; *when was the last time she had been hugged*? Her first instinct was to recoil at the touch, but she did not, could not. She was confused; was the hug for her benefit or the girl's own? Was it affection? Thanks? Relief? Self-pity? Maybe just a child craving the closeness of an adult? Did it even matter? It felt euphoric! Slowly, uncertainly, her own arms closed in and enveloped Sibylle in an embrace which brought tears to her own eyes and there they stood, weeping in each other's arms.

The morning of the fourth day was frosty, but a Spring sun in a pale blue sky brought a welcome relief to the monotony of grey clouds. Over the last few days, she had grown accustomed to a fist rattling the door at about this time, followed by Evin hesitantly but anxiously asking after her daughter. On previous days, she had opened the door a short way and thrust a pan at her so she could fetch fresh water, but on this morning, she carefully tied the scarf about her lower face once more before opening the door wide and allowing entry to the two nervous parents.

Sibylle was laying on the propped-up sheepskin with the old blanket tucked under her arms. The girl's skin was still pale and her face seemed ashen against the swathe of blue cloth which acted as a bandage around it. In contrast, her eyes were bright and shone with returning health, albeit from within dark rings of fatigue.

Evin was about to run towards her daughter when she

grabbed hold of the younger woman's wrist. When she saw the frown of confusion, she shook her head sternly, no.

"P'ague," she rasped as best she was able.

"She still has it?" Jacin enquired coldly, "I thought you were curing her?"

She nodded solemnly. Had she made a mistake letting them in? Perhaps she should have waited a few more days, but Sibylle had needed to see her parents, to see that she had not been abandoned, that she would still be loved, despite the treatment she had endured. Was still enduring.

It was a few seconds before either of them seemed to notice the bandage about Sibylle's face.

"What... Her face," was all Evin could manage, not understanding.

She tried to prepare her voice, to enunciate the word as carefully as she could.

"'otten. R- Rotten."

She could tell by their faces that they understood, but it did not stop her face flushing red with frustration at her own inability to voice what they needed to know.

"My God." She thought Evin might swoon, but in contrast, Jacin was quick to temper and turned towards her with an accusatory finger.

"If you have hurt my daughter..."

She held his eyes with her own steady gaze and was quickly satisfied when he turned away.

As Evin sat down beside her daughter, Sibylle enveloped her in a hug.

"Are you alright my dear? How are you feeling?"

"Well, mama," came the croaky, muffled reply.

"What's wrong with her voice?" Jacin' question was stern and cold. He still eyed the old woman with distrust and a curl of his lip.

"She has been ill Jacin, leave her be," Evin soothed.

"Don't you tell me what to do," came the clipped reply. "Take that cloth off her face," he snapped.

She knew what was going to happen and yet she was perfectly calm. As Evin removed the bandage and erupted into a mournful wail, she closed her eyes and waited. It took two heartbeats for the blow to come, sending her crashing to the floor and causing the scarf to slip down around her neck, revealing her face.

"God in Heaven woman, what have you brought into our house?"

Her head was pounding like a drum. As she turned over onto her hands and knees she could see four hands on the ground before her where there should have been two and two identical streams of drooling blood.

She heard a child's high-pitched scream and a shout of "Stop it!" and although she knew a second blow would come, she was not ready for it when it landed in her midriff, lifted her from the floor and sent her sprawling onto her side, gasping for breath.

Through a churning haze of pain, she heard a slap against skin followed by Jacin' voice, incandescent with anger, ringing in her head: "How dare you strike me!"

A thud, then Sibylle screamed again as something heavy hit the floor. She opened her eyes, squinting through tears and trying to force the two images before her together into one. She closed one eye and there, on the floor lay Evin, motionless.

The door slammed open and a muffled voice said something she did not quite catch. She turned her neck and through one eye, made out the blurry shape of the cleric. Jacin was standing over the fallen body of his wife and Sibylle was screwed up into a ball screaming, her hands over her ears. As she tried to blink away the blurriness, Jacin pointed an accusatory finger in her direction.

"I accuse this woman of using witchcraft in the treatment of my daughter. And I accuse my wife of engaging her services by making a fell pact with her."

V

She must have passed out.

She remembered hearing another blow fall along with a growled "Shut your mouth!", then more voices. She remembered being dragged outside and bundled down some steps, somewhere cold. Then nothing.

When she woke, she was in darkness. A thick, inky blackness which panicked her momentarily and made her touch her eyes, just to make sure they were still in her head.

The floor was earthen, but compacted to a hard surface which, without her sheepskin, spread cold into any part of her body in contact with it. She cautiously crawled through the darkness, pausing every so often to reach out for something, anything, around her. She had not gone far before she reached a rough wall of stone and mortar. Using the wall, she hauled herself to her feet with a grunt of effort. She had been laying on her bad hip and it fought her all the way to a standing position. The darkness disorientated her to the point of dizziness, so she kept the wall to her left as she clumsily walked along it, one hand brushing the cold stone for guidance and the other outstretched in front of her. After five steps, she came to a corner and followed the wall around. Another corner, then another five steps but this time the wall gave way to a wooden door. She fumbled for a latch or some means to open it but found nothing except iron bands and rounded rivets. She pounded the side of her fist against the wood, but the sound was muted, telling her the wood was thick and heavy. She completed her circuit with a fourth and final stone wall before stumbling haphazardly back round to the door. At least the wood was not cold.

"Ay! Allo?" She shouted, but her mouth was dry and her voice sounded gruff which quickly brought on a coughing fit.

Heck, heck, heck, heck.

She spat phlegm and wearily sank to the ground. Her side throbbed and she winced when she touched her ribs. The skin was probably black and yellow from the kick he gave her.

Heckkk, heck heck.

She could feel her hand shaking as she wiped snot from her face. Her breathing had become ragged and shallow. She knew she was beginning to panic, but the part of her mind that clung to rationality had always been strong and quickly sprang to the fore. She was alone in the darkness, but where? What clues did she have? The stone walls. Was she underground or above ground? Only one building in the village was grand enough to have a cellar and that was the chapel. If she were above ground, which building would have a windowless room? Maybe a pantry or a grain store? She cut through her fear and tried to think back to when she entered the village. None of the houses looked big enough. No, she was sure of it; she was in a cellar under the chapel. If she were to be accused of witchcraft, it would be the obvious place they would think of to keep a witch.

Kept under the eye of God to prevent the accused from influencing their tiny minds, she thought joylessly. How little they understood of true religion.

As she sat there in the darkness, she made a conscious attempt to take her mind off her immediate predicament.

Her face was bruised and swollen where Jacin had hit her and her ribs were sore, but she was certain nothing was broken.

She began to try and piece together what had happened. She remembered Evin laying still on the ground; was she dead? No, surely not if Jacin accused her as well. Unless he had not realised it? *No,* she sighed inwardly, *cowards who beat their wives do it to dominate, not kill.* And what about Sibylle? She had not admitted it to herself until now, but she had grown fond of the girl. She saw so much of her own spirit and determination packed into such a tiny body. It was unusual for one so young, so what had happened for her to be like that? Had her mother taught her never to give up? It would make sense bearing in mind her own brush with death as a young woman. Maybe it had come from Evin but in a different way; seeing her stand up to Jacin's violence for example; it was likely that she had been on the wrong end of that violence herself during her young life. Or maybe she was just born stubborn. Whatever the reason, Jacin did not appear to offer the love a father should. Why? Because she was not the son he had wanted maybe? There were plenty of fathers like that, she knew.

As the time passed, the darkness began to move and she noticed a haze of grey on the ceiling. She squinted to see it more clearly, then stood. Sure enough, it was morning's light finding its way through a grating in the ceiling, an arm's length above her. A beam of light hit what she now knew was the western wall of her cell and marched only half way down its stone surface before stopping, but it was far enough for her to view the whole of her cell in a dingy light through dancing particles of dust. The stone walls held no interest for her, but the door was not quite what she was expecting. Where she had thought in the darkness that it was just solid reinforced wood, she could now see a smaller, rectangular hinged hatch near the bottom, almost flush with the wood of the main door and just large enough to pass food through. How had she missed that when she had been sitting virtually on top of it?

Bustling over towards it, she pushed at the little area and hammered it with the side of her fist, but it felt as solid as the rest of the door. Was this room built as a cell? Beneath the chapel, of all places? With growing frustration, she stood under the grate in the ceiling and called out several times, but there was no answer. She stood still for a few moments and listened to the silence.

A cock crowing, but nothing more.

Damn them all! How dare they do this? After what she had done for that girl. She should never have come! Her sudden flush of anger was violent, but borne from frustration, she knew.

She shouted again, then a second and a third time even louder, letting her rage fill her lungs and limbs with its mighty vigour.

She stopped and listened. Was that a voice she had heard?

Her heart was pounding in her chest and ears, but she was sure she had heard something. She held her breath and cocked her head to one side.

There, again!

She knelt by the door where the little hinged section was and listened again.

"Hello?"

It was faint, but wasn't that Evin's voice?

"Allo?" She called back hopefully.

"You're alive! I thought they might have killed you. Oh God, what's going to happen to us?"

She sat up with her back to the door. She was calm again as she contemplated the question. A trial perhaps? She knew all about witch trials from bitter experience, but nowadays they were something eminently more dangerous. They had become farcical shows for the public which the accused rarely survived. Not intact, anyway.

Evin continued to talk and ask questions, but she was no longer listening. As angry as she was that she had returned to this accursed village, she knew, deep down in her aged heart, that she had had no choice. As much as she fought against the very concept of destiny, she knew that if she had the choice again, she would do the same thing. This woman, a mother, the girl whose life she had once saved, had sought her out and found her despite her efforts to remain hidden. After all those years, they should all have thought her dead, but not Evin. As she thought it through, she realised that it was these little nuances which, when Evin had found her in the forest and asked her to come, were the little individual reasons which collectively left her unable to resist. But at what cost? She had succumbed to Evin's hope and determination and saved Sibylle, but was it to be at the cost of her own life? Were her years of knowledge and experience and hardship for nought, other than to save two village maidens? No. She refused to accept that as her destiny. Not after the life she had lived. Events may well have brought her out of the forest for a reason, but she would not give up her life for such a seemingly small price. Not until she knew she had been abandoned. Not unless She willed it!

She was unsure how long she sat there in the company of her own thoughts, but the light in the cell had grown a little stronger by the time she heard footsteps outside the door. Evin was shouting and screaming, her fear barely veiled by the mask of outrage she was showing to the outside world.

The shouting stopped abruptly. Cocking her head to hear better, she made out the muffled sound of two sets of footsteps before Evin began again.

"Please! I have done nothing wrong. Let me out! Where is my husband?"

The unmistakable crack of a door bolt was followed by two male voices, but she could only make out the words of the voice she identified as the village cleric.

"Jacin accused her, Silas."

Silas. That name. . .

A muffled voice, presumably Silas.

"The witch is in the other cell."

The witch. She sighed and stared up at the grate in the ceiling where the light shone through. It was as though she had already been found guilty.

"No, please! Don't go! Let me explain!" Evin's panicked voice again as the door banged and the bolt shot into place.

She heard footsteps approaching her own cell and instinctively backed off towards the eastern wall and out of the light. She could hide her face more easily here.

The bolt cracked and the door opened. The cleric strode through, his black robes swirling a cloud of dust from the floor. His face was severe, but she was more intrigued by the large, plain wooden cross which hung a on a thin, knotted rope around his neck. *Justifying his actions by hiding behind a god*, she thought with repulsion.

Behind the cleric was another young man of similar age, but it was there that the similarities ended. He was dressed for the city; leather boots over blue leggings, a white shirt with puffed sleeves under an ornately embroidered jacket with brass buttons, all complemented by an ill-fitting feathered hat. His clear complexion made him somewhat comely, but his face was partly hidden by an extravagant moustache and a short, pointed beard. Beneath the hat, dusky blonde hair fell to his shoulders in unruly curls. His eyes were heavy-lidded, but that failed to hide the emptiness in their pale blue depths. No doubt he had caused many a maiden to flush in his time. She would wager that he had caused his fair share of hurt, too.

"And this is the accused witch," the cleric said, giving her a stern glare.

"Is it now." The other man's voice was quiet, little more than a whisper. There was a familiarity about him that she could not quite place.

"What do you have to say for yourself, witch?" He continued, his nose wrinkling in disgust as he looked at her along its length.

She spat on the ground in reply. She would not give them the satisfaction of hearing her try to speak.

"This one will be tougher, but we might not need her confession if the blacksmith's wife is honest with us. Put her to the question first. But let this one hear it," he added, flamboyantly waving a hand in her direction.

"But, aren't we going to wait for the witchfinder, Silas?"

"Goodness, no. He will put her in a sack and throw her in the river to see if she sinks. That won't get us any answers now, will it?" Silas paused for a moment. He seemed to be struggling with what to say; his head cocked to one side, his mouth widened and his lips peeled back from his teeth, but for just a few moments, no sound came out. He languidly raised a hand and then, just as he jabbed a long finger into the cleric's chest, the words finally burst forth. "You are a cleric of God and the spirit of all that is good in this village. I am comfortable that you should put her to the question. Of course, I will humbly witness and document it for you." He bowed his head at the word 'humbly', as though to emphasise it.

She could see the cleric was not happy at the prospect of his allotted task and yet his mouth hardened into a line. He did not like it, but would not argue, she knew.

As Silas and the cleric left her cell, she stepped forward into the warm light. She wondered again about the young man. Silas. Wasn't that the name of the village custodian last time she had been here? He had those similar heavy eyelids and blonde hair, she recalled, but he had been a fair, honest man. Could this possibly be his son?

Whether he was or not, having now met him she was acutely aware of the danger both she and Evin were in. What would Evin do under torture? A part of her, that human part that had sprung back to life over these last few days, told herself that there was nothing to worry about. No crime had been committed; no witchcraft had taken place. There was nothing to confess and therefore justice would win through. But there was another part of her. There was the survivor; the part of her which had done whatever it had needed to do to survive for so many years. That part of her was not so sure. The survivor in her had heard the fear in Evin's screams; it had looked into Silas's eyes and seen nothing behind them. The survivor in her tugged at her sleeve; it whispered in hear ear: she was not a villager in need of protection, but an outsider. An old crone. A drain on society with a disfigured face who could not speak.

Her instincts screamed at her to heed them and yet she now realised what the last few days had meant to her. She had not been shunned, but instead she had been sought out. She had been needed by two fellow human beings. She had been recognised for her skills instead of being spat upon and reviled. She had been accepted for the first time in years, albeit by two young women she had rescued from Charon's boat. She had allowed hope into her heart and she was as surprised as anyone that even Jacin's accusation had not extinguished that.

No. Evin had shown faith in her. It was her turn to show faith in Evin. Perhaps Jacin would recant his charges when his anger calmed. He would realise his daughter's life was worth more than her looks and tell this Silas that he had been mistaken. She had been forced to leave the last time she was in Godstown, but there was little she would not give for the same outcome now.

She had to hope. It was all she had left.

VI

In the hours that followed, she was sure Evin had exhausted herself. She had pleaded, threatened, screamed, sobbed with self-pity and shouted in rage. Only when she had finally fallen silent for some time did Silas and the cleric return.

A bolt at the bottom of her door was kicked aside and the little hatchway was swung open. She did not even attempt to look out. She would not give them the satisfaction of even knowing that she sat beside it. Instead, she closed her eyes and listened.

Evin let out a petrified whimper as the two men entered the other cell. Despite her attempt at fearlessness, she could feel an ever-tightening knot of dread in the pit of her stomach.

"Where is my husband? Where is Jacin? You must let me speak to Jacin!"

"You have been accused of aiding and abetting a witch. The cleric here will ask you some searching questions which I will document." Silas's tone was breezy, as though making small talk with a neighbour.

More footsteps shuffling along the passage, followed by Silas's voice again, exasperated this time as he snapped instructions.

"Place the table there. No, the other way, so I can see, idiot. I want a chair. With a cushion. Not a peasant's stool, you dolt! Give her the stool; we are not heathens. You can place those on the table. Put the rope in the bucket for now."

"Why in God's name have you brought that?" She could almost imagine the Cleric sweating as he asked the question. "This is a witch trial. No blood can be spilled."

"Oh, don't be such a fickle-puss. The witch is in the other cell. We are merely gathering information here and I just want to give you as much opportunity of gathering it as I can."

"You mean the accused witch –"

"I'll hear nothing more of it. Besides, it might not come to that. What do you think, my dear?"

The knot in her stomach was quickly rising towards her gullet.

The witch.

Silas's words rattled around her head. She spat on the ground as her distaste for this man grew by the moment. Her fate was entirely in the hands of Evin, she knew.

"I said, what do you think?" Silas had not raised his voice, but the words were icy cold and cut through her musings like a knife.

"She is innocent. We are both innocent. I just needed her to heal my daughter." Evin's voice was quiet and tremulous and she had to strain to hear.

"Heal her with witchcraft?"

"Of course not! She is just a healer."

"Then how did you come to know of her?"

"She healed me when I was young."

"Are you saying you were touched by witchcraft as a girl?"

"No, of course not. I –"

"Then what?

There was silence then. She could hear her heart pumping in her chest as the grim realisation of why she was being allowed to hear all this began to dawn on her. It was not entirely a means to intimidate her as she had originally thought. Yes, that was part of the show; to hear what would befall her sooner or later, but the main reason was to break her. Silas had said it himself, that she would be hard to break. This was his sadistic way of showing how hopeless her situation was. It was a show of Silas's irresistible power in the village, the futility of her situation and, ultimately, that if she confessed, she could be spared the questioning and he would be spared the trouble of having to document his cruelty.

"Proceed with your work," hissed Silas. It was subtle, but she noticed the eagerness in his voice.

To her, what followed seemed to last for an eternity. In reality, the light had barely moved along her cell wall. A series of scuffles, cracks and nervous commands from the cleric were interspersed by whimpering and gasping and the same question repeated over and over: 'Did you bring a witch to this village to heal your daughter?'.

She found herself morbidly wondering what sort of means the cleric was using to 'encourage' Evin. Perhaps a beating? With a blackjack maybe, something that would not break bones too soon. The sounds were consistent; she pondered whether Evin's relative silence was a consequence of her being used to such treatment. In fact, how far would these two amateur witchfinders be willing to go with a village resident? Was there a limit before the other villagers would say enough is enough? Surely they would not support accusations against their own families and community. Would they?

No. The chance of escalation would be too much of a risk. But what if they could channel their fervour against an outsider? Someone old, ugly and for whom they had no sentimental attachment?

She spat the sour taste from her mouth and wiped her chin with a sleeve.

Her distraction ended abruptly with a wail from the other cell which reached a crescendo and turned into a long, agonised scream.

She pressed her gums together. She told herself it was resolve, but deep down she knew it was to stop her jaw from trembling. She found herself absently picking at a loose thread in her woollen sleeve, pulling at it little by little, unravelling it slowly, purposefully, in the same way that two men were busy unravelling Evin in the other cell.

As the scream trailed away, the same question was asked again, but there was a tremor in the cleric's voice this time.

"Did you bring a witch to this village to heal your daughter?"

"No," came the strained reply, "No, no, no, no, no," the words become faster, more urgent, then blurred into a single sound as Evin tore into a second scream.

"My, my, it's thirsty work is it not? That will be enough for now. Let her have a little rest while we quench our appetite, shall we? We are not monsters. Let her consider her position while we consider how best to confirm that she is telling us the truth. Hmm?"

"Yes, Silas." The cleric's words carried more than a hint of relief.

As the footsteps receded down the passageway, she realised she had a chance to speak to Evin.

"Allo? E-in?" She called, as loud as she dared.

"You A'right?"

She had a long, nervous wait before Evin replied.

"Just leave me alone. I should never have found you." The words were bitter, pained, angry, petulant.

"I sayed your daugh'er. I sayed Si'ylle!"

"And look what you did to her! Maybe she would be better off if she had died. Maybe we all would be."

"No! She is n'er 'etter off dead. Ne'er!"

"Have you been happy being alive all these years? Existing alone, without anyone? Because that is the life you have probably cursed Sibylle with. She will be pushed away. Shunned. No man will take her as a wife and if she does not bear children she will be cast out. Is that what you wanted for her?"

She was stunned by the vitriol. Of course that was not what she wanted for the girl, but it had never even crossed her mind when she had been saving the girl's life. She had always been a survivor, at any cost, and she assumed that to be human instinct. Was it not the case? Was death better than a life of hardship? How could she answer such a question? Was the thread better off cut?

"Li'e is a'ways 'etter than death," she replied, eventually. "A'ways."

"But she is so young. How will she survive?"

"You cane an' you hound 'e. Re'e'er? You 'egged 'e to sa'e her!" She desperately needed to point out how Evin had found her and begged her to save Sibylle, but she was taken aback, flustered and the sounds barely made any sense to her own ears. Speech was probably the one thing she had given up on over the years and now, she was acutely aware of how wrong that had been. But Sibylle's scars were not nearly as bad as hers. Sibylle would be able to speak almost normally so why would Evin think that her daughter would be spurned like she was?

If she could have smiled, she would have then. Just listening to her own thoughts; when had she become such an optimist? Had the girl influenced her so much? Maybe she had always been an optimist. She was a survivor; could she have survived so long with a pessimistic mind? Probably not.

"Maybe I was wrong. My mother's love blinded me to the future she would live if you saved her." Evin's words were ravaged with misery and she had to strain to hear them.

She had no answer to that. None that a grieving mother would accept or appreciate, anyway.

She was still mulling it over when she heard Silas and the cleric return. Silas must have been in the doorway of Evin's cell when he began to speak, his voice loud and clear to make certain she heard what he was saying to Evin.

"We have been talking about how best to make sure you are telling the truth."

A whimper from Evin.

"Hush my dear, there is no need for that. You might be pleased to know that I have been lectured on the power of mercy and to see if it is true, I have graciously agreed to give it a chance. Therefore, if you answer me truthfully now, you will be immediately released. You will be absolved of any crime you may have committed in the eyes of God and in law. You will be free to go back to your family. Before you agree or otherwise however, I must tell you that this pulls against my sense of justice and my better nature, so the offer will only be made this once. You have just one opportunity, my dear. Just one."

There was a long pause, whereupon she found herself holding her breath.

"So. Do you solemnly swear, in the name of God, before the cross upon which Christ died, to tell the truth?"

"Yes." Evin's replied was strangled, almost inaudible.

"Excellent. Did you bring a witch to this village to heal your daughter?"

"I did."

"Thank you. It seems that you are right. Mercy is a powerful weapon after all. Release her and let her be on her way."

No! No, no, no! How could Evin betray her like this? As the pitter-patter of bare feet ran down the hallway, she beat the floor with her fists in a rage befitting of the Furies themselves!

VII

She was tense and shivery as she sat in the semi-darkness at the back of her cell. She hugged her knees to her chest for what little warmth it offered, but her jaw and hands would not stop shaking. It was more than just the cold, she knew; she had only had a cup of water to drink since she had been in the cell and her stomach had stopped growling for food hours ago. Her throat was parched, she was hungry, she was tired, but she was used to suffering all those things and never more so than during her recent illness.

The sun had set, but it must have been a cloudless night as moonlight beamed through the grate turning what little colour there was to black and white and shades of grey. It was a full moon tonight she remembered and by the amount of light flooding her cell, it must be huge.

She had been thinking on her fate for hours. Silas had not even gloated over her. He knew she had heard everything; she had betrayed herself by her reaction and he had simply bid her goodnight with an infuriating smugness and shut the little hatchway.

Betrayal. She felt so many things, but this was the one feeling which sat proudly upon the pile of all the others. Evin had betrayed her. The cowardly bitch had saved herself by condemning the very woman to whom she owed her own life as well as her daughter's. What sort of woman could do that and live with herself? What sort of woman could betray such faith, loyalty and kindness and go back to the husband who had accused her and placed her in this position in the first place? How callous must a mother be, to return to a daughter for whom she saw no future whilst leaving the woman who had cured her to the mercy of a rope or the flames? How could a mother like that ever look at her daughter again without the stabbing pain of shame and guilt?

She deserved better. Sibylle deserved better. Her first reaction had been a deep regret for ever being cajoled into returning to Godstown, but as she thought longer and harder on it, she realised to her surprise that was not true. If she had not come, Sibylle would have died with plague and possibly Evin, Jacin and the entire village alongside her. She was not sorry to have saved the life of the girl. Sibylle was strong-willed and probably more capable than she ever was to lead whatever life her scars might dictate for her. She deserved her chance to make that life for herself, no matter what it might entail. It was not for others to deny the girl that chance, even if she were destined to remain a maiden.

She seethed and shivered as she grimly rubbed her gums together into a raw, red mess while her numb fingers tugged at the hairs on her legs.

The maiden. The mother. The crone.

The sudden thought took her by surprise. It had been so long since she had worshipped that she had completely missed the auspicious nature of that magical triangle. How could she have missed what was in front of her face? Perhaps she had lived alone for so long, she had even forgotten to look.

The full moon was ascendant, her pale radiance a rare sight to behold.

She could not deny the omens were there, lined up in a row and waiting on her whim. Perhaps the Goddess was showing her that it was long past time she worshipped once again. How long had it been. . .? She could not say for sure. Would not the Goddess have abandoned her in that time for more attentive subjects? No, she realised with growing excitement. Of course not! All this time she had been worshipping through her medicines, her potions her tinctures; oh, she might not have been saying the words, but she had been worshipping through her actions for years without even thinking on it. Indeed, she herself was a living symbol of Her power, patiently waiting since those days in Colchis and Athens to be called upon once again.

With this profound realisation, her excitement began to push aside her rage and she doggedly pulled herself to her feet. She dropped her shawl to the floor and allowed a steeliness to wash over her and flush her veins with renewed confidence.

She took a small leather pouch from her skirt and laid it on the ground in front of her before peeling off a fur jacket, a woollen dress, a smock, her boots, a woollen undershirt and two underskirts until she stood hunched and naked. Her hand no longer shook as she reached once more for the pouch and removed a brick of chalk. She hobbled a few paces across the cell until she was bathed in the white moonlight which streamed ever brighter through the grate. She stood there for a few moments, statuesque, her eyes closed. She breathed deeply and held the breath, then slowly exhaled, flushing her mind of the anger, the hatred, the bitterness which had been poisoning it.

When she was at peace, she looked down upon herself. The bruises on her torso appeared stark and black in the moonlight but beneath them, her breasts, torso and arms were covered in ancient writing, pictograms and intricate patterns, all painstakingly tattooed into her skin upside down, so she could read them herself. She moved her withered breasts aside and angled her body so the moonlight fell upon a diagram on her sunken abdomen. It was a double circle, with a strange looking wheel within the inner circle. Ancient writing filled the gap between the inner and outer circles. The wheel part of the diagram was symmetrical, intricate and labyrinthine, interlaced with strange symbols where dead-ends were depicted. At the centre of the wheel was a six-pointed star which resembled a wheel of flames.

Hekate, see me now.

She concentrated on the words, repeating them in her mind over and over until they were all that existed. Her skin began to itch as though she were crawling with ants, but it did not last long before a cold, raw energy flushed through her. It had been so long that she had forgotten how the moon's power felt on her skin! In that moment, she felt more alive than she had for many, many years. She felt strong, indomitable.

It took her a long time to accurately reproduce the diagram from her belly onto the cell floor. When it was finally complete, she patiently studied passages of writing on her body; some lines on her left side; both thighs and finally her right side, committing each passage to memory. Although she would recite them in her head rather than aloud, she needed to be certain of them to keep the flow of energy intact. This process did not take nearly as long as the diagram had. Although it had been a lifetime since she had last needed to recite them, the tattoos were enough to trigger her memory of the ancient tongue. *Like a mother remembers the lullaby she was sung as a child to sing to her own daughter.* She would have smiled if she were capable.

She made a last check of the diagram to make sure the circles were closed and every letter and symbol were as clear as they could be. The only thing she was missing was a blood offering, but she had faith in her Goddess. After all, it was She who had led her here and the Goddess's faith must be a mirror of the disciple's. An offering would come, as soon as she was able.

With fervent exhilaration, she carefully stepped into the diagram, one foot either side of the star of flames. She closed eyes and stretched out her arms, then recited the first passage in her head. Then again. And again and again and again and a sixth time, until six flickering tongues of orange flame burst forth from the star between her feet. She could feel the flames licking at her legs, singeing the hairs there and threatening to scorch her skin, but she had known what to expect. Fear would have broken the ritual, but she had performed this before and was as wise to the dangers as she was respectful to the reward. Despite the heat, she stood firm and resolute as she began to recite the second passage.

It was at the end of this passage, just before the third, that the ritual demanded a sacrifice. She knew that if the Goddess were unyielding, the ritual would end here in the flames at her feet. Despite the possible consequences, she was confident that she was performing Her will, but she needed to keep her composure nonetheless. Now that she had the attention of the Goddess, She would be scouring her thoughts and if she harboured any doubts it would likely be seized upon by the Goddess as weakness and lack of faith.

As she finished the recital in her head, she stood and waited. She could feel the Goddess testing her as the heat from the flames reached her thighs, but she defiantly refused to let her concentration be teased away. Instead, she allowed the Goddess to play out her little game, doggedly remaining statuesque as a blister grew on the side of her swollen left knee. When the flames eased after a few moments, she knew the trial was over, but there was no break in the ritual for self-satisfaction or recovery. Instead, she immediately recited the third passage.

In the past, it was at this point that the she would stand beneath the bleeding sacrifice and bathe in its warm blood. For this impromptu occasion though, she decided to make a solemn oath to the Goddess of an offering beyond the likes of which she had sacrificed in the past. She made the oath with fire, holding her right hand over the six dancing tongues of flame while her left hand reached above her into the moonlight, her crooked fingers splayed as best she could manage. The flames flickered higher and higher until they licked at her palm. Her hand shook with the pain and she held her breath for the effort it took to hold it there. She could smell her own flesh cooking, but still she was resolute. The flames caressed the gnarled skin between her fingers and ate into her calluses, but still she would not move away, though she pressed and rubbed her gums together until they bled yet again. Then, after what seemed an eternal agony, the flames died away to flicker about her feet once more. She stifled a gasp and sucked in as much air as she could. She was dizzy from pain and the sudden rush of air into her lungs made stars appear in the corners of her vision. If she fainted now, she would be finished, but somehow ancient steadfastness and strength of mind saw her through. She struggled through the pain to picture the last passage of words in her mind's eye, the passage that would close the ritual. All she needed to do was to get through that, to read the lines in her head. She quickly used another deep breath to centre herself, to buy herself time. The entire fabric of her being clothed the Goddess with her worship and suddenly, there they were! As she regained her composure, the words spilled through her consciousness. As she thought them through, she could hear her own voice booming in her head; confident, demanding, powerful, like she had been in her youth!

The words ended and there was silence. She felt her heart beating hard in her chest.

Once.

Twice.

Thrice.

The pain in her hand came racing back and hit her full force. Her head was spinning with all her efforts and she felt herself falling. *No! Not now, not after everything. . .*

She was gone before she hit the floor.

VIII

She was woken by something scuffling beside her, tickling her face. Everything felt heavy. Her limbs did not want to move, even her eyelids did not want to open. Something brushed against her nostril and she rolled away, using the muscles in her face to tighten and loosen the skin in a lazy attempt to scratch her nose.

There was a numbness to her body, as though she were an ethereal presence trapped somewhere beyond existence. She sensed something beside her and with all the effort she could muster, she rolled her head and opened one eye. There, beside her face, were the beady black eyes of a black rat. It sat on its haunches as it cleaned its face with delicate clawed hands, paying her no mind whatsoever. As she moved to sit up, the creature scampered away out of sight. Her eyes were still struggling to open, not because of their heaviness anymore, but because of the brightness around her. She noticed wisps of mousey brown hair fall around her face as propped herself up and winced as a shot of pain ricocheted through her torso. She grabbed at her ribs only to suck in her breath once again at the tenderness in her fingers. Squinting down, she looked for the cause of the soreness and realised she was missing two fingernails on her left hand. She shook the long fingers as if she could shake off pain in the same way as water. She reached for her hair and rolled it between her fingers. It felt fine and healthy, unlike the coarse grey she had become used to.

Gradually, she became aware of her surroundings. She realised she was not on the floor of her cell, but somewhere much brighter. The sun streamed in through an open doorway and the smell of burning wood filled her nostrils. There was a bed in one corner with something on it. No, it was some*one*. A noticed a pail of water nearby and crawled towards it to peer in. It was Evin's face!

A shadow fell across her then and she was aware of someone standing in front of her. A booted foot hit her hard in the hip, once, twice, then a third time just under her ribs making her gasp for air.

"Get up you lazy bitch! Make yourself useful and bring me some breakfast, then go get some water for the trough."

She recognized the voice but could not quite place it in her confusion.

"Now! Or do you want me to add to those bruises of yours?"

She was distracted by a whimper from the bed just before a bucket caught her on the side of the head. She was already disorientated and now the world spun around her. She wanted to lay back down again, but something within told her that would not be wise, so instead she gritted her teeth and pushed herself to her feet with an ease that surprised her.

"Mama?"

That was Sibylle's voice.

Her heart raced and a thousand thoughts sprang up at the same time, clogging her mind with their multitude until a single thought pushed its way to the surface past all the others.

It had worked!

She was standing by the hearth, cold and full of grey ash. Next to the hearth was the bucket which Jacin had just thrown at her and there, stabbed into the ground beside the bucket, were her scissors; the ones she had used to save Sibylle from her putrefaction.

It took no effort to bend down and tug them from the ground. Oh the joy! Her back felt supple, her hip sturdy, her knees young. Other than the multitude of bruises on her body and the injuries to her fingers she felt strong. She stood for a moment with the scissors as she breathed deeply, deeper than she had for months without causing a coughing fit.

She turned to Sibylle. The girl was still pale and wore a bandage about her face. Sibylle was staring at her, head cocked to one side like a bird, a quizzical look in her eyes. *Mama. She had spoken the word so well!*

She touched her own face gently, with the tips of her fingers at first. Nose, lips, she was whole! Dare she speak back? She was nervous but anxious to try.

"Call. Your. Fath-." She spoke the words slowly, carefully, until she bit her tongue on the last word. *Teeth! How many years had it been?*

She wiped away some blood that was tickling the back of her ear after the blow from the bucket. Then, with a newfound resolve – or was it her old resolve? – she hid the scissors behind her back, gripping them hard.

"Father?" Sibylle's voice was uncertain, fearful, but then "Father!" Much more confident.

The sound of a tool being dropped onto brick, followed by a curse, then Jacin was in the doorway, a poker in his hand.

She had not expected that. His face was ruddy with anger and his eyes smouldered with contempt.

"I thought I told you to fetch water?" He pointed the poker at her as he spoke the words in a low, chill voice. "Do you need me to tell you again?"

Had he always been like this? Was this everyday life for Evin and Sibylle? Or an overreaction to his daughter's disfigurement? Thinking fast, she bent and picked up the bucket with her free hand. She dared not speak, for fear of stumbling over her words and angering him further. What on earth would she say to him anyway? Instead, she lowered her head in obeisance and moved to walk past him, but just as she approached, he held out the poker and stopped her.

"What is wrong with you this morning?" His voice was suspicious.

She was close enough now that she thought he might see the scissors behind her back. Should she answer? For the few moments it took to think, she stood there, head bowed, half expecting another beating. Sibylle had seen her pick up the scissors; would she ask about them? From the corner of her eye, she could see the girl edge back towards the wall. Wide eyes told her that the girl sensed something was about to happen.

She hoped she would not disappoint.

With as much surprise as she could muster, she threw the bucket up in the air towards the ceiling. Jacin turned and ducked. The arm holding the poker came up instinctively to deflect the falling bucket and that gave her all the opening she needed. She swung the scissors with all the strength she could muster at Jacin's throat, but his movement and her wild swing combined to frustrate her and the blow landed in the fleshy patch on the underside of his jaw instead. She froze for a moment. The bucket fell away harmlessly, Sibylle gasped and Jacin turned to face her, a picture of surprise.

The scissors had not penetrated their whole length, but by the way he hissed and the muscles in the side of his face twitched, she guessed they had entered the roof of his mouth, pinning it shut.

She backed away slowly and watched as the anger in his eyes evolved to murderous wrath. She would have to earn her sacrifice to Hekate this time.

As she backed away past the hearth, Jacin wielded the poker towards her to keep her at bay while he tried to pull the scissors from his jaw. She was running out of room and although he was struggling to remove the implement, it was only a matter of time. She was nearly able to touch the wall behind her when Jacin pulled harder on the handle of the scissors. The attempt failed, but more importantly he winced in pain as a gurgling gasp rattled in his throat.

It was the opportunity she needed. Darting to her left, she ran across the cold hearth and overturned the kettle towards her assailant. Jacin dodged the rolling kettle easily, but then she kicked up the white ash in his direction once, twice before picking up the discarded bucket and swinging it with both hands into the white cloud. The clunk told her it connected with the poker rather than the man and the bucket clattered away as she lost her grip.

But maybe the Goddess was smiling on her again. There, to her delight, the poker bounced across the ground towards her. Without hesitation she entered the white cloud of ash and grabbed the poker with both hands. She lunged with it at Jacin and heard a muffled cry as the point sunk into him. She gritted her teeth and kept pushing, trying to ram the poker through him and finish him off, but just then, a white hand burst through the swirling cloud of ash and grasped her by the hair, snapping her head backwards violently. They fell to the floor in a tangle before Jacin rolled onto his back behind and beneath her, she with the back of her head against his shoulder. He grasped her throat with thick, brawny fingers and squeezed while she clawed and scratched like a maddened cat, unable to see for the ash in her eyes.

She felt like her throat was in a vice and she tore at his fingers, but her strength was no match for him. She reached back with her other hand, desperately trying to scratch at his face, his eyes, but she had forgotten that she was missing two nails and her fingers had little effect.

Ash was in her mouth and nose and she tried to gasp for breath, but his fingers were unforgiving. She was weakening, she knew, but if she did not try, it would be over. He would either kill her or give her back to Silas for whatever he deemed to be justice.

Her free hand found the rounded handle of the scissors and tried to push them up further into his mouth, but the awkwardness of the angle and her ebbing strength would not allow it.

The effort became too much for her and her hand hit the ground. She was still trying to blink away ash when stars appeared in her vision and everything turned red behind her eyelids. This was it. She was either going to pass out or be killed. In that moment of realisation, all she could feel was regret. Regret that she had failed, that Sibylle would have to live with this ogre of a father, that the poor girl would likely face a short life of misery.

A muffled cry behind her was followed by a warm, wet sensation at her shoulder. Had he stabbed her? Was she too close to unconsciousness, too numb to feel it?

The fingers at her throat relaxed and she gasped in air and ash, immediately coughing it back up again. Beneath her, Jacin was motionless, but something loomed over her and she flung her arms out to ward it off.

"Wait, stop!" Sibylle's voice.

There was movement followed a few moments later by a dark shadow before her. As she desperately tried to push it away a small hand took her wrist and cool water splashed her eyes. She felt around in front of her and took the wet cloth, rubbing her eyes with it to clear them.

She squinted to see and there, kneeling beside her was the blurry outline of Sibylle. Something was on the floor beside her and she rubbed at her eyes again. It was Jacin. The poker had skewered him through the chest and his shirt was soaked in crimson, bright against the whiteness of the ash. She looked at Sibylle with what she hoped was a smile.

"You. . .?" She was still panting for breath.

The girl nodded, fearful and trembling.

Without a second thought, she pulled Sibylle into her arms and hugged her tightly. Sibylle did not respond at first but then, slowly, looped her thin arms around her shoulders. They stayed like that for some time and she soon found herself blinking away tears. In times past, she would have told herself that the tears were due to the ash in her eyes, but if Sibylle ever asked, she would be honest and tell her they were for the want of human affection once again.

Thank you. Praise be, Goddess!

"Fank you," she said after some time. The words felt cumbersome in her mouth and sounded strange.

"I need to go. Back to de forest. Sibylle, will you come wiv me?"

She held the girl's shoulders and watched for her reaction. A layer of ash coated her hair, face and arms. The streaks of her tears and the dirty bandage round her face gave her a ghastly, otherworldly appearance.

The girl did not take long to think before nodding, yes.

"Then pick up all your clothes and put them on. Go, quickly!" Her speech was coming easier now. She patted Sibylle's shoulder and the girl ran to her bed and pulled on a dress, a shawl and a cloak over her nightdress.

She knew they did not have much time. She looked around hastily, picking up the herbal kit she had brought and placing a foot against Jacin's jaw as leverage to wrench the scissors from his head. She pulled on her own cloak which she found in a corner and her old sheepskin which was being used as a blanket on Jacin and Evin's bed. Finally, she found half a loaf of bread and a few meagre vegetables and pushed them inside her bag and picked up the bucket. She needed a new bucket and it would make for a good excuse if she was asked where she were going.

When they were ready to leave, she took Sibylle by the shoulder and leaned in close to her.

"Whatever you do, keep walking. If anyone calls for you, ignore them. You keep walking beside, me, understand?"

Sibylle nodded obediently. She took a quick look out the doorway. The morning was still very young. Although Jacin had lit the furnace, it was still heating up and nobody was about. In fact, the only signs of life were the chickens and the black rat which now sat brazenly upon Jacin's chest. She looked down at Sibylle.

"Put your hood up." As Sibylle obeyed, she did the same.

"If I say run, you run."

The girl nodded again, but this time there was fear in her eyes. Hopefully it would not come to that. The girl was still weak from plague.

Almost instinctively, she placed a kiss on Sibylle's

forehead. A simple thing, but it made her feel awkward until she saw the large smiling eyes staring back up at her.

"Come on."

She placed a protective arm around Sibylle's shoulders and they were on their way. They kept their heads down, eyes glued to the track in front of them. They held their breath until they were beyond the arch, then cut up the bank and plunged into the trees as soon as they could.

Only after they had been travelling for a few more minutes did she begin to relax and slow the pace.

Sibylle slipped her small hand into hers and for a moment she flinched away, but then smiled down at her and took hold of the youngster's palm. There was so much she would have to get used to again! Companionship above all.

As they walked, she began to get excited about their new life together. She would have to teach her about the Goddess, of course. That must be one of the reasons she was here; part of the divine plan. She would make a book of the ritual, something she could share with and teach to Sibylle.

She had been lost in thought for most of the journey when Sibylle spoke up.

"Can we stop for something to eat please? I'm hungry."

"Of course, my darling, of course."

She was so used to her own thoughts and company. Another habit she would need to change.

They sat opposite each other across the trunk of a fallen tree and ate the bread she had picked up in silence. The air was refreshingly warm and a hazy sun found its way through the tall pine trees which made up this part of the forest. Surrounded by birdsong, she was happy to be back in her own habitat. Sibylle kept staring at her as she chewed her bread. It annoyed her, but she did not want to start off on the wrong foot. She knew communication would be the key if this was to work and it was she who would have to change the most, to accept that she was no longer alone.

"What is it child?" She asked, "Why do you stare?"

Sibylle looked uncertain.

"Go on, you can ask," she said, softer this time. Her voice had sounded harsh in her head before.

Sibylle swallowed her mouthful of bread.

"Where is my mama?" Her look was questioning rather than accusatory or fearful.

Honesty.

"She has become an old, bitter woman in a cell under the chapel." It was all the girl needed to know.

"What will happen to her?"

"I don't know," she said quickly as she looked around the forest, anywhere to avoid the girl's gaze.

"You're ly-ing," the words had a sing-song tone to them.

She studied the girl for a moment and decided the question had a genuine interest for the truth. This was it. Would Sibylle turn and leave her so soon? If she lied again, she was sure Sibylle would know. But if she told the truth. . .

"She will probably be executed as a witch." The words blurted from her, almost before she had decided to say them.

Sibylle looked at her sternly and she held her breath.

"Are you a witch?"

Some might call me that. I would say I simply follow a different religion."

She could see Sibylle think about that for a few moments before accepting it.

"And what is your name?"

She looked at the girl and smiled.

"Medea, my sweet. My name is Medea," she smiled.

Bedlam

I

It was a bright, sunny afternoon in July when Dr William Westcott, in as jovial a mood for as long as he could remember, stepped down from the hansom cab outside the gates of Bethlem Royal Hospital for the insane. "Bedlam", as it was traditionally nicknamed in common society.

Paying the driver with a generous tip, Westcott lifted his medical bag and swung his cane from under his arm. He paused for a moment to listen to the song of a nearby blackbird then, with a sprightly skip, approached the gleaming iron gates. As usual, Westcott attracted the guard's attention by rapping the head of his cane against the stone sign which hung there.

When Albert Foley stepped from the gatehouse with a cheerful greeting, a smile graced Westcott's lip. It was not a beaming smile which creased the cheeks, narrowed the eyes and formed crow's feet at the temples like some people might offer; instead, Westcott's smile used the muscles of the mouth alone. His good mood was therefore hidden from all but the closest of observers beneath a thick bush of a moustache and a neat, greying beard which passed his throat.

'Good afternoon, Foley.'

'Best of the day to you, Dr Westcott. Looks like being a fine one.' Foley offered his own near-toothless grin.

'I wasn't expecting you today, sir. It is Friday, isn't it?' Foley paused to think, scratching at his head with a long iron key attached to an oversized keyring.

'Indeed, it is my good man. But one should endeavour to surprise every now and again, wouldn't you agree?'

'Well, that's very kind of you, doctor. I hope it puts the recipient in as genial mood as yourself.'

Foley's grin broadened further as he opened the gate just enough to allow Westcott entry, then locked it again behind him.

'Thank you, Foley,' Westcott called back. 'Enjoy your afternoon. I shouldn't be long!' Westcott waved his cane in the air goodbye as he began his march along the gravel drive towards the hospital building.

The grand old building that was Bethlem Royal Hospital stretched from left to right before him. It had taken three years of construction before finally opening its doors in 1815. At nearly 600 feet in length, it was a behemoth of bricks and mortar, as imposing now as it had been then. In the centre, an impressive, pillared entrance stood proudly beneath the high dome of the hospital chapel. To the east and west of the entrance were two long galleries, each three storeys high, above a basement. At the back of the building, behind the galleries, cells for the patients stretched the full length of the building.

Westcott skipped up the few steps between the pillars, then through the lavish entranceway into the cool marble interior of the hospital's reception area.

'Good afternoon, Dr Westcott.' A friendly, gravelly voice away to the left echoed dully amidst the ringing of shoes on a chequered stone floor.

Westcott headed towards a rosy-cheeked bearded man dressed in a grey woollen uniform standing behind a wooden desk.

'Good afternoon, Stapleton. How is your boy doing?' Westcott greeted the man as he leaned his cane against the desk and placed his medical bag on the floor.

'Young Will is doing well thank you sir.'

'Good. The diarrhoea has stopped?'

'It has. And the whole building was whitewashed just this Tuesday gone. No cases of cholera since my Will, I'm happy to say. Professor Bentwith paid him a visit only yesterday and commented on the timely manner of it all.'

'Excellent. If they don't come and install a lavatory before the end of the month, you make sure to let me know. In the meantime, make sure your boy keeps drinking plenty of water.'

'I will, Doctor. Professor Bentwith said it should be boiled first.'

'Hmph. Yes. I'm sure he did. Now, I must sign in if you please.'

Stapleton completed his own parts of the visitor's book before spinning it around to face Westcott. Westcott took the pen, filled it with ink and signed with a bold, flowing script.

'Anything I can do for Mrs Bentwith, you let me know, Doctor,' Stapleton half-whispered conspiratorially.

'I certainly will Stapleton. And thank you.'

'No, thank you, sir. Thank you.'

Westcott retrieved his bag and cane and headed for the back of the entrance hall. A tip of his hat to the orderly Rasmussen at the door was followed by another short exchange.

'Good afternoon, Doctor. We don't usually see you on a Friday,' The burly guard's voice was surprisingly soft, with a thick Norwegian accent.

'A change is as good as a rest, my good man. I thought I would surprise Mrs Bentwith.'

'Super,' Rasmussen replied in his native Norwegian. 'You picked a beautiful day for it.'

A nod to Rasmussen as he passed through the door, then Westcott paused as the key turned in the lock behind him. He stood in a plain corridor which stretched from east to west, with several doors on the north and south sides in each direction. At either end of the corridor was a wider, airier gallery.

Westcott turned left towards the west wing, where the female patients were accommodated. He could see a mixture of patients and nursing staff in the gallery ahead of him with a smattering of orderlies blending in, almost unseen by the untrained eye. Most patients here were short term; sufferers of mild hysteria or admitted by family members whilst recovering from some personal tragedy. There were a few longer-term patients; mostly those suffering from more benign conditions, such as imbecility or melancholia. The gallery was awash with sunlight from the south-facing windows, as good as any tonic when it came to mental healing, Westcott believed.

Just before he entered the main gallery, Westcott opened the last door on the northern wall to his right. Behind it were two flights of stone stairs leading down to the basement. It was cool here and dimly lit, with only a single, flickering electric lamp to light the way at the turn of each flight of steps. Despite the faint hum of electricity, the silence was strong enough to cause the *Clack! Clack! Clack!* of Westcott's cane to echo up and down the stairwell as he walked. Upon reaching the basement, he vigorously cracked the cane three times against a sturdy wooden door. A brief chill ran through Westcott as he listened to muffled footsteps on the other side. Then, with a bang which almost startled him, a metal plate snapped across and a face appeared at the newly formed square gap near the top of the door.

'Dr Westcott to see Mrs Bentwith,' Westcott stated formally, recovering himself well.

The joviality he had felt upstairs was already on the wane following his walk downstairs. By contrast to the galleries upstairs, the basement of the hospital was dingy and damp with little thought for comfort. This part of the hospital was home to the patients who had been declared criminally insane.

'Good afternoon, Doctor. We don't usually see you on a Friday.'

'Good afternoon, Schultz. Would you let me in please?' Westcott's tone was suddenly clipped, on edge.

'Right you are, sir.' The metal plate clanged back into place. A faint rattle of keys, the grind of a lock in obvious need of oiling, and finally the door creaked its protest as it was pulled open. Schultz stepped aside to allow Westcott entry into a small dingy chamber with a second door on the facing wall.

'What brings you here today?' Schultz asked affably as he locked the door behind Westcott to seal both men into the little room. Only a chair and small table offered the gatekeeper any crumb of comfort.

'A surprise for Mrs Bentwith,' Westcott replied cordially.

Both doors were wooden and reinforced with steel, but the second door only needed three heavy bolts to be slid across to open into the ward beyond. As Westcott stepped through, Schultz spoke again.

'I think she's in the bath house this afternoon, Doctor.'

Westcott paused and half-turned.

'Is that so? Is that not something you normally oversee, Schultz?'

'It is,' Schultz admitted, sheepishly rubbing at the back of his neck, 'But I'm not allowed down there today, sir, so I'm still here on security.'

'And pray tell, who is overseeing Mrs Bentwith?'

'A new fellow. I don't know his name, sir.'

'Hmph. Thank you, Schultz.'

'A pleasure as always, Dr Westcott.'

The door closed behind Westcott with a loud bang, followed by three metallic *clunks*. He unwittingly hurried his step, perturbed by the unusual news. As he removed one of his gloves, a frown furrowed his brow and, for the first time in the months since he had been visiting the female ward for the criminally insane, he did not have a word for anyone as he passed through the dank, dismal area ironically called the day room. Entirely distracted by something he could not quite put his finger on, Westcott barely noticed Mullins lift his cap in greeting, or the electric lamps flicker and darken behind their protective grills.

He finally lifted his eyes from the cold floor in front of him when young Jeanette stood directly in his path, holding up a rag doll. With his introspection suddenly interrupted, Westcott blinked at what Jeanette was holding.

Although only six years old, the girl's mother had been committed to the ward for murdering her husband while she was pregnant. Jeanette had been born in the ward for the criminally insane and had spent her entire life there. She was small-boned, sickly, with sallow skin and lank, thinning hair. It had been Westcott who had suggested that she be taken upstairs to visit the melancholic patients each week. He hoped to bring some cheer to the patients and give the youngster a good dose of sunlight at the same time. The orderlies had been surprised by the marked improvement in the girl's general health since.

'That is an exceptional doll, my dear,' Westcott said softly, almost fearfully. His eyes became fixed upon the lop-sided toy made from leftover fragments of cloth as it was being waved at him on the end of Jeanette's thin, pale arm. Westcott took a sudden, involuntary step backwards. Something triggered inside him, a flashback of jumbled memories, which made him gasp aloud. In his attempt to disguise his reaction, Westcott's final words were clipped and hurried.

'You must give her a name. now excuse me, I must find Mrs Bentwith,' whereupon he hurriedly stepped around the girl.

As he removed his other glove, Westcott was suddenly aware of the numerous other people wandering around him in the semi-darkness, like phantoms in an unwanted dream. *Like denizens of Tartarus*, he thought gravely, *Unable to escape their tortuous afterlife.*

His old friend Lupo suddenly came to mind, twisted and bloody. Westcott tried to blink the vision away, to bring himself back to the present. As always, but not without difficulty, Westcott finally, resolutely, pushed the image aside. He did not have time to dwell on such mournful thoughts.

He hurried on through the day room towards a corridor which echoed with the sound of dripping water. He paused to catch his breath, then wiped perspiration from his forehead with an already damp hand. He frowned, looked down, then back at where he had come from. Where was his left glove?

'Hey! You can't go down there!'

It was the voice of Mullins from the day room which distracted him. Westcott's brows sank low over his eyes in a brooding temper. It was enough to make Mullins pull up short, alarm clear in his eyes.

'I- I'm sorry Dr Westcott, b-but we have been asked to keep this corridor private this afternoon.'

Then, as an afterthought: 'Are you alright, sir?'

Westcott glanced over at where Jeanette stared after him, her head cocked in puzzlement. He took a last fruitless look at the floor around him for his missing glove before answering.

'By whom?' There was a low rumble in his voice now, akin to faraway thunder on a stormy day.

'By this letter. From Dr Jennings, sir,' replied Mullins, taking a piece of folded paper from his pocket.

Westcott snatched the letter from him and unfolded it with a snap of his wrist. It took barely moments to read:

To Whom it may concern,

The bath house is off limits to all comers this afternoon due to an experimental treatment taking place for certain inmates. This applies to staff as well as visitors.

Sincerely,
Dr A. J. J. Jennings, FRCPsych

'You damned idiot, Mullins, this isn't Jennings' writing! To begin with it's left-handed. It's not even dated, so how do you know it's referring to today?'

Mullins scratched his head, flustered.

'Because, it was, er, given to me today, sir?'

Westcott stared at the orderly for a moment. There was a part of him that wanted to verbally incinerate the man for his foolishness, but bigger worries were on his mind.

'Is Constance Bentwith down there?'

'She is sir. With that new sickly looking fellow. Erik something.'

'Damn it!' Westcott muttered the words under his breath as he screwed up the letter and pocketed it.

'Go fetch Jennings himself,' Westcott barked. 'Now!' He added when Mullins just stood there wide-eyed. 'And look for my glove on the way!' He shouted as an afterthought.

Mullins hurried through the day room as Westcott strode up the corridor towards the suite of rooms known as the bath house. The sound of water grew louder as he approached the corner of the corridor where a flashing light juddered and blinked from one of the rooms on his right.

Electric lights not working properly. Again. It will never catch on, he thought briefly.

Westcott marched round the corner to find a small man standing outside one of the bathrooms to the right of the corridor. He held one end of a length of thick, twisted wires. The other end lead away up the corridor, firmly secured to the wall. Instinctively, perhaps with a modicum of surprise, Westcott paused and watched for a moment.

The bathrooms were merely wet rooms with a drain at the centre of the floor beneath a copper bath. The doors to the little rooms could be locked from the outside and in place of windows, vertical iron bars allowed the supervisor to ensure patients were behaving and not harming themselves. The man in front of Westcott was looking through one such viewing window into the bathroom beyond. He was dressed in the grey woollen uniform of an orderly and was so engrossed in what he was doing that he was oblivious to Westcott's presence.

As Westcott watched on, he jumped with alarm as something hit the iron bars hard. An arm shot from between the bars, straining every sinew as it tried in vain to reach the orderly who stood just beyond the grasping fingers. Westcott frowned. Despite the gloomy light, the skin certainly looked the right colour for Constance, that Mediterranean olive brown. Was she having one of her dangerous episodes?

The man chuckled to himself as he lifted the wires and momentarily touched them to the iron bars. A flash of blue light and the arm disappeared instantly.

Westcott blinked with shock as a small cloud of smoke rose to the ceiling and began to dissipate.

'Come on, do it again. Come on, here I am!' The man goaded whoever was in the bathroom with a sinister glee.

Westcott had seen enough.

'You there! What are you doing?' He demanded as he strode forward waving his cane.

The orderly twisted round, clearly surprised by the challenge.

'Who are you? I'm not to be disturbed,' the orderly countered, brandishing what Westcott could now see was a fistful of copper wires encased in rubber wrapping.

'I mean it!' Desperation was already in the man's voice as he slowly backed away from the marching figure of Westcott.

Westcott was within just a few feet of him when Constance Bentwith slammed herself against the bars again, fingers grasping for the man's collar. With teeth bared, her black hair plastered about her face and wearing a sopping wet linen smock that clung shamelessly to her skin, the woman was the very embodiment of madness itself, like a raging banshee.

The orderly reacted to her immediately, catching her arm with the copper wire and sending her hurtling backwards where she hit the copper bath with a dull clang, before landing heavily with a wet slap.

Westcott was upon her tormentor in an instant. With cane raised, his first blow was to the side of the knee. The man dropped to the ground with a gasp as the second blow landed firmly against his temple and the third rapped his wrist, causing the man to drop the wire onto his own leg. A flash of blue and the man went rigid, made a strange squealing noise which he could not quite seem to get out of his throat, then fell to the ground as an infant flame caught hold in his woollen trousers. Westcott readied himself to apply another blow to the head, quickly realised it was unnecessary, then used the cane to deftly flick the cable away. After a brief pause to make certain the man's fight was done, he batted out the flame with his bare hand.

With his opponent unconscious, Westcott immediately turned toward the bathroom, peering beyond the iron bars.

'Constance? Constance!' He could hear the concern in his own voice.

Constance was laying in two inches of water caused by a broken tap beside the wall. She was soaked through, and Westcott could see burn marks on her arms caused by the electrical cable.

He slowly pulled the bolts on the door and entered the bathroom. He knew he had to be careful. There had been several side effects to her possession by a devil. As well as becoming entirely mute, she suffered extremes of emotion, especially anger. She had also become inhumanly strong, and injuries healed at an exceptional rate. If Constance did not recognise him, she was more than capable of killing him, he knew.

'Constance?'

Westcott's voice was low, barely above a whisper. A ridiculous thing when trying to wake someone or attract their attention, he knew, but his mouth was dry, and a deep dread swirled in his stomach.

Constance twitched, causing a drip of water to run down her bare arm.

'Constance?'

Another step forward and Constance rolled into a crouch in the blink of an eye. Even though her face was shadowed by twisted clumps of dripping wet hair, Westcott could see her lips were parted in an inhuman snarl. It was a vision which offered a chilling reminder of when the parasite – the devil – had been inside her.

'Constance, it is me, Dr Westcott.'

He had just enough time to say the words before she pounced at him. Side-stepping her lunge with relative ease, Westcott used the cane to block a clawed hand as it swept at his leg. Knowing her strength, Westcott parried her hands once, twice, then a third time in quick succession. As she over-reached herself with the next blow, Westcott took her leg away from under her to send her sprawling into the water on her back. With the grace of a practiced fencer, he quickly placed the foot of the cane against her chest, between her breasts.

'Constance, stop!' The command was unnaturally loud and rang throughout the bath house. Then, in a calmer, more cordial tone: 'Remember your breathing.'

Breathing heavily, Constance paused her assault. Without moving the cane from her chest, Westcott lowered himself to one knee in the cold water and removed his hat.

'Constance, I am your friend. Breathe with me. In. . . Out. . . In. . . Out. . .'

As he spoke, Constance breathed. As she breathed, she relaxed. Westcott removed the cane from her chest and placed it on the floor beside him. As he talked her through the breathing exercise, he brushed the hair from her face until he could see her jaw begin to soften.

'You must tell me what has happened,' Westcott said to her eventually.

With that, Constance threw her arms around the doctor and hugged him tightly.

II

Westcott helped Constance into one of the other, drier bathrooms. There, he perched her on the edge of the bathtub with a blanket around her shoulders while he emptied water from his shoes and tried to dry himself.

'Do you recognise that fellow?' He asked her, wringing out the bottom of his trousers as he nodded towards the man laying in the corridor.

With shoulders slumped, Constance nodded her head slowly. Water continued to drip relentlessly from the straggled tips of her hair.

'Why haven't I seen him? Is he new here?'

A slow nod of her head was the only reply.

Westcott knew Constance would offer nothing; that he would have to ask questions of everything he wanted to know. Replacing his shoe with a squelch, he stood in front of her and began to rub the blanket vigorously over her thick black hair.

'We must get you dry, or you'll catch your death.'

Westcott paused his task when she began to sign something to him.

Have you seen Charlie?

Westcott sighed. Not an impatient sigh, but something akin to pity, or perhaps regret.

'Not since I asked him to visit Stapleton's family for their cholera. I hear that he has thrown himself into liquor and his work.'

Did you give him my letter?

'I did. Though he did not read it while I was present.'

It hurt to tell her the truth, but Westcott knew she was likely to pick up on any mistruth. He needed to change the subject back to the present.

'I am afraid I must press you about the man laid out in the corridor, my dear. He is obviously sick with something. How long has he been working here?'

I saw him the other day. That is all.

'Did you notice anything suspicious?'

Only that he was looking at me. It was nice to have someone looking at me again.

A faint smile crossed her lips at the memory.

Westcott finished rubbing her hair and replaced the blanket around her shoulders. Her face was drawn and her lips pale, a shadow of her former self. Something else for him to worry about.

'There. It may need a damned good brush, but at least you won't catch a chill.'

'What the Devil is going on here? Who is this?'

The words were strong and authoritative. Before replying, Westcott slowly turned to face the newcomer, his fists settled onto his hips.

'I was hoping you could answer that very same question, Jennings.'

Westcott's words simmered with barely controlled fury as he glared at Dr Jennings and a shocked-looking Mullins. Jennings was a relatively young man for his position, in his early thirties. He stood over six feet in height with a slim build and an open, affable smile which Westcott had always warned Constance to be wary of. "Let us say, it belies a mind which is both overly confident in his own abilities and yet less than capable in a practical sense. A horrible pairing of traits for any would-be doctor, let alone the head of medicine in the criminal wing of an institution for the insane," he had told her when Jennings was appointed to the position soon after Constance had been admitted.

Yet, despite Westcott's criticism, Jennings was already

making a name for himself. He had placed himself at the forefront of psychological medicine and had hinted at several secretive experiments to support his claim.

Jennings had recently been accepted into the Theosophical Society, a worldwide esoteric cabal of truth-seekers intent upon greater wisdom and the understanding of God. Knowing this, Westcott had quickly moved to dangle the proverbial carrot of his own secret society, The Hermetic Order of the Golden Dawn. Even more exclusive than the Theosophical Society, the Golden Dawn's aims were the same, but that is where any similarities ended. The Golden Dawn was shunned by almost every other esoteric organisation for their use of rituals in their attempt to contact beings from other worlds, or "planes of existence" as some preferred to call them. It was an enterprise deemed far too cavalier and dangerous for the Theosophical Society.

Making the offer to Jennings had been a risky move. Westcott failed to mention that, during those dark events of the previous year involving the arcane books the Demonologica and Maledicta, Constance's possession and his friend Lupo's death, he had gained traumatic first-hand experience of the dangers of ritualism. Because of those experiences, Wescott's confidence in the Golden Dawn's more ambitious ritualistic efforts had evaporated in a matter of months. Unfortunately, his society co-founders William Woodman and Samuel Mathers did not see it that way. They had heard the stories of other-worldly beings, and those same stories had only served to fuel their hunger to experience such things for themselves. For good, or for ill.

No doubt eager to experience wonders beyond the veil, yet unaware of Westcott's changed stance on ritualism, Jennings grasped the opportunity of membership with both hands, but Westcott laid out some ground rules. His acceptance into the

Golden Dawn would be on the strict condition that he leave Constance alone. It was a proviso Jennings had accepted with alarming enthusiasm.

All this was at the forefront of Westcott's mind as he faced Jennings in the bath house.

'Whatever do you mean?' Jennings was suddenly indignant.

'One of your orderlies, laying in the corridor there, was electrocuting Mrs Bentwith. I want to know where those instructions came from.'

Westcott's words seethed. As he waved an accusatory finger towards the corridor where the man lay, he could feel a red rash climbing his neck and slithering through his whiskers, a sure sign that he was livid.

Jennings ambled over to the prone man, then leaned over him. His smile turned upside down with disdain.

'Mullins, do you know him?' Jennings asked.

'I've seen him around the last few days, sir. The name is van der Steen. Erik van der Steen, I believe.'

'I hired van der Steen myself and I can assure you, this is not him. Van der Steen is a young fellow, full of vigour. Whoever this is appears somewhat sickly.'

In his astonishment, Westcott quickly aimed both barrels of his anger at the younger doctor.

'You are saying that this fellow is not even an employee? Then who the Devil is he man? And how in hell's name did he manage to gain staff access to this building, let alone the criminal wing?'

'It is something I will look into. Mullins, fetch Weaver, would you? Get this man upstairs to room 5, there's a good fellow.' There was no concern in Jennings' voice whatsoever.

The decibels rose quickly as Westcott's fire burned ever hotter.

'Oh no you don't! I want some time with him first.'

'So sorry, Dr Westcott, are you an employee here? Hmm, no, I do not believe you are. Therefore, I will handle this.'

Jennings' prideful smile almost sent Westcott into meltdown. And yet, when he spoke again, his voice was soft and controlled.

'Of course. A word first if I may?'

While Mullins left to search for Weaver, Constance watched on as Westcott led Jennings by the elbow towards the corner of the bathroom. She was unsure whether they knew she could still hear them. She suspected Dr Westcott did, despite his whispered words.

'You listen to me, Jennings. I don't like you and I am pretty sure you feel the same about me, but as far as your esoteric future is concerned, I may as well be your god. That young woman behind us is my ward while she is in here. Do you understand? Your position in the Golden Dawn is mine to give or take as I see fit. Let me make it very clear that my generosity can flip on a whim depending on what you do now and in the future. Have I made myself clear?'

Westcott poked Jennings' chest with a forefinger as he spoke. To his credit, Jennings was unperturbed.

'You misunderstand me, Dr Westcott. Once the fellow is secured in room 5, he is all yours to speak to.'

'Don't feed me that claptrap! You and I both know that's not what you meant. Now get out and give me five minutes with the man here. I don't need the likes of you listening from behind a door.'

'Of course. Give Mullins and Weaver a shout and they will be along as soon as you are finished.'

Jennings turned and left without even a glance at Constance. Westcott's fiery gaze followed him the whole way.

'I am sorry about that, my dear. Damned fellow does like to overstep the mark,' Westcott apologised to Constance.

I have dealt with worse than him, she signed back.

'Yes, well, just remember that is why you landed in here in the first place.' Westcott's words softened a little.

Do you really think I am insane, Doctor?

The question was out of the blue and caught Westcott off guard.

'Now is not really the time, my dear,' he flustered.

Do you? She persisted.

Westcott paused and thought for a moment before looking her in the eyes.

'The truth is, I do not know. At the time you were admitted it was the only way we could prevent you from being tried for murder. But the more we have spoken and grown to know each other since then. . .'

Westcott suddenly became reflective, his eyes staring past her at something which wasn't there.

'Possibly. Quite possibly. You are impulsive, you have extremes of mood, you lack empathy. And yet, now you are free of the devil which took hold of you, you have done the right thing despite those traits. No, I am in error. You do not do the right thing, but you do things for the right reasons. One should never kill, but I know you killed to protect your friends and family. It is ironic that the police tried to accuse you of the Avery Place head mystery purely for the similarity that it was a severed head. If they had realised it was your housekeeper Mrs Simpson's head, you would have been done for. There would have been no saving you. Of course, the police do not know about the Bamfrys' butler, Hammond, and we are better off keeping it that way.'

Westcott's eyes suddenly refocussed, boring into her, judging her.

'I assume still that the episode of Hammond's death was

the devil's doing as well?' There was the faintest hint of an accusation in his tone.

Constance curled the corner of her lip into a little smile but kept her face low so her tangled hair shielded any tells she might give the good doctor. She was not going to fall for that bait.

When he realised he would get no reply, Westcott turned his attention towards the corridor with an unsatisfied huff. Constance followed silently to watch him kneel beside her tormentor. She watched the doctor hold two fingers to the man's wrist and then to his throat. Finally, he put his ear to the man's chest and mouth.

Her assailant was in his fifties, she guessed. He had a drawn, haggard appearance. The bones of his cheeks pushed at waxy sallow skin and his lips seemed to draw back from the few stumps of rotting teeth that remained. Constance could smell something odd about him, something corrupt beneath the stale smoke, body odour, wet wool and boot polish.

She sniffed the air.

Without any thought for Westcott going about his business, Constance knelt the other side of the man and inhaled deeply.

'What is it?' Westcott asked, quizzical at her interest.

Pushing the doctor aside, Constance shuffled around the prone man. She breathed deeply over his mouth, his nostrils, down to his throat and towards his chest. Leaning in close, her hair fell about her face and covered her attacker's body as she inhaled again, inches above the man's chest. Then, suddenly upright, she signed her explanation:

Corruption. In his chest. This man is dying.

'I know he's dying my dear, he has just received a jolt of electrical current which I fear has ruined his heart,' the doctor replied.

His tone, as though explaining death to a child, raised her ire as well as her resolve.

I mean he was dying anyway, despite all that. Electrocution or not, there is something in his chest. He does not have long to live.

'Is that so?' Westcott murmured the words, his eyes narrow with curiosity.

Constance could feel his gaze but ignored it as she continued to take in the intoxicating scent of the man's illness, breathing in the fumes of the corruption which was slowly killing him. She was interrupted only when Westcott began rifling through the man's pockets.

'Quick! Search him. I doubt Mullins will wait long before sticking his nose in.'

Working as quickly as they could, Westcott and Constance went through the orderly's pockets and placed the contents on his chest. A tin of cigarettes, a box of matches, a pocket watch, a purse with a few coins, a dog-eared photograph, a handkerchief, a ring with three keys, and, lastly, exactly the sort of triumph Westcott had been hoping for: a tatty folded note.

Wescott glanced at Constance, then along the corridor where he expected to see Mullins and Weaver any second. He unfolded the note hastily. Constance read the contents over his shoulder:

Francis,

I thank you for your trouble.

When the job is done, I shall deliver £10 to your wife and son.

Forever grateful,
G.

Westcott had just enough time to shove everything he had removed into his own jacket pockets before Mullins led Weaver along the corridor carrying a stretcher between them.

'Sorry Doctor,' Mullins said with sheepish regret, 'We have to take this gentleman up to room 5.'

Westcott stood back beside Constance.

'Is he alive?' Weaver asked without concern.

'He is. Though we believe he is not long for this world.'

Constance spat on the man, drawing a look or puzzlement and surprise from Mullins.

'A proper lady you are, aren't you? I'll finish my errand then it might be time to get you back to your cell Mrs Bentwith.'

'Mrs Bentwith will return to her cell when we are finished,' Westcott remarked icily.

'Right you are, Doctor. I suggest you see that you're finished by the time we get back then.' Mullins was undaunted as the two men placed the stretcher down, lifted the man onto it and left.

When they had gone, Westcott noticed the goose pimples standing proudly on Constance's arms.

'Damn it, you will catch your death. Come along, you need to get into some dry clothes.'

As he followed his ward through the day room towards her cell, Westcott's mind was a whir of activity. Who was this man Francis who had been posing as Erik van der Steen? The note, if it was related to his attempted electrocution of Constance, suggested a benefactor, someone lurking behind the scenes hiring what might be a dying man to do his dirty work. But why Constance? Westcott was aware of three victims of Constance Bentwith: The Bentwiths' housekeeper Mrs Simpson, Lord and Lady Bamfry's butler Hammond, and Constance's own maid Mary O'Connell. He suspected there may be more but had never received an adequate reply to that question. Sometimes, he accepted that there were things it was perhaps better he did not know.

As he waited outside the cell for Constance to change, Westcott's eyes skimmed across the population of the gloomy day room. Old and young, able and disabled, lucid and confused. An underground place where the law, the medical world, and general society placed people they did not know what to do with. And yet, he knew they had done the right thing to send Constance here. While she was alive, there was always a chance for release.

That reminded him. The surprise he had come to deliver. Westcott reached into a jacket pocket and retrieved the handkerchief filled with biscuits he had brought as a treat for her birthday. One corner was sodden, and the biscuits were crumbled to pieces. Hopefully she would enjoy them anyway.

III

The footprints were deepest in the soft mud beside the trickling stream. Bold impressions set close together with scuffs of loose mud; she knew immediately it was a man, walking with a heavy load. A few brief snuffles and she no longer needed the prints to track her quarry, though she need not have bothered picking up the scent. This man had done nothing to cover his tracks. She was nearly running by the time she had followed the trail up the bank, out of the forest, across a second fast-running stream and around the perimeter of a ripe cornfield.

A warm wind tousled her fur as the sun emerged from the clouds. Insects left their hiding places, darting this way and that, while birds broke into song again after the rude interruption of the afternoon downpour.

She allowed none of this to distract her from the hunt as she followed the footprints round the base of a steep hill. When she stumbled upon a structure just fifty strides ahead, she abruptly checked her run and slinked beneath a hanging bramble.

The construction was round, made from stone and wood, with straw neatly arranged on the top, sloping down from a high centre. A thin wisp of white smoke drifted lazily from the highest point, dispersed instantly by the strong breeze. Voices carried on the wind as two children and a woman ran from the structure to greet the man she had been following. He released a bundle of wood from his back, placed his hands above his hips, stretched backwards, then dropped to one knee to greet the children with open arms.

The family were dressed in crude roughspun tunics. She noticed the man wore pieces of tough hide under his feet, strapped into place by thin lengths of leather which criss-crossed up his legs, halfway to his knee. It seemed an odd thing to do, to cover his feet so he could not feel the ground beneath him.

The man untied the rope which held the bundle of wood together then ducked inside the little dwelling. He returned almost immediately holding a long wooden tool with a thick, flat head at one end which gleamed in the sunlight. He wore a smaller version of the implement at his waist, she noticed. Placing a piece of wood on an old stump, the man raised the tool above his head then brought it down hard, splitting the wood in two. It was a fluid motion borne of years of practice. The children picked up the pieces and ran them inside, emerging again seconds later to repeat the process until all the wood had disappeared.

This tool bothered her. Could it cleave through fur as it did wood? She would have to take care not to find out.

As dusk approached, the wind changed. The scent of smoke was on the air, filled with grease and earthy flavours. It was not long before a hide was pulled across the entrance of the dwelling and fixed into place from within.

Rising from beneath the bramble, she padded forward. She was cautious at first, keeping low to the ground, then quicker as she approached. A rich mix of aromas beset her nostrils: burning wood, rotting flesh, deer hide, mouse, and from somewhere off to her left, something deeper, more caustic.

Her cunning was suddenly to the fore. She thought back to the implement the man had used to cleave the wood. Did she want to be inside that little space with the man and his tool? He was obviously strong. Ever cautious, she turned and padded silently away, towards a shallow pit filled with the acrid scent of decay and excrement. Layer upon layer of subtleties bombarded her nostrils, both old and fresh alike.

This is where she would lay in wait.

It was nearly dawn when she was stirred from her slumber by a woodpecker hammering a nearby trunk. The morning light was still very faint, but her vison was excellent, allowing her to see into the thick shadows with ease.

When a sound came from within the little dwelling, she was suddenly on her belly, low amidst the late-summer brush.

One of them was coming.

She sniffed the air.

The youngster, the boy.

He approached at a run, chubby legs still clumsy with age. Standing on the edge of the pit, he lifted his short tunic and began to urinate.

Her instinct kicked in.

Three, four, five paces and she pounced. Her claws gripped the child as she sunk her teeth into its throat. The taste of blood filled her mouth, hot and sticky. Something cracked between her powerful jaws. Her prey went limp. She shook her head. A piece of warm flesh tore away and she gulped it down greedily. So engrossed was she with her food that she did not notice the man until she heard his anguished cry. He was nearly upon her as the shiny head of the long tool swung down towards her neck. She twisted to one side in sudden desperation, but too late.

She watched on from up amongst the trees as the man hacked over and over at the body of the wolf. It was only when the woman and second child joined him that his fury began to abate. That was when she descended towards them, all three looking at her in puzzlement and wonder.

The man stepped protectively in front of the others. His naked torso was slick with blood, still steaming in the cool of the morning. He was the one she entered. A moment of confusion, then she found herself looking down at the long tool, caked in fur and grue.

An axe, she suddenly knew.

She looked towards the woman. Her eyes were filled with tears and horror. She clutched the second child to her breast and backed away.

'No, no, Gaius, no!'

She understood the words but took no heed as she lifted the axe and stalked after her own family. With a sudden burst of energy, she closed in and swung the weapon.

Constance slowly opened her eyes. Despite the blurriness of sleep and the gloom of her cell, she could still make out an outline. Light grey against the darker shadows of early morning, hunched back, knees bent either side of his long, emotionless face. White eyes glowed faintly from black sockets. Long, smooth fingers clasped his lower shins as usual. The vision had an unearthly radiance amidst the murky surroundings of the dying night.

Natharlep.

With a bored sigh, Constance blinked, and the devilish apparition was gone.

As usual. Until the next time.

In some ways she still missed the devil – the parasite, as Dr Westcott had called it back then – which had seduced her and lived within her. It had only been for a few days, yet those few days had apparently turned her life upside down. There had been a sense of comfort while he had been inside her. Natharlep had been like a warm blanket. He had protected her, absolved her of any decisions. He had engulfed her very being and shielded her from the harsh realities of life.

Not that there had been many harsh realities, as far as she could recall. She vaguely remembered Katherine's death, Richard Kramer's mission, and of course her husband, Charlie. Dear Charlie. Other than him, her memory of the Spring of 1889 was sketchy at best. A memory would return occasionally, usually triggered by one of Dr Westcott's mesmerism sessions. Dr Westcott was always seeking out those memories to trigger some sort of emotion in her, whether it be sorrow, pity, fear, happiness; but they never did.

With a soundless sigh, Constance rolled over onto her back. The air was cool and the straw-filled mattress lumpy. The blankets scratched her skin and the bed creaked as she moved. Yet despite all that, despite the intensity and realism of her nightmares still being fresh in her mind, she found this to be the best part of the day. Very little light could enter her tiny cell, and everything was still quiet. It was her daily opportunity to think, without the hubbub of her surroundings or the distraction of the other inmates. "Patients", as Dr Westcott called them.

This morning, Constance found herself pondering what Dr Westcott had told her the day before. "Impulsive." "Lack empathy." He had made it very clear that he believed she may be insane.

She pondered that notion for a moment. Madness. Lunacy. She didn't feel particularly compelled by the moon. Would she know if she were? Was it something she should be aware of? She had been incarcerated here for, what? Months? A year? Nothing inside her suggested she should think of herself as mad. At least, not what *she* would define as madness, anyway. It raised another question: What *would* she consider to be madness? Uncontrollable mania? She briefly pondered the other inmates of the criminal wing. Sally had regular fits of mania whereby she needed to be restrained for her own safety as well as the safety of those around her. Constance certainly considered her to be insane. Rose liked to eat her mattress. But was that insanity? Or compulsion? Did it just amount to the same thing? What about Florence, who liked to lick anything and everything?

With a deep sigh of exasperation, Constance allowed herself to think back to all the deaths she had been responsible for. Some people referred to them as murders, but she had never seen it that way. There was her maid, Mrs. Simpson. The Bamfrys' butler, Hammond. The scoundrel in Whitechapel. That two-faced Mary O'Connell. It was her death which had forced her friends to have her admitted to this God-awful place. But when all was said and done, the only killing where she had no control over her actions had been Mrs. Simpson's. That poor woman's loss had been Natharlep's evil doing. And yet, strangely, that was the death she regretted the most. Did the fact that she was responsible for three deaths without being able to blame a devil inside her make her the definition of insane? No. Surely not. There had been a reason for each and every one of them; Killing Hammond had saved her husband, Charlie. She would do that again in an instant. The man in Whitechapel? That was his comeuppance for the evil he had been about to commit. As far as Constance was concerned, that man's death had saved many other women from mistreatment and misery. She would happily kill him again too, given the chance. And finally, there was Mary. It was true that she had made Mary suffer. Even so, her only regret was that she had liked Mary. She was good company. But Mary had used Constance, and the outcome of that had been Lupo's untimely death. Constance considered herself fortunate that Dr Westcott came to visit at all after that debacle. Would she kill Mary if she could make the choice again, with the benefit of hindsight? Yes, probably. To protect her loved ones. But not in the manner she had. Given her time again, she would be more clandestine about it.

Constance frowned as she thought about it. Mary's death had been a spur of the moment act. It had been committed in the heat of temper and a burning desire for vengeance. But now, looking back, she felt that she should have planned it. Of course, the ability to plan proves a sound mind. So maybe she *had* been insane at the time?

As daylight slowly crept into the little cell, specks of dust swirled in the air above her. It was an unfortunate reminder of the smoke from Charlie's pipe.

The muffled sound of shouting interrupted her thoughts from another cell across the day room.

Agnes.

Constance knew her expletive-laden tirades were aimed at the orderlies but that did not make it any easier to accept the broken silence. Constance groaned inwardly at the ruckus. She could even hear the creaking and banging of the bed frame as Agnes wriggled and writhed, as though laying upon a hot skillet.

Now, that would be a fine sight to see.

Constance instantly snapped her eyes closed, then conjured a mental picture of Charlie's handsome face. It was a trick Dr Westcott had taught her, to remove such horrid thoughts as quickly as possible.

Perhaps one day Charlie would come and visit, to give her a new memory to remember. How long had it been now? Was he so disgusted by her actions? To begin with, Dr Westcott always tried to bat such questions aside. "Of course not, my dear! He is simply playing the game. Excelling at the part of the bereaved husband. By staying away, he avoids arousing any suspicion of underhand measures regarding your incarceration." As far as Constance was concerned, if it were true, he need not play the part quite so well. Or he could at least write. Nowadays, the good doctor gave a decidedly more honest response. Like yesterday, when he admitted he had not seen Charlie for a while.

The morning bell broke her thoughts, followed by the customary rattle of keys in the door at the far end of the day room off to her right. She sat up, stretched, then moved her head from one side to the other, causing the bones in her neck to crack, loud and satisfying.

During her first week of incarceration, she had erupted into a rage when Charlie had not visited. The orderly, a stocky man with a thick neck and bald head had threatened her with solitary confinement if she did not calm down. When she had broken his fingers, six more orderlies had entered with truncheons. Despite her strength, it turned out she was no match for so many of them. Since then, Dr Westcott had helped her to curb the worst excesses of her emotions by using mental imagery, breathing exercises and mesmerism. He had paid particular heed to what he called her tolerance threshold; that point where her blood ran so hot that she could no longer control herself.

Was that the tipping point for her insanity, she wondered?

Her thoughts were distracted when an orderly unlocked and opened the door to her cell, allowing a draught of cooler air to raise the hairs on her skin. She quickly became drawn to a disturbance to her left in one of the cells on the opposite side of the day room.

'Orderly? Orderly? There's something wrong with Polly!' The voice was stringy, worrisome. It was Maggie.

Constance could almost taste the fear and confusion in the young woman's tone. At the age of thirteen, Maggie had been the youngest to have been sentenced in court to the ward for the criminally insane. By her own account, which she was not shy to tell, her father came home drunk one evening and believed her to be his long-dead wife. When his attentions became amorous, Maggie had hit him with the nearest thing she could find: an iron. It had killed him instantly. She would have gone to the gallows if it were not for a sympathetic defence barrister who had convinced the judge that she must have been rendered temporarily insane by the shock of her father's attempted assault.

Polly by contrast was the eldest in the dormitory at sixty-two years. She had been incarcerated in Bedlam for thirty-two of those years. Once a respectable nanny, she had fallen into a melancholic episode. She had begun to ask ominous questions, like whether a woman could be sentenced to death. One day she went to the kitchen, picked up a knife and smiled sweetly at the cook when asked what she was doing. She then proceeded upstairs, cut her poor ward's throat, then promptly asked her employer to press charges against her, which of course he did. Her plea to the judge that he send her to the gallows had horrified him. In his eyes, such a request could only be borne from insanity. In a strange twist of fate, it had been Polly who had taken the young Maggie under her wing in Bedlam.

Constance watched the furore unfolding round Polly's cell. She could smell the stale scent of death in the air and knew the old woman had passed. She watched as two orderlies pushed their way to Polly's bedside before one hastened to fetch Dr Jennings. When Jennings finally arrived several minutes later, Constance warily watched his every move with a grim countenance.

As far as the inmates were concerned, Jennings may as well have had horns and a forked tail. Dr Westcott's warnings aside, Constance had heard tales amongst the other inmates that his cutting-edge cures were very often just that: with the use of a scalpel. The story went that Angry Agnes had never been as angry as she was now before Jennings had tried to cure her. Rumours circulated that Jennings had removed her 'tainted' blood and replaced it with that of a calm, pure soul. Constance knew it could not be true. She remembered seeing Charlie use a transfusion contraption in the past and she recognised the marks the needles left on the skin. Agnes had none. But something had happened, and whatever that was, apparently it had been enough to tip poor Agnes over the edge. Something had pushed her mind over the precipice it had been balancing on before that fateful day Jennings had taken her away. And it was not just Agnes. There had been other stories: that he used sensory deprivation for prolonged periods, binding the eyes and pouring wax in the ears to concentrate troubled minds; or how he experimented on the deceased and dissected their brains. There was even a tale about bodily mutilation which had piqued Constance's interest when she first heard it. That was until she heard the more persistent rumours which related to a part of the anatomy she had no desire to let Jennings anywhere near. And after yesterday's experience in the bathhouse, the tales of how Dr Jennings experimented with the effects of electricity on patients were a little more poignant today. Strangely, she had thought nothing of it before.

Constance could barely control the snarl in her lip as the doctor declared poor Polly dead and told the orderlies to remove the corpse to the mortuary. A buzz of consternation rose amongst some of the inmates which Jennings did nothing to calm as he stalked out of the day room almost as quickly as he had arrived.

The day was off to a bad start, but at least it had been something to break the dreary monotony of life in the hospital. A regular day was rarely eventful: wake up and be freed from the cell. Look up at the windows in the day room to see whether it would be a bright or dingy day. Attend the dining room for breakfast. This was always a thick porridge of oats and raisins which could be eaten with a spoon or fingers, depending on the inmate. Mornings were for needlework, except Fridays when groups of six women at a time were taken to the bath house to bathe. The needlework was usually repairing uniforms or other clothes, but sometimes mail sacks or coal sacks. The afternoons were usually occupied by some sort of activity, perhaps crochet work, basket making or similar. Occasionally, selected women would be taken from the group for what Dr Jennings called therapeutics. These were the times when Jennings would select one or two patients before disappearing with them for a few hours. After the afternoon sessions there was a dinner of soup with vegetables followed by lights out, when the women were locked in their cells for the night.

Constance knew she was lucky in the afternoons. Her therapy was exclusive and always with Dr Westcott when he came to visit. Jennings had taken up his position on the ward just a few weeks after Constance was admitted, and Dr Westcott wasted no time putting him in his place. Despite that, Jennings had still subjected her to several sessions of ice bath treatment, "to let you know who runs the show here", she remembered him saying. It had been three weeks before Dr Westcott's influence finally paid off. Since then, he had made certain Constance was excluded from any more of Jennings' therapeutic sessions. Oh yes, she had seen the way Jennings looked at her. His eyes gleamed with something between loathing and curiosity. She always tried to catch his gaze when she noticed him looking. He hated that.

Reminiscing on those dreaded ice baths, a chill shiver seeped through Constance. She could have avoided them, of course. She could have thrown the orderlies around the room, broken their bones, torn them limb from limb, but, back in those early days, Dr Westcott had been almost beside himself with worry that she would lose control and succumb to just such an urge. Yes, that was what he had called it: an urge. He had told her 'If you allow yourself to be ruled by raw temper or base urges, especially in this hospital, you will hang. As surely as night follows day. There will be nothing that I, nor anyone else will be able to do to change that outcome a second time. So be careful, Mrs Bentwith. Remember your breathing and learn to recognise when you are about to be impulsive.' Dr Westcott had said those words in such a sombre, earnest tone, that they had stayed with her all these months later. She had not deviated from them one bit. Not until yesterday, when the dying man had electrocuted her over and over.

Yesterday's events had shown just how important Dr Westcott's breathing exercises really were. He had started training her even before Bedlam, although there had been greater urgency after her committal. The exercises were designed to be used just at the point when she began to lose control of herself. He had taught her to recognise the symptoms: clammy palms, short breaths, feeling flushed, uncontrollable shaking. Dr Westcott likened the exercises to another revolutionary new breathing technique designed for birthing mothers to control their pain. She had employed the exercises numerous times over the months, especially after she had first entered Bedlam. It had undoubtedly saved the lives of others, therefore presumably her own too.

Constance's thoughts were broken when an orderly arrived. An aging man with a round, angry face and thick sideburns. She had only seen him in the last month and his mistrust of her had always been plain to see.

'Come on. The doctor wants to see you,' he mumbled. His face reddened further as he spoke.

Are you new here?

Constance signed the words slowly for him. The orderly just stared, uncomprehending, then turned away. Knowing the rules about touching an orderly, Constance snapped her fingers twice, ignoring his obvious outrage as she signed the question again.

Are you new here?

'Oh. You're the dumb one, aren't you?'

Mute, Constance signed in reply.

Her eyes narrowed. There was something off about him. Something he was hiding. She could smell the sweat on his palms and the back of his neck and there was a strain to his voice.

'I've not been taught it yet. Now get along with you.'

The orderly waived his truncheon towards the end of the day room and looked around distractedly while he waited for her to lead the way.

'Devil!'

Constance ignored the outburst from young Sarah Green, a suspicious girl in her late teenage years who had recently been admitted for paranoia and imbecility. Sarah was another who constantly eyed her with mistrust, shouting at her as she passed. "Devil" was her favourite, but also "wicked, wicked woman" and even "Satan" from time to time, often spitting at her too. Strangely, the behaviour did not annoy Constance. To begin with she was surprised and puzzled. Did Sarah know something of her background? As time went on, Constance lost interest in that question. Nowadays, she was simply amused by her own apparent notoriety.

An orderly opened the door at the end of the day room as Constance approached. She sauntered through into a cool corridor, past several doors on either side. The corridor turned to the right, then continued for a few more steps until she stopped at a heavy wooden door at the end.

'Wait there, Missy,' the orderly snapped. 'Turn around and show me your hands.'

Constance did as she was bid, holding her hands in front of her. The orderly took a pair of heavy iron cuffs from a hook on his belt and secured them to her wrists tightly, pulling on them to make certain they were secure. With a final wary glance, he knocked on the door.

'Come,' came the muffled reply from the other side. Jennings' voice.

The weasel of an orderly opened the door and Constance stepped through into the corner of an office.

Jennings sat behind a broad, oak desk so highly polished that it shone with the light from the window to her left. An inkwell and pen sat in the centre of the edge furthest from the doctor. Two polished boxes of papers were neatly positioned, one on each corner of the desk, to either side of the inkwell. A small brass handbell sat within easy reach of him. Beyond those four items the surface of the desk was bare. An overly-full bookshelf filled the wall to her right. On her left, two green wingbacks sat beneath the window with an occasional table between them. In the far corner beyond the furthest chair stood a cabinet of small drawers with a decanter on top. Against the wall behind her was a lavish, marble fireplace.

'Thank you, Weaver. You may wait outside.'

'Yes sir,' came the prompt reply as Weaver departed.

Jennings, his fingers steepled beneath his chin, looked at her thoughtfully until the door closed.

Constance hated these things. It was not the first time she had been here and to her mind it was simply a declaration of superior position from the doctor. On prior occasions she had been reminded of where she stood and how her life was in his hands, a classic show of perceived power from a man who made himself drunk on such ideas. After his dressing down from Dr Westcott yesterday, she was resigned to hearing more of the same.

'Mrs Bentwith.' Jennings shifted uncomfortably, then drummed his fingertips against the desk, leaving dull prints on its mirrored surface.

Despite his authoritarian demeanour, Constance could smell an undercurrent of fear oozing through the man. Not that she needed to smell it. Why else would he have her handcuffed?

'I am going to put a stop to this ridiculous situation we have. I will be writing to Dr Westcott to tell him that he is no longer welcome here and that I will take personal responsibility for your continuing medical referral and rehabilitation.'

Constance stared at the man, confused. All this because Dr Westcott threatened him yesterday? Was Jennings such a small man that he could not accept his dressing down?

'You may leave,' Dr Jennings said, interrupting her thoughts.

Constance began to sign a reply, then rattled her bonds in exasperation when they restricted her movement.

'I am not releasing you from those until you are back in the day room. I know all about your temper.'

He was certainly not helping that temper. Constance stepped forward, banged her palms on the desk, then lifted her hands again, holding them towards him for release. Dr Jennings instantly pushed back in his chair, snatched up his little bell and rang it vigorously.

The door to the office slammed open. Constance turned to see Weaver, Mullins and two other thick-set scowling orderlies stalk into the room holding heavy wooden truncheons.

Constance turned back to Dr Jennings, raised her hands to sign to him, then stumbled to the ground as something struck her hard across the cheek. Dazed, she turned to see Weaver standing over her with his truncheon readied again. As she blinked away stars, the two heavies took an arm each and lifted her roughly to her feet. She barely had time to notice Mullins' shocked face in the background before Weaver drove his truncheon into her midriff. The blow knocked the wind out of her, and she would have fallen to the ground if she were not being supported.

In the corner of her eye, she could see Jennings rise from his seat and step around the desk.

Now you feel brave, she thought sardonically.

'We shall call this the first lesson learned,' he said with a rush of delight in his tone.

'Westcott is not the only man in the Golden Dawn. It turns out his co-founder Samuel Mathers is far more accommodating to the wishes of new recruits, and he welcomed me without condition. Now, if you have nothing to say, Weaver, Schwarz, Mikkelsson and Mullins here will see you back to your duties in the day room. The next time I send for you, I suggest you remember who you are, where you are, and show a little more respect.'

Constance raised her aching head and glowered at the doctor. Visions of him impaled through the eye with his pen sprang vividly to mind, but she could not yet even grasp her breath let alone try to free herself. Instead, she meekly allowed herself to be marched from the room.

IV

'Mrs Hodges? Where the Devil have you put the morning post?'

Westcott rifled through the mess on his desk, displacing wads of paper so haphazardly that the rug was soon buried beneath piles of newspapers, letters, coroner's reports and medical books.

'Mrs Hodges?' His waning patience caused him to drag out the last syllable into a long, rising note of frustration.

'It's under Lupo, on the table by the chaise longue,' came the distant, equally exasperated reply.

Westcott turned and immediately saw the pile of half a dozen envelopes beneath a disembodied and preserved human hand.

'Well, I never,' he mumbled to himself as he lifted the hand, retrieved the post and sat on the chaise longue to glance through the envelopes.

The Zoological Society. . . Commissioner Monro. . . A Cairo post mark. . . Each envelope was discarded in turn until he singled out the fourth. He absently dropped the remaining two letters without even looking at them as he opened the envelope with undue haste and unfolded the letter inside:

My dear William,

I thank you for keeping me up to date with Connie's condition and current circumstances. It saddens me to learn that even my wife's incarceration and recovery can be put at risk by the poisonous tentacles of the Hermetic Order of the Golden Dawn and your continued in-fighting.

I have met Dr Jennings on several occasions. He is an arrogant and petty man as I am certain you already know. His interest has always been his own advancement. If you had thought to ask me about him before brokering a place in the Golden Dawn, I would have told you how unwise it might be.

I regret, I am up to my eyes with work and will therefore be unable to visit either your good self or Connie any time soon. You will just have to dream up a new plan alone, as you tend to do.

Yours,
Charlie.

'Damn it!' Westcott's words were louder than he intended, full of vexation.

'Your language has become so much more difficult to listen to recently.'

Westcott jumped. He had not seen Mrs Hodges in the doorway.

'My apologies for the language, Mrs Hodges. I had thought you to be elsewhere.'

'No excuse. A clean tongue reflects a clean mind.' Then, without the sharpness: 'What is it that upsets you so?'

'Bentwith has turned down both my own invitation and my request to visit his wife now that I cannot. To add insult to injury, he also sees fit to lecture me.'

Westcott passed the letter to Mrs Hodges, leaned back on the chaise longue, and wearily rubbed his face as she read it.

'Can you blame him?' She asked, unsurprised.

'For not visiting his wife?'

No, for mistrusting the Golden Dawn. I mean look at us. Look at you. Mr Woodman is increasingly sick and withdrawn. You have tried to change the Order's direction, and before you say anything,' Mrs Hodges held up a hand to stop him, 'I understand why. I am here with you, am I not? But you must understand that for most of those members who have not been through what you have, they hunger for it. They long for that little glimpse of another world; that proof that there is something beyond the veil.'

Her expression turned to sympathy as she looked at him. When she continued, her tone was softer.

'Put yourself in Samuel Mathers' shoes. He is hungry for power. His close colleague has seen something, been part of something for which he has been striving for half a lifetime. If you were him, would you not at least want to try?'

'But the danger –'

'Is beside the point. For him, and for all those who side with him, it is the experience they crave.'

'Are they all idiots?' Westcott blustered.

'It is why many of us aspired to join the Golden Dawn in the first place, William. It is why you helped found it. Nowadays, it is generally the sole purpose of all whom

Mathers recruits. Unfortunately, your perceived success is also your potential downfall. It is an added carrot that Mathers can dangle in that recruitment process. Yes, we still use rituals of the right-hand path, but from a thrill seeker's point of view it is like comparing east-end gin with lemon water. One will certainly make you drunk and maybe even kill you, the other merely gives a passing hint of the flavour of its fruit.'

There was a pause in the conversation as Westcott looked up at his colleague, housekeeper and confidante.

'Why are you not interested? Why don't Florence Farr, Agatha, Ramees Ibrahim, Yeats, all the others want the same thing? If devilry and corruption is what you desire, why do you all side with me and not with Mathers?'

'Because I dislike gin,' Mrs Hodges replied flippantly. After a brief pause, she continued with a hint of annoyance: 'William, sometimes you really are the most obtuse man. It is because we are truth seekers, not thrill seekers. Our membership is based upon the betterment of human understanding. You have glimpsed that through your own experiences, which, being intelligent people, we all accept your word as being dangerous and therefore unwise to repeat. On a personal front, I would also like to think we do not hold the same jealousies which some of Mathers' people do.'

'Jealousies?'

'The need to be one of those who has experienced the other side,' Mrs Hodges replied with a sigh. 'Besides, it is not all about devilry and corruption, as you put it. Our appetite for other-worldy experiences is well nourished by rituals which use the right-hand path. Less eventful, perhaps, but they still show us glimpses of the unseen world around us.'

Westcott tugged at his whiskers while he thought about her reasoning. It did make sense. How could it not? Until he had experienced the dangers and horrors of devils and possession and golems for himself, he too would have been one of those whose curiosity would be champing at the bit to see it for himself. Unfortunately, to see it was one thing; to experience it was something entirely darker and more disturbing. Perhaps he should use Constance Bentwith's current predicament as a warning. He had been reluctant to even continue using the safer rituals of the right-hand path but had decided them to be a necessity for advanced learning. In the back of his mind, he also knew the need for his followers to be able to protect themselves should they need to, and the rituals of the right-hand path were perfect for that.

With these thoughts, Westcott's attention came full circle. He needed to regain access to Bethlem Royal Hospital. If Charlie was not willing, then who? After what he had seen in the bath house and read in the note he had found in the orderly's pocket, he honestly feared for Constance's life.

With a flash of inspiration, Westcott was quick to his feet. Stepping to the coat rack, he rifled through the pockets of his jacket to pull out various items and place them on his desk.

'What on God's green earth is all that?' Asked Mrs Hodges, suddenly inquisitive.

'It is what I took from the orderly. The other day in the bath house after he had electrocuted Mrs Bentwith. I took it from his pockets and had no time to return it before more orderlies came to cart him off.'

The pair of them looked at what he had thrown on the desk. A crumpled letter, a dog-eared photograph, a pocket watch, a tin of cigarettes, a box of matches, a purse, a ring of keys and a handkerchief. Mrs Hodges picked up the letter and unfolded it carefully before scanning the contents.

'Paid to do what?' She asked, puzzled.

'I wondered if it were to harm Constance,' Westcott replied gravely.

'What makes you say that?'

'Because on the day, someone had left a letter with one of the regular orderlies, Mullins, telling him not to let anyone into the bath house.'

'I am sorry doctor, but I do not see the connection.'

'The letter claimed to be from Jennings, but it was not Jennings' handwriting. In fact. . .'

Westcott left the thought unsaid as he excitedly returned to his jacket. He deftly rifled more pockets until he finally pulled forth a ball of paper which he held aloft.

'Eureka! The very letter!'

Westcott straightened out the letter supposedly signed by Dr Jennings as he walked to the desk, then placed it beside the first letter, To Francis, signed G. The writing matched!

'As I suspected! Both letters written by the same hand, and a left hand at that.'

'So, it seems the man you need to speak to is the man they carried away in Bedlam. As you are debarred from the place, how do you propose to do that?'

'The man I need to speak to, Mrs Hodges, is the man who hired him. The fellow who wrote these letters and has the initial G.'

'But surely you cannot find him without the man he hired?'

'I have an answer for that as well, Mrs Hodges. Now, I think we shall require tea.'

V

The cell was so overcrowded they could not even sit. Men and women alike, shoulder to shoulder, the children either standing on the bench at the rear of the cell or held in their mothers' arms to avoid suffocation. It was sticky and hot, the air heavy with body odour, stale breath, excrement, straw, and that one smell which always lingered beneath the others: the acrid scent of death. She looked around the confined space. The haunted terror on most of the faces told her who was resigned to their fate. A few were still hopeful, but they had been the later arrivals, crammed in just yesterday by vicious guards who knew how to wield a bayonet. Those few late arrivals still spoke of courage and how the revolutionaries merely wished to instil fear in them. There were some who even now, in the heat and appalling conditions, still sported their wigs, their coats buttoned to the neck, cravats neatly arranged, bosoms powdered to stave off the moisture of sweat and fear. Those prisoners were mainly the older generation, holding waspish, perfumed handkerchiefs to their noses to disguise the heady aroma of inevitability which surrounded them. The wailing of the children was a constant background music. Their hunger, discomfort, tiredness, fear; only exhaustion brought a pause, whereby they would fall asleep leaning against whoever stood beside them.

A door clanked open beside her, and a squad of soldiers spilled into the room where the cell stood. A half dozen of them held bayonets and pikes towards the iron bars which held the prisoners while a corporal unfastened the lock on the cell's gate.

As murmurs of hope and mistrust ran around the cell in equal measure, those that pressed forward were escorted through the gate until ten men, women and children stood in the little room outside the cell. "Where are we going?" asked one fearfully as the corporal locked the gate again. "To freedom," the corporal replied.

As the soldiers marched the prisoners out of the room,

she decided to follow. She could sense the hope and fear amongst the little group, neither emotion able to dominate the other as they were herded away. A mother kissed her child's head: 'It will be alright, little one.' The words were calm, reassuring. A man demanded to be told where they were being taken. The only response was the butt of a musket in his back, followed by a ripple of laughter from the soldiers.

Outside, the sun shone brightly. Relief washed over the prisoners as they felt fresh air on their faces. They breathed deeply, relaxing a little as they crossed themselves to give thanks to God. It was only when they were ushered into the back of a straw-strewn cart that they began to sense something was amiss.

She followed closely, floating on the summer's breeze. Close enough to enjoy the looks of confusion turn to alarm when they rounded a corner into a huge square dominated by a wooden platform at its centre. The prisoners defended themselves vainly against fruit, vegetables, stones and worse, thrown at them from a tumultuous crowd of thousands. Soldiers held back the raucous mob on either side as the cart approached the platform. There were people as far as the eye could see and as a roar of expectation spread throughout the throng, the noise was deafening. It took a surprisingly long time for one of the male prisoners to finally notice the tall, wooden structure atop the platform. Eyes wide with terror, he began to scream hysterically. A guillotine!

At the foot of the platform the crowd parted eagerly. From here, the prisoners could see the heavy, shining blade being hoisted, the thick, fresh straw scattered around a wicker basket and the black-masked figure of the man who would part their bodies from their heads.

She was particularly interested in the individual reactions. The screaming man aside, a few of the older men stiffened their backs, ready to meet their deaths with dignity. One woman tried to leap from the cart, only to be caught by the soldiers and dragged up the steps of the platform to be the first to use Dr Guillotin's apparatus of death. She thought the reaction of the children to be especially interesting, their open bewilderment belied their innocence when it came to the business of death.

When the first woman had been strapped to the plank and manoeuvred into the machine, a curiously expectant silence fell across the crowd. In that moment, she enjoyed the briefest whimper from the condemned, as it carried on a ripple of wind. When the blade fell, a magnificent cheer went up. Thousands punched the air in triumph, even throwing their hats skyward in celebration of a life lost.

It was then that one of the younger boys darted from the back of the cart and into the crowd. Soldiers followed, struggling to push their way through the mob as the populace cheered and whooped at their afternoon of entertainment.

She decided to give chase herself. In amongst the throngs of people she darted this way and that, tracking her prey by the push and pull of the crowd's movement as the boy charged through. It was a simple thing to catch him and force her way inside, pausing for a moment as she familiarised herself with this new vessel. Someone caught her by the wrist. Without thought, she broke the man's fingers and pulled herself free. Onwards she ran, until she spied a knife tucked into a man's belt. She pulled it free without a care of being caught. As the man turned and began to berate her, she pushed the knife up into his throat. Blood dripped, then drizzled, then fell in torrents. Others began to reach for her, but she was slick with blood now, making it easier to wriggle from their grasp. On the occasions where she was unable to pull free, the knife snicked through the air, cutting and stabbing, this way and that, finding victim after victim until as much blood soaked the square as the platform itself.

When Constance opened her eyes, two black pits of darkness gazed back at her, inches from her face. A white fire burned in each of those pits, far away, like tiny bonfires at the end of two long, black tunnels. Natharlep was sitting on her chest, leaning over her, staring directly into her very soul.

When she blinked, the vision was gone.

Despite the sporadic shouting and banging from other cells, it was several minutes before the morning bell rang and a few minutes further before her door was finally unlocked.

Although she had the relative freedom of the day room and beyond to the breakfast room, Constance continued to lay on her bed, staring at the ceiling. How many days had it been since Dr Westcott's last visit? Four? Five? She could not recall him leaving her for so long. Had Dr Jennings made good on his threat?

The thought of being alone left her with a strange, empty feeling. She did not sense that anything bad had happened to Dr Westcott. Would she know if it had? When she concentrated, she had a rough notion of what Charlie was feeling. She could tell if he was at ease, in pain, tired. But Charlie was different to Dr Westcott. Charlie was the man she loved. She knew that from her memories of the years before Natharlep. There was a connection between them, a link that she could not even explain to herself, let alone to others. But Dr Westcott was different. She thought of him as a caring paternal figure, a man she could trust, who had answers to all her questions. But where was he?

Several minutes passed before the orderly named Stapleton poked his head around the door. There was an air of restlessness about him, but Constance did not even think to care why.

'Good morning, Mrs Bentwith.' Not quite a whisper, but he kept his voice low.

She glanced at him and then back at the ceiling.

'I have some news about Dr Westcott.'

Her interest suddenly piqued, Constance pulled herself up and round so she was sitting on the edge of the bed, her movement lithe as a cat.

Stapleton did not often do the morning locks. Usually only when Mullins was not around. Dr Westcott had told her how he and Charlie had helped the Stapleton family recently so she knew he was someone she could trust. She was, however, puzzled at the scent of sweat from him so early in the morning.

'Dr Jennings has banned him from the hospital grounds. Won't even let him through the gate. So, he found me last night and asked me to give you this.'

Stapleton checked over his shoulder, scratched at his beard, then produced an envelope from his sleeve. He held the envelope out to her, waiting patiently for her to take it.

Constance reached out an arm, took the envelope and sniffed it gently. It certainly bore Dr Westcott's scent, despite being up Stapleton's sleeve. She opened it, unfolded the contents, and read:

Dear Constance,

I regret that my frank words with Dr Jennings have resulted in me being debarred from entering Bethlem Royal Hospital. Be comforted in the knowledge that I am working to find a solution.

I am determined to discover the identity of the man who was electrocuting you. I have some clues and will follow them to their conclusion.

In the meantime, if you should need anything, please pass your letters to Stapleton.

Sincerely,
William W. Westcott.

Constance gave Stapleton an uncertain half-smile. Damn that man Jennings! How dare he?

'Do you have a message for me to return to the doctor, Mrs Bentwith? Dr Westcott was keen that I should ask.'

Constance's mind was a whirl of thought. How long would it take for a solution? Could there even be a solution? Clues? The letter said "clues". Did he have clues other than the note that he found in van der Steen's pocket? What was she to do in the meantime? Who would help her to control herself?

The uncomfortable smile beneath Stapleton's whiskers told her that she was letting her self-pity show. Recovering quickly, she signed for a pen.

'I assume you'll be wanting a pencil, Mrs Bentwith,' Stapleton said, virtually ignoring her signs.

He passed Constance a stubby piece of lead pencil from his pocket. She turned the letter over to its blank side and began to write.

My dear Dr Westcott,

I will miss you terribly.
    Please do keep me updated.
    If you happen to see Charlie, please tell him I love him.
Now would be a wonderful time for him to finally visit.

Yours,
Connie.

With that, she folded the paper, returned it to the envelope and passed it to Stapleton.

VI

Constance enjoyed a rare moment of peace as she sat outside her cell in the day room soaking up the last of the afternoon sun. There was very little chatter which would normally reverberate around the day room, with most inmates concentrating on making ashtrays from clay on temporary benches at the end farthest from her cell. Constance had declined the activity, preferring to sit alone and perform the more mundane task of darning socks instead. Although the clay work was a rarity for the inmates, she hated how it managed to get everywhere and found herself cleaning little pieces of clay from her fingernails and skin for days afterwards. Also, she knew her tolerance threshold had been much lower than usual in the days since Dr Westcott had been gone, so she thought it best to stay away from everyone as much as possible. To avoid any "unnecessary dramas", as Dr Westcott would say.

There was something about these little tasks which she enjoyed. The sort of chores she had always passed to her housekeeper, she took on readily here. There was something about the dexterity with the needle which helped keep her mind free from the jumble of thoughts which normally tumbled through her head. It was relaxing, peaceful and helped her to remain calm.

When four of Dr Jennings's burly orderlies arrived to escort her to what they referred to as a treatment room, Constance dropped what she was doing and accompanied them without fuss. They marched her along the same corridor towards

Dr Jennings office, then through a door on the left just before the corridor turned to the right.

This room had changed since Constance had last been here. Two high windows allowed the afternoon light to brighten something akin to a drawing room, albeit a very spartan one. A fire in the grate made it almost uncomfortably warm, perhaps to make up for the lack of character in the decoration. A portrait of a young Queen Victoria hung above the grate against a tired wallpaper of green and white stripes with gold edging. Two comfortable chairs sat either side of the fireplace on a rug so worn and faded that it was hard to make out the pattern. But that was where the similarities to a drawing room ended. The remaining three walls were bare, sporting a heavy coat of shiny pale-green paint. The door she had entered through in the corner of the wall opposite the fireplace was made of the same heavy iron as the cell doors back in the day room. But what intrigued Constance most, and was probably meant to frighten most inmates, was the wooden table between the living area and the heavy iron door. It sported a stained, darkened surface with a hinge in the middle which could raise one end. Buckles fastened to thick leather straps hung from various points along the length of the table. A flash of memory made her pause momentarily. She had seen a table very similar to this one in the theatre at University College years ago, when Charlie had given her a tour. It was an operating table.

'The doctor said you should sit down,' Mullins said to her, not unkindly. 'He'll be with you soon.'

As Constance took a seat by the fire, all the orderlies left the room except Mullins. He stood by the door picking at a fingernail while they waited in silence.

What was this this strange double room supposed to achieve? Was it for the benefit of Dr Jennings or her? Was she meant to be cowed by the presence of the operating table? Was the chair and fireplace supposed to put her at ease? Constance pondered these thoughts as she stared into the flickering flames. What plausible reason could there be for such a contrast? She had been in the room before, with Jennings' predecessor soon after she had been admitted.to Bedlam. The table had not been here then. It had just been a comfortable room. She remembered Dr Westcott telling her that it was designed to put patients at ease so they would feel more comfortable, therefore more likely to speak about their histories, their ailments, their woes. Why would Jennings change that? At least she had not been handcuffed this time.

She was so deep in thought that she did not hear Jennings' presence until she caught sight of his feet by the fire. At least he had the intelligence not to startle her. The last person to do that had walked away with a dislocated jaw and three teeth lighter.

'What do you see?' Jennings asked, a soft smile twisting his mouth at the edges.

Constance must have looked puzzled because he followed up his question.

'In the flames. What do you see?'

Devils from other worlds, pleading with me to let them in, Constance signed back at him.

'I am sorry, Mrs Bentwith, you will have to slow down. Even after all this time, I am still learning.'

Just flickering flames, she signed slowly, sighing inwardly that her attempt at humour had fallen flat.

'Does fire hold any special meaning for you?' He continued.

No.

'I am aware your friend was consumed by fire in extraordinary circumstances. I believe her husband also had a life-changing brush with flames. Yet it does not disturb you?'

Should it?

Jennings declined to answer. Instead, he looked long and hard at Constance before seating himself beside her in the second chair. He crossed one leg over the other and clasped his knee.

'I see two ways we can treat you, Mrs Bentwith. The first is to treat the trauma of your past. If you had committed your crimes following a psychological breakdown, that would probably be the best option but, for me, it would be a waste of time. I know enough of your history to understand that you did not, in fact, suffer a breakdown. What you suffered was, I surmise, infinitely more traumatic. The overwhelming loss of control of all physiological function to another sentient being. This brings me to my second proposed treatment. We must aid your recovery by helping you learn to speak again. The ability to communicate normally with others will banish any feelings of dissociation from society. After that, your mind can begin the healing process.'

Constance stared at him. What on earth was he talking about? Feelings of dissociation? Learning to speak? Healing her mind? She wondered whether they should swap seats and perhaps Dr Jennings should be the inmate.

'You look confused, Mrs Bentwith.' Jennings spoke the words as though she were one of the imbeciles back in the day room.

How do you know so much about me? She signed slowly.

'Your friend Westcott had to give me a certain amount of information before I would allow him so much freedom of the building,' was the smug reply.

Constance watched as he gave a little self-satisfied jaunt of the head. His thumbs rolled over each other continuously above his knee.

'Now, some questions if I may,' Jennings continued, sweeping her query aside.

'Are you aware of what happened to you before your committal?'

Yes.

'Did you play any part in the, erm, unfortunate deaths which occurred?'

No, she lied.

'Hmph. So, you were aware of what was happening, but did nothing?'

Constance barely dignified that with a response. Instead, she simply pushed herself back into the chair and glared at Jennings.

'A conversation is a two-way street, Mrs Bentwith. I am merely trying to establish whether you were the driver, the horse, or the cart whilst you were under the influence of this devil.'

Constance, unimpressed, raised an eyebrow. These questions only served his interest in the esoteric, not her welfare or rehabilitation.

There followed a few moments of silence as the pair engaged in a silent battle of wills. She assumed Jennings did not like her for her friendship with Dr Westcott. To his credit, if that were truly the case, it did not show in his face. Eventually, Jennings sighed, shifted in his seat, then tried a different tack.

'Let us start again, Mrs Bentwith. Are you able to describe to me your time with something else inside you?'

Which part? Constance decided to play along, to see where this would go.

'Were there different parts?'

He grew within me like a parasite. Ever stronger until I had no more control.

'Very interesting. And I assume the deaths occurred after he had taken complete control?'

Constance nodded slowly.

'But of course.' The patronising tone was not lost on her. 'And, at what point did you become mute?'

I do not recall ever speaking.

That surprised him. He rubbed a hand across his jaw thoughtfully.

'What do you think happened to your sense of speech?'

I cannot say how I lost something I do not remember having. Dr Westcott believes the devil took it with him.

She noticed his nostrils flair at the mention of Dr Westcott.

'You keep referring to the devil as "he". How do you know?'

Constance shrugged her disinterest as Jennings' frown turned to puzzlement.

'And how is it possible that the creature could take such an innate sense such as speech?'

It was at this point that Constance felt that familiar pull of impatience. She stood abruptly. She barely noticed Jennings recoiling into his seat as she stalked to the fireplace, leaned her hands against the mantelpiece and began the breathing exercises which served so well to douse her temper. It did not take long to wrestle back control, whereupon she turned to face Jennings with an accusatory tilt of the head. From the corner of her eye, she could see that Mullins had one hand on the door handle. The other gripped his truncheon so tightly that his knuckles were white.

Do you plot to make me lose control, Doctor?

The words came fast, she knew. Probably too fast for Jennings.

'My, my. Please sit back down, Mrs Bentwith,' was all Jennings could manage in reply. He began to regain his composure, but she could smell a fear that had not been there before. For the sake of cordiality, she sat back in the chair.

You ask questions which are meaningless. You repeat a process I have already undertaken with Dr Westcott. You will never be the doctor he is. Let him in. I promise you, you will never even know I am here.

Constance made sure the signs were slow enough that Jennings caught every word.

'An interesting request, but we both know that is not the case, do we not?' The incident in the bath house proves that beyond any doubt, methinks.'

I was the one being attacked. The orderly was using electricity to shock me. Besides, I hear he was not even an orderly. Do you allow entry to the criminal wing for anyone, doctor?

That made him bristle, a satisfying sight to see.

'I do not appreciate your humour, Mrs Bentwith. Besides, Westcott broke the man's wrist and left him with a nasty burn, so now neither of them will be re-entering the criminal wing.'

Who was he?

Constance had the bit between her teeth now.

'Even if I knew, it would not be information I would share with a patient.' The words were blunt and clipped, but Jennings quickly steadied his tone. 'He is still in a coma upstairs. I do not expect the fellow to see out the week.'

She was unsure whether that last piece of information pleased her or not. Dr Westcott thought he had been hired by someone. But who? Jennings? Why? Out of spite? It did not feel like his way of doing things. What would he have to gain by the subterfuge? Surely he would just send in some heavy-handed orderlies like he did the other day. Besides, she had the feeling that he was telling the truth.

Are we finished?

The conversation had become a bore.

'In a moment.' Jennings stood and took a long, flat piece of shiny metal from his jacket pocket.

'First, please open your mouth, Mrs Bentwith.'

Constance did as she was bid. Anything to get out of the room and back to her cell.

Jennings leaned over her and placed the metal object on her tongue, pressing it down. It was warm from his pocket and tasted of iron. Jennings peered down her throat, removed the implement, then used both hands to feel the front and sides of her throat.

'Hmm. Can you say Ahhh,' he asked after a few moments.

Constance merely shook her head.

'You are simply not trying. Like this,' Jennings opened his mouth wide and let out an 'Ahhhh', touching his throat as he did so. 'Vibrate your throat here. Ahhhhh. Now you try.'

Constance opened her mouth in a parody of what she had just seen. Nothing.

Once again, Jennings held a cool hand to her throat.

'Vibrate your vocal cords, Mrs Bentwith.'

Nothing.

'Perhaps you are not trying hard enough. We will work on it in future sessions. Or perhaps we can look for a surgical solution.' His tone was clipped.

You are wasting your time, doctor. You cannot repair something that is not broken.

'Nonsense! We shall get to the bottom of it. Westcott is no authority on these things, you know. He is a coroner who deals with the dead, whereas my speciality is the living. It so happens that we are fortunate enough to have a fresh cadaver. I shall use it to discover more about the nature of your affliction. Mullins, perhaps you would be good enough to show Mrs Bentwith back to the day room please?'

Constance was quick off her seat and almost at the door without even a glance at Jennings. Mullins, slow in his duties, caused her to wait before exiting. When she was finally into the corridor beyond, she did not pause, even when she heard Jennings' words drift from the room behind her:

'Perhaps we shall reconvene early next week.'

There was a hint of satisfaction in his voice which made her dislike the man even more.

VII

'When thinking about our bodies, I find it useful to keep in mind the puppeteer. I see plenty of puzzled faces amongst you. But think about it. Grayson, if you could raise the cadaver's arm, please? Now, if I reach in... And... Grasp the tendon here... And here... Apply a firm tug to both, and... Voilà! I can open and close the fingers and thumb in parody of a wave. So, when you think of the human body, liken it to a puppet, with the strings on the inside rather than the outside. Thank you to my worthy assistant, Grayson, and thank you all. That will be all for today.'

A furious rapping noise filled the little round theatre as the crowd cracked their knuckles against the wooden rails in front of them, then died as quickly as it had begun. The students shuffled their notes, replaced their top hats, then filed silently up the steps towards the exits at either side of the auditorium.

All except for one.

'Dr Westcott. How good of you to come, but surely you already have some mastery of the topic of tendons and movement?'

'Good morning, Bentwith. Indeed, I do. Though I do

not remember the tutor being quite so hands on back in my day.'

Wescott headed down the steps, lifted the rail, and stepped through into the centre of the operating theatre. He extended a hand of greeting towards Charlie Bentwith. Charlie, without humour, lifted his arms to demonstrate that his hands and forearms were smothered in blood and pieces of dead flesh. Westcott withdrew his hand.

'Thank you, Grayson. Can you give me a few minutes, old boy?' Charlie asked. Grayson nodded, wiped his hands on a piece of cloth, covered the cadaver and most of the operating table with a crisp white sheet, then left via a richly varnished wooden door at the rear of the operating floor. As soon as the door closed, Charlie spoke.

'Perhaps we can dispense with the formalities until after I have washed up?'

Charlie's smile was forced. Not so long ago that smile would have been a full-blown ear-to-ear grin and a wink.

'Please do,' Westcott replied, unsure what else to add.

There was a brief, uncomfortable silence as Charlie went to the sink, picked up a bar of carbolic soap and began scrubbing it vigorously up and down his arms. Meanwhile, Westcott lifted the edge of the sheet with his cane and peered with interest at the cadaver beneath, its right arm opened from elbow to wrist by a neat incision.

'Is this a social call, old boy?'

Westcott considered his reply before speaking. He had already decided that honesty was the only way this would work.

'Partly. How are you?' Westcott dropped the sheet and dragged his attention back to the matter at hand.

Charlie did not look up from his scrubbing.

'Oh, you know. Cutting out kidney stones and playing

with corpses by day, going home to an empty house at night. I believe you know exactly what it's like, hmm?'

Westcott had not been expecting the barbs so soon. He certainly did not appreciate the dig at Lupo's loss, but at least Bentwith was engaging with him.

'Indeed, I do. Although Mrs Hodges lives in as a housekeeper now.'

'Excellent! Congratulations, Westcott. Have you just come here to gloat that you are now less lonely than I?'

Westcott knew he was going to have to play this differently if he had any chance of getting to the end of the conversation he wanted to have. More direct, perhaps?

'Not at all,' he said. 'I'll come to the point. Do you know a fellow named George Simpson?'

Charlie finally looked round as he rinsed his arms under the tap.

'I do. Here to drag up old memories too?'

'Unfortunately, yes. Is he by any chance related to your old housekeeper Mrs Simpson?'

'Her husband. What's this about, Westcott?' Charlie was suddenly interested as he dried himself on a nearby towel.

Westcott felt a sudden weariness wash over him. It was as though he had known the answer all along, but the vain hope that he was somehow wrong had kept him going. Now, his head ached with a fatigue and sadness he had not felt since Lupo's death.

'Charles, can we sit down?' Westcott headed for one of the benches in the front row of the auditorium, uncaring whether Charlie followed him or not.

'Westcott? You're scaring me old boy, what has happened?' The heavy dread in Charlie's voice was good to hear. It told Westcott that the younger man still cared, even if he didn't show it.

'I believe George Simpson has attempted to have Constance killed.'

'What? Is she alright? What happened? Why didn't you tell me man!' Charlie flung the towel aside and stalked towards Westcott, standing the other side of the rail with hands on hips. The reek of absinthe about him made Westcott wonder whether he had been bathing in the liquor, but now was not the time to pull him up on that score.

Westcott sat, placed his cane beside him and held up a hand to slow the other man down.

'Someone posed as an orderly and electrocuted her in the bath house. Constance is fine. I arrived just in time and subdued the fellow. I found this in his pocket.'

Westcott reached for the note he had taken, signed by the mysterious G. Charlie devoured the contents eagerly.

'Mrs Hodges and I have performed a divination ritual with it.'

'A what?'

'You may remember, you helped perform a divination with the golem's arm, when we were tracking the whereabouts of Magrit.'

Charlie's eyes flashed with anger at the mention of the woman who had almost killed them all in the summer of 1889. Despite killing Westcott's companion Lupo, she had been spared death. Like Constance, they had committed her to Bedlam, except Magrit was in the more comfortable part of the hospital, directly above the criminal wing where Constance languished.

'I remember all too well. And what did your divination tell you?'

'It led me to a room on the outskirts of St. Giles. I traced the landlord who gave me a list of tenants. He also told me that one tenant had left a few days prior. He was able to give me a name: George Simpson. I put two and two together and here I am.'

'A veritable detective these days Westcott. A magical Sherlock Holmes.'

Westcott refused to bite. Instead, he continued with what he had to say.

'Dr Jennings has shut me out of Bethlem. Samuel Mathers has his claws into him, and the idiot is doing everything Mathers says. Therefore, to ensure the safety of your wife, I will need your help.'

'What do you suppose I can do?'

It was less proactive than Westcott had hoped, but at least it was not a "no".

'In the short term, we need to warn Constance that there is likely to be another attempt on her life. In the long term, to ensure Constance's safety, we need to depose Jennings from his role as Head of Medicine for the criminal wing.'

'Oh, not too much then. Shall I start a petition?'

'That will not be necessary.' Wescott brushed off Charlie's sarcasm with a raised eyebrow.

There was another uncomfortable pause until Charlie flung out his arms and snapped:

'What then? What can I do that the great William Wescott cannot?'

Westcott refused to bite.

'Charles,' he said, gravely, 'Do you know what anger does to a man? I mean prolonged, unrelenting anger. I am not talking about a fleeting pique of temper. Do you?'

'What are you talking about, man?' Charlie was nearing exasperation.

'Anger. The deadly sin of wrath. It changes a man, Charles. It pushes friends and loved ones away, it skews our ability to think straight, it makes us do things our natural conscience would not normally even consider. And all the while, it gnaws at its host from within, eating at him from the inside out.

'All those traits which Constance showed when she was corrupted by that devil, they are irresistibly creeping into you now. The anger will slowly take control until one day there will be nothing left of the old you. Charles Bentwith as we all knew him will disappear.'

'Dear God, a sermon now?' Charlie flung out his eyes in exasperation.

Again, Westcott held his patience.

'Holding on to anger is like grasping a hot coal with the intent of throwing it at someone else; you are the one who gets burned. It is one of the teachings of Buddha, an ancient Eastern religion.

'You are using your anger for the purpose of keeping your grief buried deep inside you. You are now at a fork in the road of life, Bentwith, and I will do you the courtesy of divining your future, depending on which road you take.'

'Is this going to be more of your Golden Dawn mumbo jumbo?' Charlie sneered, his lip curled with contempt.

Westcott ignored him. He glanced at the floor and sighed a deep sigh. When he spoke again his voice was soft, almost caring.

'You can embrace that anger, if you so wish, and take the left-hand path. Your remaining friends will shun you as they become unwilling to suffer your ire any longer. They will give up on you as a lost cause. As you become increasingly lonely, you will look for solace in drink. By the staleness of your breath, I suspect you have already set out upon that journey. From the lesson you have just given, I can see you still enjoy your work. Your students hang on your every word. But your loneliness will make you bitter and you will no longer be able to hide your true self. You will be passed over for promotion and then pushed aside when drunkenness makes your hands shake. At that point, you will no longer see the point of rising from your bed in the morning. You will die early, alone, probably at home, and no-one will find your corpse until they break down the door.

'Or you can turn right at the fork. On the right-hand path, you let go of your anger. You release your grief, your hurt, the emotion of what you have seen, what you have been through and the horrid things you have done. Embrace it all as a part of your growth. Learn from it. Discover a better version of yourself. Your friends, your wife, we will help you move on and become a better, stronger man for the experience.'

Westcott paused for a few moments to allow his words to sink in.

'Your wife needs you, Charles. I need you. I suspect you have had no contact with Kramer since he left London.'

He decided to stop there. He knew he had overstepped when Charlie's nostrils flared with renewed anger. Westcott took up his cane and rose to leave. Suddenly, having said his piece, he was his old, brash self again.

'Think on it Bentwith. But do not take too long or the next time you see Constance she may well be in a wooden box. Or, if Jennings has his way, on a table under a sheet. Like the fellow over there.'

With that, Westcott turned and skipped up the stairs in a manner that belied his uncertainty.

VIII

Mrs Hodges had just served up a breakfast of eggs, ham and tea. She always ate with Westcott when she could, when he didn't hide himself away in his study. They did not always talk, but the company was good for them both.

'It's a fine morning again. Perhaps we could go for a walk in the park before it gets too hot?' Mrs Hodges asked. She was determined to instil a little more summer brightness into Westcott. He had been brooding more than usual recently.

'Yes, perhaps,' he replied listlessly after finishing his mouthful.

He was distant again. She had noticed a slump in his shoulders ever since he had been banished from Bethlem. Dark rings under his eyes told of a man with the weight of the world on his shoulders. Mrs Hodges knew there was only one topic he would be interested in.

'He just needs some time, William. Perhaps if we divine for George Simpson's whereabouts again? Finish your breakfast and I will fetch the crystal and maps.'

'Perhaps,' He said again, 'But that will not solve the problem of Jennings. There is hardly any point saving the poor woman from potentially being murdered, only to see her killed or maimed in one of his ridiculous experiments.'

Mrs Hodges frowned her own frustration. The predicament with Constance Bentwith was distracting Westcott from his ongoing tussle in the Golden Dawn.

'You can only solve one problem at a time, William.'

'Oh, really? Where in the ancient texts does it state that?' Westcott replied flippantly.

'Don't be obtuse. You know perfectly well what I mean. One solution will lead to others.' Mrs Hodges was having none of it. Then, softer:

'We need someone who has Samuel Mathers' ear. Someone who can send titbits of information without being suspected.'

'That would be delightful, wouldn't it? If only we had a man or woman who is unknown to Mathers, does not mind the occasional trip to Paris, and buys into the unfortunate consequence of being murdered if their duplicity is ever discovered. Or even worse: their reputation ruined.'

Mrs Hodges pursed her lips, unimpressed.

'There is no need for sarcasm, William,' she scolded frostily.

A sharp *rap-rap-rap* at the door broke the conversation. Mrs Hodges rose abruptly to answer it while Westcott sipped his tea, acting for all the world as though he had heard nothing. Moments later, she re-entered the dining room.

'Someone to see you, William,' she stated with a tone of happy satisfaction.

She stepped aside and in strode Charlie Bentwith, his hat and cane still in hand.

'Thank you, Daisy,' he said quietly with a half-smile in her direction.

'Daisy. . .?' Westcott voiced his confusion, teacup halfway between saucer and lips.

'My name, William,' Mrs Hodges replied as she rolled her eyes at Charlie. 'I'll get you a fresh cup, Charles.'

'Hmph! Well, I never,' Westcott mumbled, surprised.

'Thank you,' Charlie murmured, somewhat in a daze.

'Well, don't just stand there Bentwith. You can take a seat.' Westcott tried to tone down his impatience but failed miserably.

'To what do we owe the pleasure?'

As Charlie removed his jacket and sat, Westcott was careful to notice his appearance. Dishevelled hair was nothing unusual, but a creased collar would never have been worn a year ago and the black rings around bloodshot eyes told of too many late nights with a bottle of liquor. He had shaved, at least, and his shoes only wore the road mud from this morning's venture; no old or dried-on stains. Perhaps there was still a gentleman in there somewhere after all, fighting to reach the surface again.

'I have been thinking about what you said the other day,' Charlie began. Then: 'Thank you, Daisy,' when a cup was placed in front of him and tea poured from the pot.

'Well? What of it? Yes please, Mrs Hodges.' Westcott pushed his cup in her direction. Mrs Hodges dutifully topped up the cup with tea and added a fresh sliver of lemon with a pair of silver tongs before passing it back.

'I, I cannot allow –' Charlie took a moment to swallow his emotions and steady himself. He took a sip of tea, exhaled a long, shuddering breath, then started again.

'You are correct. I cannot continue along the path I am on. The idea of Jennings –'

Charlie's voice caught in his throat and he clapped a hand to his mouth. His eyes welled up with tears. Mrs Hodges was beside him in an instant with a handkerchief and a comforting hand.

'Don't you worry now Charles, you're with friends here.'

'Thank you,' Charlie tried to smile through a strained voice.

He took a few moments to pull himself together. He tried to lift his teacup, but his hands shook so violently that he immediately placed it back onto the saucer. He half-smiled up at Mrs Hodges as she patted his shoulder, calmed himself with three long breaths, then continued, his voice stronger this time.

'You are right. I need to change the path I am on. What do you need of me?'

'Excellent, Bentwith. I think I can speak for Mrs Hodges as well when I say that we admire your courage. In fact, we were discussing just before you arrived what we need to do to see Jennings deposed from his position at Bethlem. You might just be the man to help us achieve it.'

'Really? How so?'

'How would you like to join The Hermetic Order of the Golden Dawn?'

IX

It was late on a muggy, sticky evening when the train finally pulled into a busy Gare du Nord station. The sun was low, giving the Paris sky a vivid reddish-purple shade, not unlike London on some evenings. It was the perfect backdrop for the tall silhouette of Gustave Eiffel's new iron tower which dominated the skyline of the French capital.

Charlie Bentwith exited his cramped carriage and stepped onto the smoky platform. He paused to light his freshly packed pipe, then picked up his suitcase again and strolled towards the exit. A hustle and bustle of Frenchmen tutted and frowned their way around him, but Charlie was more intent on admiring the cinched waists and shining fabrics of the more well-to-do French women he passed, supplementing the tipping of his hat with an occasional wink, whenever he caught an eye.

As he approached the concourse, Charlie noticed a man standing perfectly still amongst the hubbub of travellers. Of average build, an overly tall top hat gave the illusion he was taller than his true height. The gentleman was sharply dressed. He stood with confidence, feet planted, resting both hands upon a cane in front of him. A pair of round wire-rimmed glasses sat above a sandy moustache on a face which wore such a strikingly sombre expression that Charlie wondered if the fate of the world might be on his shoulders.

Charlie puffed on his pipe as he approached.

'Mr Mathers, I presume?'

'Indeed. You may call me Adeptus Exemptus, Mr Bentwith.'

'You can just call me Charlie.' Charlie grinned broadly through a puff of pipe smoke and held out a hand of greeting. Mathers ignored the hand entirely, swung on his heel, and stalked off across the concourse.

'I have a carriage waiting, but you will need to extinguish that pipe before you enter it. I cannot abide the smell,' Mathers stated flatly without pausing to see whether Charlie was following or not.

'Where are we going?' Charlie tried to keep his tone affable, despite the pace.

'To my offices where we can talk. You can spend the night there. If we come to an accord, then we can initiate you at the temple on the morrow.'

'Ah, right,' was all Charlie could manage before emptying his pipe on the footway and mounting into a small but comfortable carriage.

Charlie had no idea where the carriage was headed. He tried to keep his bearings but was soon hopelessly lost as they turned this way and that on their journey through the shadowy streets of the city. He made several attempts at conversation on the way. Mathers' answers were always polite, yet somehow managed to smother any opportunity for small talk almost immediately. When they finally dismounted the carriage, only the dim flickering candle of a nearby streetlamp and the carriage's own lantern lit the ornately carved mahogany door that Mathers approached.

Three knocks, then two, then another one, after which Mathers turned and offered a humourless but pleasant smile while they waited. A few moments later Charlie heard bolts being drawn. The door creaked inward to reveal an ostentatiously furnished reception area with winding staircase to the rear. It took a few seconds for Charlie to notice the diminutive man who had opened the door.

'My associate. May I introduce Hans von Kürnberg, Hans, this is Charles Bentwith, the fellow I spoke to you about.' Mathers introduced them.

'Good evening, erm. . .' Charlie held out his hand but left the greeting hanging, unsure how to address the German.

'You may call me Hans.' Hans reached up to shake the hand of a bemused Charlie.

'Ah-hem. And you?' Hans prompted when Charlie failed to reply.

'Oh, um, Charlie,' he said finally with a friendly smile.

Hans stood roughly the height of Charlie's shoulder. He was immaculately dressed in a grey Parisian suit with a sky-blue cravat which was barely noticeable beneath a long, perfectly groomed beard without moustaches. His thin hair was neatly oiled to either side of what was already a broad head, making it appear broader still.

'Hans is one of my most loyal associates in the Golden Dawn,' Mathers explained as he led the way to a room left of the spiral staircase. 'Like us, he believes Westcott has gone too far, trying to curb the use of rituals; the very ethos upon which the founding of this order was based.'

Mathers led Charlie through an ordinary looking door into a lavish office. The wall to his left was full of books. In front of him, a portrait of Mathers wearing Egyptian-style ceremonial robes hung between two floor-to-ceiling stained glass windows featuring various occult symbols. Upon the wall behind him there hung an array of antique maps showing the world, Europe and several locations in Asia and the Far East in more detail. But the most interesting was the wall to the right. It was a blackboard from floor to ceiling, covered in chalk diagrams of circles, pentangles, seals and excerpts of writing in languages which were far beyond Charlie's understanding.

'Please sit,' Mathers broke Charlie's wonder with the offer of a stiff-backed chair beside an occasional table with a chess board set upon it. The rows of pieces stood ready for a new game.

'Do you play?'

'I am afraid I never learned, old boy,' Charlie replied, then winced inwardly at his overfamiliarity.

'The sport of gentlemen. You should learn,' Mathers scolded, with a smile which carried no warmth.

'I have taken the liberty of arranging a light supper which should be ready shortly. In the meantime, I would very much like to discuss the contents of your letter.'

The man was certainly to the point, thought Charlie.

'Of course. It is why I am here, after all,' he said, accompanied by what he hoped would be a warm smile. 'What would you like to know?'

'You mention that your wife is a victim of William Westcott's obsessions. I am of course aware of the goings on, but perhaps you could give me some background.'

'Certainly. You are no doubt aware that in December of '88 my friend's wife, Katherine Kramer, became sick and died.'

'Indeed, I am,' Mathers interrupted. 'Tell me the story in your own words.'

Charlie gave the other man a long look, wondering just how much he already knew about the events of that winter and the Spring of 1889. Dismissing the worry, he gathered his thoughts and began.

'Katherine scratched herself on a book. I say on a book, but it was a little hook hidden in the spine. To begin with we believed – when I say we, I mean her husband Richard and I – we thought she had an infection. But when Richard saw some strange goings-on between Katherine and a swirl of smoke, we realised it was something else entirely. Her temperature kept rising and she died, burning to death while giving birth to some sort of horrific devil creature.

'Shortly after Katherine's death, my own wife Constance took ill with similar early symptoms. Westcott was recommended to us. He put her through an experiment where he mesmerised poor Connie, and the result was to manifest something dark and ugly within her. It was after this that things came to a head. Connie had an unfortunate incident with our housekeeper, then I was alerted to her presence at the house of Lord Bamfry, the Dean of University College London where Richard and I worked. It transpired that Connie had been playing with the same book as Katherine, a book called the Demonologica which interested Westcott intensely. It is one of seven diabolic tomes. I am sure you have heard of them, full of witchcraft and other-worldy delights. Anyway, I found her at the Bamfry house, where Lady Bamfry tried to blackmail me. I got into a scrap with their butler who fast became one of Connie's victims. Let us just say, it ended badly for the Bamfrys.

'Connie had apparently been cured of her devil following a ritual performed by Westcott, Kramer and Lily Lefèvre, now Kramer's second wife. I was not present for the ritual, so am unable to vouch for the authenticity of what I have been told. Ever since, Connie has been mute and borderline insane. The Spring of '89 saw more horrors when a young woman named Magrit summoned a golem using another of the diabolic tomes: The Maledicta, the book of curses. I had the displeasure of getting up close and personal with this creature once or twice. I recall it knocking me senseless on one occasion and I also had the proud job of examining its disembodied arm which appeared to be two different arms that had been stitched together.

'Anyway, would you believe that Connie's new companion, Mary O'Connell, was in the pay of this Magrit. She used Connie to steal dolls which Magrit imbued with life. We met the tiny army in your temple in London. That is where Westcott's friend Lupo met his unfortunate demise, at the hand of the golem and Magrit's strange army of animated toys.'

'I liked Lupo. He was a good man. Very loyal to William,' Mathers interrupted.

'Loyal indeed. Would you believe that Westcott now uses Lupo's preserved hand as a paperweight?' replied Charlie.

Surprisingly for Charlie, Mathers gave no reaction to that grisly news. Trying not to squirm, he decided it best to move on and continue his tale.

'Magrit gave herself up. For what reason, we could never fathom. Connie killed young Mrs McConnell for her duplicity in the affair. That is when Westcott and Kramer had her committed to Bedlam and told me it was for her own good. To keep her out of the hangman's noose, they said at the time.'

'You do not believe that?'

'I believe Westcott was so intent on using his rituals that he gave no thought for the consequences. I believe he damaged Connie beyond repair then had her locked up when she became too difficult for him to control. A trial would have implicated him, so he convinced Kramer and Lily that it would implicate them too. They aided and abetted his actions then fled to the Isle of Wight like snivelling cowards.'

Charlie was shocked at just how much it had hurt to say those words. He thought they would come easily, bearing in mind the anger and betrayal he had felt at the time. And yet, here he sat, suddenly worried that the lie would stand out like a sore thumb to a man like Samuel Mathers. But if Mathers did suspect something, he gave no outward sign of it.

'Interesting,' Mathers murmured after a few moments, his forefinger pressed against his lips in thought.

Charlie decided to allow the sudden silence to play out. He did not want to appear over-eager.

'And how do you expect this little arrangement to work?' Mathers enquired thoughtfully after the pause.

'Exactly as I intimated in my letter: I will keep you abreast of the goings on in the Golden Dawn in London. I will tell you what Westcott is up to, how they attempt to thwart your takeover, and any other information you might request.'

'My takeover? When Woodman dies, I expect to be named the sole heir.'

'You might expect that, but most of your London membership have very different ideas.'

'Oh? For what reason?'

'Westcott's followers, and let's face it, most of the London members are, see you as a tyrant. A man who ignores the dangers of ritual as documented by Westcott in 1889. They believe you are a danger to yourself, those around you and the very world itself with your dogged determination to expand on Westcott's discoveries. They believe you have shunned Westcott through jealousy rather than ideology.'

The merest glimmer of a smile crossed Mathers' lips. As the light in the room darkened momentarily, his eyes smouldered with a dark blue pinprick of light which almost threw Charlie off his stride.

'I thank you for your candour, Bentwith. And what do you think of me?'

'I, I think it is Westcott who uses those around him. He

makes discoveries and then abandons those who aid him and limits those who might surpass him by trying to prevent other members from exercising those very same rituals. It seems to me to be counter-productive to the fundamental foundations upon which the Golden Dawn was built.'

That raised an eyebrow from Mathers.

'For the uninitiated, you seem to know a lot about the workings of my secret society.'

'Because your fellow founding member is more liberal with his knowledge. Especially with those who have already seen it all first-hand. Like me.'

'And he trusts you?' The question came after another thoughtful pause.

'I walked away after what they did to my wife. But I am beginning to rebuild trust again with Westcott. He needs me. I am the only other person in London not in an asylum, who can convince his peers about the dangers of what we saw.'

A light tap at the door was followed by a stern 'Come' from Mathers. Hans entered with a wheeled table full of dainty little dishes of food and a shining metal pot with steam swirling from its spout.

'Perhaps you would offer me an insight into the dangers you speak of over some supper,' Mathers said as Hans set up the table beside them.

X

'Despite my doubts, that was excellent,' Bentwith sighed as he dabbed at his mouth with a napkin.

'I find a vegan diet keeps me lean and alert and has only the slightest burden on my karma. Alcohol only serves to cloud the mind.'

Mathers slurped at his lemon tea. Since hearing Charlie's testimony over supper, he had mellowed significantly from the stiff-backed, suspicious man who had greeted Charlie at the train station.

'The only thing that worries me is making our relationship known to Westcott. I would prefer something a little more clandestine.'

'It is the only way he will not suspect anything. Any slip on my part and Westcott will be on it in a flash. By being open and making the occasional trip to Paris, I am confident he will believe me when I tell him I am travelling to keep *him* abreast of *your* plans. Of course, I will have to tell him most of the information I have, but I can be discreet with the subjects that matter. He will think I am working in his interests, when in fact I will be passing the real information to you.'

'It is a bold and insidious endeavour, Bentwith. If anything goes awry, it will be you who answers for it.'

'Then it is in my interests to make certain it does not go awry.'

'Very well. You shall stay tomorrow night as well and I will have you inducted into the order.'

'No, no, that will not do at all. That will raise suspicion. It is Westcott who must induct me. If he refuses, then I shall know he either doubts my loyalty or my ability to spy for him. It is the only way.'

Mathers shot Charlie a sly look which bordered on admiration.

'You really are an ambitious man, aren't you Bentwith?'

'Not at all. I am a simple, base, vengeful man, who has but one favour to ask.' Charlie replied flatly.

Mathers' surprise at that statement was plain to see.

'A favour you say. Why is it only now that you feel the necessity to request a favour?'

'Because it has taken this long to judge whether I should trust you or not.'

'Is that so.'

Charlie was relieved to see Mathers' thin smile was more bemused than upset.

'It is regarding a Dr Aeneas Jennings, currently Head of Psychological Medicine for the Criminally Insane at Bethlem Royal Hospital.'

'Ah! The penny drops. Your unfortunate wife in Bedlam. Very clever, Professor Bentwith. Get me on side, then submit the real price of your loyalty. What is it you ask?'

'That Jennings be held accountable for any harm which comes to my Connie. As he is clearly in your camp, I ask that you personally make him aware that he should not be part of her treatment. Also, Jennings must allow Westcott access to her. I hope that granting this favour will be the final cherry on the cake as far as proving to him that I am on his side, for the sake of my wife.'

A long pause followed. Charlie held his breath while the other man's eyes narrowed, staring at him intently. For his part, Charlie did his best to weather the storm with what he hoped was a look of stubborn defiance. Eventually, Mathers spoke.

'It is a small price, and one I can easily afford. We have an accord, Bentwith.'

XI

The return to London brought a much-welcomed change in temperature for Charlie after the muggy heat of Paris. The journey was an easy one, buoyed as he was by the outcome of his conversation with Samuel Mathers and the sense of purpose it brought for him. For the first time in months Charlie felt some pride at achieving something worthwhile on behalf of his cruelly incarcerated wife.

He was surprised at the amount of respect he suddenly had for Mathers, too. From the way Westcott had spoken, Charlie had assumed he was a crazy man, as deserving of a place in Bedlam as any of the current residents. Instead, Mathers had shown himself to be a thoughtful, calculating man, willing to barter and scheme for what he ultimately wanted: The Hermetic Order of the Golden Dawn and the power that came with it. It was a weakness that he might be able to exploit in the future.

When he arrived at Westcott's house near Regent's Park, even the brief rain shower as he stepped from the hansom cab could not dampen his spirits. Charlie was greeted promptly by Mrs Hodges and the three of them were soon sitting at the table with tea and cake to discuss his Parisian adventure.

'Other than his incessant need to conjure God-knows-what from God-knows-where, the fellow is actually quite pleasant,' Charlie stated between bites of currant bun after he had recounted his tale.'

'Indeed. A veritable charmer.' Was Westcott's arid response.

'Well, you went into business with him,' Charlie pressed.

'I set up a society to enable us to learn more about ourselves and the universe around us. It just happened to be with two mavericks if you will forgive the Americanism. In the Golden Dawn's short lifespan, it seems I have managed to experience far more than both Woodman and Mathers put together. Ironically, that is probably the sole reason why I am the sanest of the three of us.

'Does he still have that Kürnberg fellow following him around?'

'Hans? Oh yes. It will be Hans with whom I correspond.'

'I am surprised Mathers trusts anyone with that task, just in case he should miss any details,' interjected Mrs Hodges.

'I had the impression that correspondence was beneath him. He sees himself more as the thinker behind the scenes. The hand that rocks the cradle if you will.' Charlie accompanied his remark with a warm, crooked smile.

'You think it funny?' Westcott was suddenly terse.

'Not at all. I believe the pair of you are surprisingly similar. He is just a little colder in his thinking and a touch more suave in his delivery.'

As Charlie's grin broadened, Mrs Hodges hid behind a sip of tea. Westcott shifted irritably in his seat, then offered a robust response.

'This is not a game, Bentwith. The position you now find yourself in will make you responsible for people's lives, including your own. You cannot let your guard down because he will be watching. Do you think you are likely to be the only spy he has in London? One slip of the tongue, one throwaway comment, and you will risk discovering just how dangerous your suave new cradle rocker can be.'

'You think he has more spies than just me?' The notion that he might not be alone in his dealings with Mathers had never occurred to Charlie. It unnerved him more than he would care to admit.

'You've met him, what do you think?'

Charlie attempted to hide his consternation with a large bite of currant bun. The mouthful of deliciousness gave him just enough time to think and calm himself again before he replied.

'Surely he would have mentioned any allies?'

'Hmph! Of course not! He would rather keep you all on your toes, in the same way as I wouldn't tell you if I had others in Mathers' camp. He will be expecting the same information from each of you. It is how he will filter truth from mistruth.'

'Do you? Have others?'

'Why in the Devil's name would I go to all these lengths to talk you into it if I already had someone on the inside?' Westcott rolled his eyes in exasperation, uncaring of the fact he had instantly contradicted himself.

'Then how is any of this plan ever going to work, Westcott?' There was a desperation in Charlie's voice, but he was past caring.

'The trick will be camaraderie, Bentwith. Changing a one-way flow of information into a two-way conversation. Knowing what he wants from you is halfway to guessing what he is up to. Getting along well with von Kürnberg, or whomever else he trusts the task to in Paris, is a must. I will help you.'

'Then it is surely fortunate that most of our correspondence will be written.'

'It is. But he will summon you to Paris from time to time to ask you questions. To test you. Suspicion is in his nature. And I would not be surprised if he sends whichever lackey he uses for that correspondence to London from time to time as well.'

It was a sobering notion which put the three of them into a brief, thoughtful silence. It was Mrs Hodges who broke it.

'Perhaps it would lighten the mood if you told Charles about your success with Dr Jennings.'

'Ah! Yes. Excellent idea.' Westcott heaved himself from his seat, picked up his pipe and tobacco from the mantelpiece, then paced the room as he filled the bowl.

Charlie placed down his empty cup and looked up at Westcott expectantly. It was not long before his impatience overcame him.

'Well?'

'Yes. I have been speaking to Matthews. He has given me a signed letter until such time that Mathers's instructions filter through to Jennings.'

Westcott poked his pipe in the direction of an envelope on the mantelpiece.

'Matthews? What are you talking about? Who is Matthews?'

Westcott gave Charlie a long hard look as though he were being purposefully stupid.

'Henry Matthews, the Home Secretary,' Mrs Hodges explained quietly, accompanied by a smile which Charlie could not quite decide upon; was it pity or encouragement?

'Oh. Of course. Henry Matthews. Why on earth is he involved with Jennings and my Connie?'

Westcott huffed for effect.

'You are lucky that Matthews is sympathetic towards cases such as your wife's. That letter up there is an order to Jennings that, under threat of prosecution, he must allow you and I entry to Bethlem. From the time of its delivery, we are the only two men who are legally allowed to treat Constance.'

'What? How on earth did you manage that? Why would you include me?' Charlie sputtered over the words.

'You are her husband. I would like to think you will attend your wife at some point during her incarceration, despite your new responsibilities to Mr Mathers.'

Westcott's withering glare disappeared behind a cloud of pipe smoke.

'But the letter from Mathers. . . I thought that was going to do the job?' Charlie asked, confused.

'And I am sure it will. But I had no idea that you would be able to negotiate that. Don't act so hard done by, Bentwith. Think of this as my little insurance plan. In case Mathers' letter happens to go missing or never arrives. It seems we are not going to be able to get rid of Jennings in the short term, so applying pressure from a position of authority is the best we can do.'

'You don't trust me?' Charlies sounded wounded.

'Oh yes, I trust you implicitly Bentwith. But not Mathers. Sooner or later he will let you down and you will lose any trust you might have in him, too.'

Charlie considered it all for a moment, turning it over in his head. Finally, he seemed happy.

'When do you plan to deliver the Matthews letter?' He asked.

'This afternoon. No time to waste.'

'Well, bearing in mind Jennings is one of Mathers' men, I had better go and write my report of the event to Hans.' Charlie rose from his seat and prepared to leave.

'An excellent idea,' Westcott agreed as Mrs Hodges rose to see Charlie to the front door. Charlie had already turned to leave when Westcott called after him.

'Oh, and Bentwith?'

'Yes?' Charlie looked back.

'Be back here at eight o'clock sharp.'

'Whatever for?'

'Your investiture into the Golden Dawn. Can I interest you in a snifter of brandy to celebrate?' Westcott asked, pointing his pipe towards a decanter on the sideboard.

Charlie looked at the glass of dark liquid, his face a battleground between fear and longing. A moment passed before he answered.

'No, thank you Westcott.'

'Good man.' Westcott's eyes glittered with admiration.

XII

It had taken four of them to manhandle her onto the table and all six of them to finally strap her down following three blows with a heavy truncheon to stun her into submission. Constance reeled from the blows. As she fought to remain conscious, a voice from behind her said something. Sounds of movement were followed by the door clicking shut.

'Now, there was no need for all that bother, was there Mrs Bentwith? Hmm?'

Her vision swam, making Dr Jennings' eyes sparkle and dance as his silhouette leaned over her. Constance felt something touch the side of her head before Jennings lifted his fingers away, red with her blood.

'Tut, tut. There would have been no need for that if you had just cooperated.'

The same hand pushed her head back against the table. Something rough crossed her forehead, then pulled tightly, securing her head in place.

'Now, I know this is going to be hard for you, but I am afraid good therapy is always difficult. There can be no success without hardship.' She felt cold fingers against her throat. 'Can you hum for me, please?'

Puzzled, Constance could do little more than look up at the doctor. Her vision flickered between seeing double and general blurriness, despite her trying to blink away the giddying sensation.

'Hum, please. You're not trying.'

Nothing.

When Jennings took his hands away, her vision cleared momentarily. Instead of seeing a doctor upset at his patient's lack of cooperation, she thought she saw... Was that... glee?

Dr Jennings leaned over her again, holding open her eyelid as he examined her pupil. Unable to move her head, Constance strained against the heavy straps across her chest, wrists and legs. It was all to no avail.

'You may have a concussion which would make any further sedative dangerous. Therefore, I shall proceed to examine your larynx as intended, but without anaesthetic.'

The doctor disappeared from view. The sudden brightness that filled the space he had departed caused her to wince involuntarily. When he returned, a scalpel glinted in the blaring light.

XIII

'Foley? Let me in, please. I have a letter here signed by the Home Secretary himself.'

Albert Foley left his seat in the gatehouse and wandered over to where Westcott stood. He ignored the letter Westcott held towards him.

'I have strict instructions not to let you in I'm afraid, sir,' was his meek reply.

'Foley, take the letter and read it. Then please let me in, there's a good fellow.'

Foley took the letter and began to read, whispering to himself as he did so.

'Do you need me to read it for you?'

'I can read well enough, Dr Westcott,' came the reply, then more whispering.

Westcott's moustaches bristled, but he remained silent, patiently waiting for Bethlem's gatekeeper to finish his chore.

'And this is the Home Secker-tary's signature, is it?' Foley finally asked, the doubt clear in his voice.

'It is. Along with the crest of his office on headed paper. Now please let me in.'

'Hmm. It's all a bit irregular.'

'It is very irregular, I agree. I should never have been barred in the first place.'

'I don't want to lose my job over it.'

'Nobody is losing their job, Foley, I can assure you of that. It is there in black and white. I am to have access to Mrs Constance Bentwith for her continuing rehabilitation and psychological care. This letter absolves you of any wrong-doing, Foley.'

'Abs-what?' Foley rubbed his chin, uncertain.

'The letter overrides your employer. In a nutshell, this order from the Home Secretary of the British Empire is more important that any instruction given by Dr Jennings,' Westcott explained.

'Well, alright. I suppose it's not for me to stand in the way of the Home Secker-tary's wishes. But it's very irregular.'

Westcott tapped his foot as Foley wandered back into the gatehouse, then returned with the key. A quick turn of the lock and Foley pulled the gate open. Westcott stepped through, graciously thanked Foley, took back the letter, then headed up the gravel drive towards the entrance to Bethlem Royal Hospital, swinging his cane between steps.

As he entered the cool interior of the entrance hall, Westcott quickly looked for Stapleton at one of the desks.

'Ah! Stapleton. How are you?' Westcott greeted the man with a smile beneath his moustaches.

'I believe you're not supposed to be here, doctor,' Stapleton replied, confusion clear on his crinkled forehead.

'I wasn't. Now I am. A letter from the Home Secretary giving me access to Constance Bentwith.' Westcott waved the letter in the air with a flourish. 'Now will you sign me in please?'

'Certainly, doctor. Young Will is doing well. Back to cleaning machines in the cotton mill last week, he was.' Stapleton informed the doctor as he wrote in the visitor's book.

'That is excellent news. No more cholera in the block?'

'None since last I saw you, doctor. If you could sign here, please?'

The news put Westcott in a favourable mood. As soon as he had signed the book, he thanked Stapleton and skipped towards where Rasmussen was already unlocking the door.

'Thank you! Good to see you again Rasmussen,' Westcott said as he passed, acknowledging the "and you, sir" with a raise of his cane along the corridor beyond. In no time at all he was down the stairs and rapping the same cane against the entrance to the criminal wing.

Westcott wondered what Constance's reaction would be to him turning up unannounced after so many days. Would she be happy to see him? Angry at his absence? He doubted Jennings would have said anything about it. She probably felt abandoned, the poor woman. He was so wrapped up in his thoughts that when the viewing plate clanged open, it took him by surprise.

'Schultz! There you are. Would you kindly let me in please?'

'Doctor Westcott? I wasn't expecting you, sir.' Schultz glanced away, puzzled for a moment. 'Is Dr Jennings expecting you?'

'I very much doubt it. I have a letter here from Henry Matthews himself, the Home Secretary. I plan to present it to him.'

'Well, erm, I believe Dr Jennings is indisposed at the moment in his surgery.' Schultz sounded sheepish.

'With whom?' Westcott's demand was tinged with a large dollop of dread.

'With your Mrs Bentwith,' Schultz replied. 'It's just taken six of us to get her in there.'

'Good heavens! Let me in, now!'

Schultz was already rattling his keys without bothering to close the viewer. In seconds, Westcott was through, but Schultz wanted to lock the first door before opening the second into the day room.

''For God's sake, man, no time for that. Get it open!'

A flustered Schultz turned and slid the bolts.

XIV

The tumult from outside distracted Jennings.

'Weaver? What is going on out there?'

Weaver poked his head around the door to the corridor beyond for a few moments.

'Begging your pardon, doctor, but Dr Westcott 'as arrived and demands to see you immediately. Mullins is telling 'im you're indisposed.'

'Westcott? What in God's name is he doing here? He's barred from these premises! Wait here with Mrs Bentwith while I go sort it out, there's a good man.'

Jennings put the scalpel back on a nearby table and left. The noise from the corridor beyond became muffled as the door slammed closed, then was followed by the click of a lock as Weaver turned the key.

'Good afternoon, Mrs Bentwith. Constance. I don't believe you know me.'

Weaver sauntered into view. A pudgy-faced man with thick sideburns and a clean-shaven lip and chin. He disappeared behind her briefly, where she was unable to see him, then the table swung upwards to put her in a forty-five-degree seated position. The sudden movement made the room swim around her as her eyes struggled to adjust quickly enough.

'It looks like we 'ave a few moments alone before your Dr Westcott arrives. Oh, dear, you look puzzled, my dear. Let me introduce meself. My name is George. You see, you knew my wife, Flora. Flora Simpson. Ah! You recognise the name. I see it in your eyes. That's good. You see, Flora went missing while she was your 'ousemaid. You replaced her with a young Irish lady. When I asked 'er about it, she couldn't tell me nuffin. 'Owever, a few months ago, I received an anonymous letter with a Paris postmark.'

Simpson paused his speech as Constance wriggled against her bonds. His smile told her he was enjoying the show. He picked up the discarded scalpel, then continued.

'As you're a captive audience, let me give you the gist o' the letter.'

As he recited the letter, Weaver used his best, high class accent.

'I regret to give you this news in such a detached manner, but it has come to my attention that your unfortunate wife has been murdered. The culprit is, I believe, her employer, Mrs Constance Bentwith, who currently resides in Bedlam. Should you wish to learn more, or avenge yourself for her death, I suggest you contact my associate, Mr Francis Heathcote.

'Blah, blah, address, closing.

'It is a letter which gave me many a sleepless night, I can tell you. You see, I always assumed my Flora 'ad left me. Perhaps for a softer man, or even the bottom of a cup of gin. Yes, I put a roof over 'er 'ead, but I was never the best of 'usbands. Then this letter arrived, and everything changed. I decided to apply for a job 'ere under the name of John Weaver. I wanted to put a face to the name, you see. And what a pretty face it is. Is that Mediterranean colouring? Very exotic.

'It quickly became obvious that it would take someone with more cunning and under'andedness than me to do you in. So, I 'ired 'eathcote with the little money I 'ad saved. It turned out I was on duty on the day in question. When Mullins told me to 'elp 'im with a stretcher, I thought, this is it! I'll get to carry your murderous corpse out of 'ere. But no. There you were. Still walking around and breathing. Saved by that pompous old bastard out there. When I went to see 'eathcote in room 5, 'e wasn't there. I've 'eard no more from 'im, so maybe 'e's dead. Squirrelled away to Jennings' mortuary for dissection per'aps.

'I was wondering what to do after that. I was even thinking about forgetting the whole thing and leaving this 'orrible place, but then this opportunity falls in me lap and 'ere we are. God 'as sent me a window of opportunity, Mrs Bentwith.'

Simpson delivered the final sentence with a particular conviction. As he rotated the scalpel in his left hand and tested it's point with a fingertip, there was a banging at the door.

'Weaver? Let us in!' Westcott's voice.

Simpson glanced towards the locked door and smiled a sad smile.

'It doesn't look like God will keep the window open for very long, does it Mrs Bentwith?'

Constance tried to wriggle. She pulled against the restraints until her head pounded and her vision blurred yet again.

'Per'aps I'll see what's inside you, like the Ripper did to all those poor women.'

'Weaver? Unlock the door. Now!' Jennings this time. 'Schwarz, get the spare keys from my office!'

The door rattled on its hinges as someone flung himself into it.

Simpson, relishing the moment, placed the point of the blade against the hollow of Constance's throat, He tapped the cold metal against her skin, twisting the blade in his fingers while he searched for the fear in her eyes.

With a sudden snap, Constance broke the leather strap restraining her left arm. She grasped her assailant's wrist with lightning speed, reversed it with a loud *snap*, then plunged the scalpel into the man's own throat.

Simpson's triumphant eyes grew wide with shock. There was just enough time for a heartbeat before a spatter of blood hit her face. Still gripping the scalpel, Simpson tugged it from his own flesh to cause an arc of dark red blood to shoot across Constance and up the wall behind her.

Simpson stared at the wall. His brows knitted with puzzlement, a sure sign that he had not yet quite understood the magnitude of what had just happened.

A second surge of hot crimson liquid drenched Constance's dress and face.

Simpson's confused gaze meandered down from the wall to Constance. Despite the restraint around her head, she managed to catch his eyes with her own as she dipped two fingers of her free hand into the warm goodness trickling down her own throat. She took pleasure in the dying man's horror as she licked them clean.

Constance was so caught up in her victory that she was unsure whether Simpson collapsed before the door burst open, or whether it was the other way around. Westcott headed straight over to her, while Jennings made his way to the dying man on the floor.

'She has killed him!' Jennings was outraged.

'While strapped to an operating table?' Westcott rebuked him. 'Look, he's even holding the scalpel which killed him! As a coroner, I would argue it's a clear-cut case of suicide.'

Westcott ignored his poor choice of words as he began to free Constance from the straps which still held her. It was then that he noticed her left hand was free. He cast a querying glance at her, only to be met with a clandestine wink and a smile. With a look that could have killed, Westcott pulled a pocketknife from his jacket and made a motion as though he were cutting the left strap, then he cut the one holding her right wrist.

With the remaining orderlies in the room, standing around the fallen body of their colleague, Westcott had cut four straps before Jennings noticed.

'What in God's name do you think you're doing, Westcott?'

'The damnable straps are so tight I couldn't undo them. What were you thinking, strapping the poor woman to an operating table?'

'I-, I-,' Jennings stammered. His arms and trousers were thick with blood where he had been tending to the now-deceased Simpson.

Leaving Constance to unbuckle the final strap which secured her head, Westcott saw his opportunity.

'You were going to operate on her, weren't you? You bastard! How dare you?'

'Westcott, I- Why would Weaver commit suicide? It makes no sense,' Jennings continued.

'Working in a place like this with someone like you who operates on the people he's supposed to care for? It would be enough to drive anyone to despair!'

Westcott spat the words, unable to disguise his disdain for the other man. In a flash of rage, he was suddenly inches from Jennings's face, his finger raised in warning.

'If you come near this woman again, I will make it my personal duty to not only have you removed from this institution, but to have you struck off from practising in this country. Do you understand me, Jennings?'

Jennings stepped backwards away from Westcott's challenge. His bewilderment was plain to see, unable to understand how things had escalated so quickly. As Westcott turned back to Constance and helped her from the table, Jennings could only watch on in puzzlement and incredulity, surrounded by his equally shocked orderlies.

Back in her cell, Constance sat on the bed as Westcott paced around angrily.

'What the Devil did you think you were doing?' He demanded, struggling to keep his voice low so as not to be overheard. 'Why did you kill Weaver?'

It was not Weaver, Constance signed impassively. She looked like a picture of hell itself with her face dripping and dress spattered with blood.

'What are you talking about?'

It was George Simpson. He told me so. He was going to cut my throat, but I managed to break the strap and...

Constance shrugged and smiled awkwardly as a drop of red liquid fell from the end of her nose.

Westcott looked at her for a moment, as though weighing up the truth of the information. There were no indicators to say otherwise.

'And why were you on the table in the first place?'

I believe Dr Jennings was going to operate on my larynx in an attempt to make me speak. If you had not come when you did, it might be him lying dead.

'I still don't understand. How did George Simpson know that you killed his wife?' It is all very strange,' Westcott pondered. He absently pulled at his moustaches while he thought it through.

I can answer that. He told me. A letter postmarked from Paris.

Westcott's eyes widened at the revelation. Could it be that

word had gotten back to Mathers? An indiscretion over-heard by one of the members of the Golden Dawn? A spy he was unaware of? Or had Mathers used some other, more other-worldly means of discovering the secret? Either way, the thought disturbed him. Especially now that Bentwith was his double-agent. How would he react to the news? Badly, for sure. He would not be able to hide his anger from Mathers and the game would be up. Westcott would lose his spy almost before he had begun. He had to think quickly.

'Your husband cannot ever know about this,' Westcott stated coolly, eventually. 'Is that clear?'

My husband has not visited since I was incarcerated here. How would he find out?

Despite using hand signals, Constance managed to por-tray her bitterness in her expression.

'How indeed,' Westcott pondered, 'How indeed.'

When he was ready to leave, Westcott crossed the day room towards the exit. The death of George Simpson had solved one problem, but how had Mathers found out about the murder of Simpson's wife? Did he have access to a police theory, perhaps? Mathers was perfectly capable of linking the deaths which he knew Constance had committed with a missing person in her employ. But had Simpson even reported her missing? Was someone Westcott trusted in the Golden Dawn a spy for Mathers? That did not add up, because only the Kramers, the Bentwiths and Mrs Hodges knew about it. Mrs Hodges? No, her counsel was too astute for her to be a mole. Besides, he had known her long enough to trust her. She had even counselled against forg-ing the Golden Dawn with Woodman and Mathers years before. Had Mathers discovered the secret through a scrying technique, perhaps?

Deep in thought, it took a moment for him to notice the tug on his jacket. Turning abruptly, he looked down to see Jeanette smiling up at him.

'Do you have a new dolly to show me?' He asked her, his voice gentle but wary.

Jeanette smiled up at him as she brought her arm out from behind her back with a flourish. Upon her hand was an over-sized black puppet, with two crude button eyes sewn to the middle finger. The little finger and thumb waggled backwards and forwards, as though the puppet were clapping its hands.

Westcott offered an over-the-top show of delight which quickly turned into a frown.

'I say, is that my glove?' With hindsight, his words were more accusatory than he would have liked.

Jeanette nodded. Her grin broadened despite Westcott's tone.

'Here,' Westcott said, rummaging in his pockets, 'Perhaps he or she should have a friend.'

With that, he pulled the remaining odd glove from his pocket and gave it to the beaming girl.

XV

The man who sat on the wooden throne was short and barrel-chested beneath a thick red cloak. Long black hair was kept neatly in place by a tall red hat brimmed with pearls beneath a gold star and feather on the front. A long, aquiline nose parted two large, wide eyes and ended above thick, well-groomed moustaches. The top lip was invisible beneath the whiskers, but the bottom lip protruded unnaturally from beneath, as though the jaw was undershot. The face was narrow; high cheek bones gave way to sunken cheeks beneath the whiskers. There was an aura about him, an earthy magnetic charisma that belied his nobility and attracted her interest from her perch high in the rafters of the banqueting hall.

The man sat at the head of a long table. Virtually every inch of the table was filled with plates of meat, vegetables, fruit, carafes of wine, goblets and plates. A younger, blonde-haired woman sat to his left. Beyond them, the hall was filled with richly dressed men, women and children, each flaunting expensive furs and silver jewellery. They laughed and gorged themselves heartily, all while the thin-faced man at the head of the table watched them with a smouldering intensity.

After several minutes, the man stood. Silence instantly fell upon the hall.

'You, my boyars, are the nobility of Wallachia,' the man stated, his voice strong and fearless.

Some of the banqueters cheered and banged their goblets against the table in applause.

'The prosperity of our motherland fills your pockets with silver. It gives you plentiful food and wine for your tables and servants to wait upon you. Prosperity makes you flabby and shy of work, while the common man fills your coffers with taxes to the point where he can no longer afford to eat.

'But that is not why I invited you here today, to feast under my roof. I invited you today, because none of you lifted a finger when my father, Vlad, was betrayed and beheaded, or when my brother, Mircea, was buried alive. Indeed, some of you even lent their hands to the task, to save your own skins. Is this the definition of nobility?'

A low murmur rippled through the crowd. A couple with their son rose to leave, only to be met at the door by guards who forced them back. Others turned a deathly white. One, already drunk, cheered and heckled from the back of the hall.

'Today, we will put everything to rights, my boyars. Today, you will make your amends to the people of Wallachia and for your treatment of my family.'

As the man spoke, she swooped down from her perch in the rafters, gliding towards him, into him, filling every finger and toe as though wearing him like a glove. Her voice sounded alien and strange as she spoke the next words; her first words for how long? She could not remember.

'Guards! Take the infirm and the infants to the dungeon. Herd the rest outside. They will see the world from high upon a stake before the sun goes down.'

The room erupted into screams as guards entered from every door. Men tried hiding under the tables, women fell to their knees to beg for their lives, infants were torn from their mothers' arms and carried off. All the while, she stood there, relishing the pandemonium she had unleashed around her. When most had finally been dragged away, she turned to the woman who sat impassively beside her. Her skin was pale, her eyes wide. She took the woman's icy hand in her own.

'Come, my love. Let us take our supper outside and dine beneath the screams of the impaled.'

Constance opened her eyes. The dark shadow of Natharlep sat at the end of her bed, emotionless as always. She held his gaze for as long as she could, returning his emotionless stare with her own defiant one until her eyes became watery and she was forced to blink. With that, the vision was gone.

A key turned in her cell door. As it swung open, another dark shadow stood in the gloom of its frame. She watched intently as the shadow entered, the changing light transforming the dark shape into the outline of a man.

'Connie?'

She knew the voice immediately.

Without a moment of hesitation, she leapt from the bed and flung herself at her husband. Clutching her tightly he lifted her from the floor, swinging her around as she breathed in his scent.

'I am sorry, my love,' he whispered eventually, his voice close to her ear and cracked with emotion. 'I promise, I will never leave you alone again.'

With that, their lips locked in a passionate kiss.

The Gentleman Volunteers

2 a.m. to 6 a.m.: The Duke of Wellington is staying at an inn in Waterloo, a town in the United Kingdom of the Netherlands near the French border. He wakes early to write letters and orders, and receives confirmation that the Prussian army, under the command of Field Marshal Blücher, will march to reinforce the Allied position today.

'Ah! Lord Grenville's fat nephew. I'm glad you're here, I have a job for you.'

Sir Arthur Wellesley, Duke of Wellington, barely even glanced up from his desk as he spoke.

'Sir Arthur,' Richard Temple-Nugent-Brydges-Chandos-Grenville, the 2nd Marquess of Buckingham replied warily. He was as yet unsure which part of the duke's greeting he should give prominence to: the slight, or the pleasure of his presence.

Half dressed in only a white shirt and his military trousers and boots, Wellington sat stiff-backed as he continued writing at a furious pace before finally placing down his pen and using a blotter. He just about managed to waggle a finger at a chair on the other side of his desk as he folded the letter and passed it to a courier.

'To Parliament. Make haste, I want it to arrive before the House sits tomorrow morning.' Wellington's voice was soft, calm, yet full of authority.

'Yes Your Grace!' The courier briefly bowed his head and left the room, off to find a horse to take him to the docks at Ostend.

Buckingham sat where he had been told, the chair creaking beneath his weight. Wellington took another piece of paper from a pile, dipped his pen, then began to write again as he spoke.

'The problem with commanding armies, Buckingham, is the paperwork.'

'The rest is easy?' Buckingham quipped nervously with a smile.

Wellington paused to glance up at him, his face solemn.

'Oh no. Never easy, dear fellow. One is sending men to their deaths. I just happen to have a distaste for the paperwork.'

'Buckingham wanted to squirm, but the legs on his chair did not feel safe so he decided to remain still.

'You asked for me,' he said instead. The quicker the duke got to the point, the quicker he could leave the discomfort of this whole situation. Besides, since the courier left, he had it in mind to get himself on the same ship back to England. Just in case Napoleon won.

'Thank you for coming. I have a job for you Buckingham.' Wellington continued to write as he spoke.

'A job? Oh no, I'm not a soldier, sir. The only reason I am here is because I cut short my travels in Prussia for fear of war. I'm in Waterloo by pure circumstance as I am staying at an inn just up the road before heading to Ostend and home. You just happened to retreat your army to the same damned place.'

Buckingham was gravely aware how much like an outburst that had sounded. He flushed crimson when Wellington paused his writing for a second time to look at him.

'And what a happy circumstance it has been,' Wellington smiled. 'Now, I must press you on behalf of King and Country.'

'No!' Buckingham blurted the word, as his nerves almost sent him tumbling from his rickety chair.

For the first time, a flash of irritation crossed Wellington's face. He placed down his pen and clasped his fingers.

'Buckingham, the circumstances of our meeting are not an issue here. In trying times such as these, I make it my business to find out who the guests might be in any town, village or hamlet where I spend the night. Imagine my surprise at the happy coincidence that someone of your pedigree happened to be staying less than half a mile away. Now that you are here, King George, parliament and I require your services. Please.'

Wellington followed up with a terse smile.

'But I am not a soldier,' Buckingham repeated, trying hard to keep an even tone.

'You were once Paymaster of the Forces. That's close enough,' Wellington countered.

'But, but-'

'I have not even told you the reason why your services are required.'

There was a brief pause. Wellington smiled kindly at Buckingham who frowned back warily.

'You're not going to make me fight in the battle?'

'Oh, good lord, no. It would be a complete waste of your talents. Besides, I have officers and soldiers aplenty.'

Buckingham relaxed slightly at that. His audible sigh of relief allowed his shoulders to slump and his belly to test the stitching in his cummerbund. However, when he rubbed a hand down his rosy cheeks, his fingers came away moist with perspiration.

'Well, that's a relief. Do you need me to carry correspondence back to London, perhaps?'

'No, I have plenty of couriers who can take to the saddle faster than you, dear fellow. This task is something more. . . Clandestine.'

'That sounds dangerous.'

'I can spare no-one else.'

'I really don't think-'

'You would be suitably rewarded.'

'With. . .?'

'You are a marquess. A title not really befitting your estate at Stowe. How does the title Duke of Buckingham sound?'

'How, what?' Buckingham was suddenly confused.

'If you complete the task I require of you, you will offer us the opportunity of winning today's battle and thereby put an end to war in Europe for many years to come. I will not only see it as a personal favour to me, but I will also lobby the King to grant you a more esteemed title.'

'And what is it you actually require of me?' Buckingham was suspicious.

'I need you to circumvent the French army to a little inn just to their south, named La Maison du Roi. There, you will find a book which I would very much like you to bring me, please.'

'A book? You want me to risk my life travelling through territory crawling with French soldiers for a book?'

Wellington held up his hands.

'Please, Buckingham, let's not be dramatic. The French soldiers will all be on the battlefield to the north, trying to kill me. Besides, you will not be alone.'

'I won't?' Buckingham's jowls shook with consternation, despite the apparent good news.

'Of course not. You will have a troop of my gentleman volunteers with you.'

Buckingham's face turned from angry red to pasty white within a heartbeat. Wellington's gentleman volunteers were known by hearsay only. There had been rumours about them for several years; a troop made up entirely by men of privilege whom Wellington had saved from disgrace and taken under his wing for only the most secretive – or dangerous, depending on who told the tale – of missions. The rumour went that Wellington was ruthless in his selection. Only those men who knew how to fight and could compliment the group were invited to join.

'Gentleman volunteers?' Buckingham's voice was suddenly high-pitched and stringy. He quickly cleared his throat.

'Uxbridge!' Wellington shouted.

Buckingham jumped in his seat, causing the chair legs to creak yet again. A heartbeat later, there was a rap at the door and the Duke of Uxbridge entered.

'Good morning, sir.' Uxbridge's greeting was surprisingly warm, but a glance towards Buckingham caused the edge of his nose to crease in disdain.

'Good morning, Uxbridge. Would you be a sport and send in the volunteers, please?'

'Uxbridge gave a brief nod of the head, then left immediately to the sound of Wellington's thanks.

'If, if you have the volunteers here with you, why on God's green earth do you need me to go?'

Wellington's eyes seemed to pierce straight through Buckingham as he smiled a kindly smile.

'How the Devil did you ever manage a life in politics, hmm? My gentlemen volunteers are a myth. An enigma for the enemy to talk about around their campfires, for French soldiers to fear. If they complete this mission, who should I say has managed the task? Knowledge of a clandestine fighting force will cause outrage at home, and I certainly don't want the enemy to stop fearing them if they fail. Therefore, succeed or fail, I need a name. That name shall be yours, Buckingham. If you succeed, Britain will acknowledge your success by your elevation to a dukedom.'

'And if I fail?'

'Then the unfortunate second Marquess of Buckingham will have been caught in the crossfire, bravely deciding to fight for his country on his return home from Prussia.'

Buckingham was finally coming to the realisation that Wellington was giving him little choice. With a knot of dread in the pit of his stomach, he decided to ask one last question.

'And, if I refuse to go?'

'Then the unfortunate second Marquess of Buckingham will have been caught in the crossfire, bravely deciding to fight for his country on his return home from Prussia.'

Wellington's repeated words came with a wry smile which paled into insignificance for Buckingham. All he could see was the cold, detached determination in the duke's eyes. The eyes of a man who had sent many thousands of soldiers to their deaths in the wars preceding this one.

Buckingham's thoughts were shattered as the door opened again. Uxbridge strode into the room, followed by nine men in uniform.

'Volunteers, two ranks, attention!' Uxbridge barked.

The men immediately formed two lines in the cramped quarters, stiff-backed, boots together, arms by their sides. They were resplendent in the uniform of the French chasseurs, Napoleon's light infantry, with a shako cap neatly balanced on their heads.

'Thank you, Uxbridge, that will be all.'

Wellington finally rose from his seat and beckoned Buckingham to do the same.

'Allow me to introduce you,' Wellington continued as they approached the men. 'This is Viscount Rothgar. He commands this merry little band when they are in the field. He has survived six duels, the last of which was illegal and took the life of a cousin of Pitt the Younger. Imagine his chagrin when Rothgar here disappeared without a trace.

'Next, we have Edward, the former heir to the Egret family estate. Unfortunately, he suffers from a malady which causes monstrous urges and is wanted for murder in four counties. You are only looking to murder Frenchmen today, Egret, is that clear?'

'As glass, Your Grace!' Egret replied immediately, his tone seemingly eager for the opportunity.

'Third, Sir Geoffrey Scott-Mansfield. A nasty piece of work. Do you remember that furore that caused such a scandal at the debutante ball a couple of years back?'

'I do,' Buckingham replied warily, staring at Sir Geoffrey with wide eyes.

'Sir Geoffrey here was the cause of it. I believe he is wanted by the fathers of at least four of the young debutantes with a view to fulfilling his obligations.

'Beside Sir Geoffrey is his twin sister, Lady Jane Scott-Mansfield. You will never see anyone shoot a rifle more accurately than Jane. Her reactions are second to none. I once saw her dodge a musket ball which hit the fellow standing behind her.

'Lastly, the bear of a man beside her is the late Baron Seaford, affectionately known as Baron Black. He has suffered four mortal wounds in his time, yet here he is to tell the tale.

'In the back row, we have the first of our George's, George Deed. Not gentry, but his ability to track a man is beyond compare. He tracked his wife's murderer for six days through rain, forest and across three rivers before strangling him to death. I saved him from the hangman's noose.

'Beside Deed, we have our second George. Do not let appearances fool you. He may appear weak and sickly, but Sir George Rutherford is a master of the occult and my direct report from the volunteers. He is the man we must thank for locating the book you will steal for me.

'Then, the fellow with the scars, we have our third George, George Saunders. As the last man to join our little troop he is affectionately known as George the Third.'

'But the man is clearly blind, Wellington,' Buckingham interrupted, aghast.

'He is. Blinded by shrapnel whilst fighting under my command at Vitoria. Show him George.'

George the Third took a brass implement from a hard leather case on his belt. He attached it to his head like an eye patch, by a leather strap with a buckle, so that the brass contraption covered his right eye. It began to move immediately, ticking and whirring with the sound of internal cogs and levers.

'The eye piece allows him to see at range. I would put money on him hitting anything with a rifle at two hundred paces.'

'But how on earth does that contraption work?' Buckingham asked, leaning in to look at the strange gadget.

'As I said, Rutherford is a master of the occult. I am certain, if you find the time and he has the inclination on this little mission, he will be happy to inform you.

'Now, you need to be careful what you say to the next man, Viscount Drummington. He may appear diminutive but looks can be deceiving. He has a horrid temper which is perfectly aligned with his loathing of all things French when they killed all three of his sons at Salamanca in 1812. That same day, I saw him beat six French infantrymen to death with the broken handle of a cavalry sabre. As you can see, he carries the repaired weapon with him. Drummington, I have been meaning to ask you whether it reminds you of your dead kin, or how much you detest Frenchmen. Which is it?'

'With respect, neither Your Grace. It's just a bloody heavy sword which serves to kill anyone who gets close enough.'

The answer amused Wellington as much as it horrified Buckingham.

'Excellent. I hope it is as successful in its duty today as it has always been.'

'Thank you, Your Grace.'

Buckingham rubbed at his eyes as though he could wake himself from a nightmare.

'Nine of them? You're sending nine men to find a book?'

'Nine men and one woman, Buckingham. You forget to include yourself.'

The jest was not lost on the gentleman volunteers, who smirked appreciatively.

'What is this book which is so important to you?'

As soon as Buckingham asked the question, the smiles faded from the volunteers' faces. Wellington clasped his hands behind his back and took on a grave demeanour.

'It will, I believe, be the difference between the allies winning the battle today and creating a new peace in Europe, or continued war with the Emperor on the French throne. Rutherford, perhaps you are best placed for an explanation?'

A sudden gloom settled over the room, as though the candles had all dimmed at the same time. A whistle of wind caused Buckingham to shiver involuntarily as Rutherford's piercing eyes peered at him grimly from the darkness beneath the peak of his shako, two red pinpricks of light just visible amidst the deep shadows of his sockets.

'The book is near mythical in nature. One of seven diabolic tomes, the Septem Voluminibus Diabolica. No one knows its true age. Some believe it was the first of the seven to be written, in the time of the great John Dee. Others that it was the last, perhaps fifty years or more after his death.

'It is a mighty tome. Over twelve inches in height, it is bound in human skin. The title was branded upon it whilst the donor still lived. In Latin it reads: Sabbatum: Foedus per Rituale, Rituale per Dominium, Dominium per Foedus. Covenant Through Ritual, Ritual Through Dominion, Dominion Through Covenant.

'The content is said to be painstakingly illuminated. It offers the user a means to strike a bargain with the Devil. Legend says that for the Devil to listen, the bargain must be sufficiently ambitious; world-changing to such a degree that it will pique the interest of His diabolic mind. If it is not, the stories say He will immediately take the celebrant's soul to hell and eternal damnation.'

There was a long silence when Rutherford finished his description. The light in the room seemed to wane further still before a warm breeze lifted the flickering flames from their wicks and the shadows were once again pressed back to the corners of the room.

'Yes. Well. That is quite the tale. And you believe him, Your Grace?'

'I do, Buckingham. Indeed, I do. We have reason to believe that Bonaparte has been in possession of the book for some years and that his spies reacquainted him with it on Elba. In just four months, he has escaped his exile and built an army of well over 100,000 infantry, cavalry, and guns. If he wins today, he will not stop south of Brussels. We will be looking at the dawn of a new French Empire with Bonaparte at its head. He will look to conquer Europe all over again.'

A restless silence fell on the room as each person contemplated that thought. It was Buckingham who broke the silence.

'No room for failure then,' he commented, his voice solemn.

'None at all,' Wellington confirmed with a half-smile which bordered on apologetic.

'A dukedom, you say?' Buckingham weighed up the offer.

'I did. I will set the wheels in motion if you are successful, and assuming we all survive today's encounter.'

'I will do it. For king and country. But first, there is one thing I will require,'

Buckingham linked his hands behind his back as he looked at the troop of volunteers. The stance caused his bloated abdomen to strain against his cummerbund once again.

Wellington was clearly surprised by the affront.

'Really? A favour? What might that be?' He asked cautiously.

'Breakfast, Your Grace. I will need breakfast.'

6 a.m.: To disguise his strength, Wellington deploys his army behind a long ridge on the Mont-Saint-Jean escarpment, to the south of Waterloo. To his south are the farms of Hougoumont on his right and La Haye Sainte at his centre. Emperor Napoleon Bonaparte deploys the French army on a slope south of these landmarks. The ground is not good for battle; thick mud made worse by constant rain.

Well breakfasted, kitted with the uniform of an officer of the chasseurs along with two pistols, shot and powder,

Buckingham was finally ready to leave. The uniform was decidedly ill-fitting, tight under the arms, far too small about the waist. Even the trousers had needed to be refashioned to fit him. By good fortune General Picton, one of Wellington's officers, had a dress tailor on site to make adjustments to his dress coat. "If I am to meet my maker today, I shall do so while looking my best," Picton had commented while graciously allowing Buckingham to commandeer the man.

While the alterations were made, Buckingham and Rothgar were briefed by Wellington and Uxbridge. The distance to La Maison du Roi was approximately five miles. He had wanted to make the journey on horseback, but Wellington had denied him "You are disguised as French light infantry. How would you begin to explain yourself on horseback?" He had asked, incredulous. Buckingham had begun to argue until Rothgar pointed out that it would be much easier for the French to spot someone on horseback. Finally seeing common sense, the argument had ended there and then.

When Buckingham finally accepted that the tailor could do no more with his uniform, he reluctantly left the inn to meet the volunteers in a barn near the outskirts of Waterloo. Rothgar had already been gone half an hour. The rain was so heavy that he was wet through in minutes as he trudged along the puddle-strewn road. Rain dripped from the brim of his shako and one of his boots was already full of water. He was well-aware he looked a miserable sight.

The volunteers were seated on rough hay bales, but at least it was dry. Rutherford and Drummington casually looked over at him. George the Third and George Deed appeared to be fast asleep.

'I say, shouldn't you stand to attention when an officer enters?' Buckingham was aggrieved at the slight.

He almost jumped out of his skin when a voice beside him answered:

'What exactly is your rank?' It was Rothgar's calm voice.

'My rank is unimportant. Wellington has put me in charge!'

No. His Grace put you here as his lackey, to take the credit we cannot in event of our success. I do not remember him saying that you were "in charge".

'The impertinence!' Buckingham was reddening already, completely flustered.

'You keep up with us, and hopefully you won't get killed. You do as I say, and hopefully you won't get killed. You do anything to put the mission in peril, and. . . Egret?'

Rothgar pointed to Edward Egret. Buckingham turned to look.

'We will make sure you get killed,' Egret responded, amused.

'Exactly that. Now, do you have any questions, Buckingham?' Rothgar's smile was deceptively charming.

Buckingham flushed crimson. This deal was becoming worse by the moment, and he knew he only had himself to blame. Wellington had known exactly how to play him: a title. It had been impossible to resist. At Stowe, he had an estate that was the envy of Britain. He had married money, but a further rise in fortunes would bring the financial stability he craved and social recognition enjoyed by his forebears. Inevitably, as always when placed in a difficult position, Buckingham decided to decline to answer Rothgar's question rather than suffer further ridicule.

The rain had eased by the time the little troop were ready to leave. They formed five ranks of two and, despite Buckingham's wish to be at the front with Viscount Rothgar, he was overruled in favour of the lean and tacit George

Deed. "We need to make sure we know where we are going", Rothgar explained, "And the only volunteer I trust with that is Deed." Instead, Buckingham trudged along in the middle beside Sir George Rutherford.

As they headed out of the little town, Buckingham was surprised that ten French infantry were virtually ignored amongst the throngs of British and Dutch officers going about their own business. Once beyond the outskirts, George Deed left the little group, jogging off ahead before ducking through some brush and out of sight, presumably on a scouting mission.

As his fear of being challenged by allied soldiers subsided, Buckingham took the time to weigh up his marching companion. Rutherford was around fifty years of age, he guessed. Iron-grey hair topped a deeply wrinkled face and as soon as they were outside the town's boundary, he slipped a long, thin pipe into the corner of his lips. His eyes were alert, but the man looked tired. Not just fatigued, but tired to the point where the weight of the world might have been on his shoulders. Buckingham decided to try his luck at conversation.

'So, George's eyepiece. How does it work?' The effort of speech made Buckingham realise he was already puffing hard with the march.

'You would doubtless not understand,' came the terse reply.

'Try me,' Buckingham insisted.

'Alright. The apparatus was built by Justus Hespe, a German watchmaker and inventor of mechanical devices. The glass lenses were manufactured by none other than the great William Parker, with his own fair hands. Inside the apparatus is a tiny prison made of glass.'

'You mean a prism?' Buckingham interrupted, proud that something from his schooldays had stuck with him.

'No,' Rutherford replied patiently, 'I mean a prison. It was I who summoned the otherworldly creature which resides in that prison. The creature reads George's thoughts, triggering the mechanics of the device accordingly. If George wishes to see something a mile away, the creature will spark the cogs which will align the lenses to set the magnification.'

Buckingham was confused.

'But that doesn't change the fact that the man is blind,' he pointed out.

Rutherford looked over at him as though he were foolish.

'The visions are relayed back in the same way. Through the mind of the creature and transferred into George's thoughts.'

'Oh. I see. I think. Very clever. Will it work for anyone?'

'It is only attuned to George.'

'Of course.'

While Rutherford was being talkative, Buckingham decided to press the conversation.

'Who taught you all these things?'

'My mother had some skill, but she died when I was young. I am mostly self-taught.'

'Is that so? Wellington did not mention how you came to be a member of his gentleman volunteers.'

'He did not.' Rutherford's demeanour was beginning to change with the more personal questions.

'It is going to be a long march. Would you care to share the tale?'

Rutherford stared at Buckingham for a few moments, his face impassive.

'I am certain His Grace would prefer his secrets to be kept secret, rather than spoken to anyone with the impertinence to ask.'

Buckingham did not reply. Partly due to Rutherford's words, but partly because he wanted to hide his breathlessness from the other man. His boots were heavy with caked mud already. The musket he carried pulled and rubbed at his shoulder. His coat chafed his arms, and he could feel trickles of perspiration running down his back. He wondered in that moment whether he had ever been more uncomfortable.

It was only a few minutes later that Buckingham heard the sound of marching feet carried on the wind from somewhere behind a line of poplar trees. Out of breath and desperately looking for a reason to rest, Buckingham spoke up.

'Rothgar? Viscount Rothgar?'

As the little column paused, Sir Geoffrey Scott-Mansfield spun round, a finger to his lips.

'Shh! Those are French soldiers you hear beyond the trees. What do you think they will do if they hear an Englishman over here?'

'Y-You will have to shoot them?' Buckingham stammered.

'Before the battle? It will attract the entire army!'

By now, Rothgar had turned to join them.

'What on earth do you want, Buckingham?'

'I- I just need a short rest. To empty a stone from my boot.'

Rothgar looked him up and down, his face a mask of disdain.

'What on earth has Wellington given us? We have barely marched a mile, and unless we are quiet, keep ourselves to ourselves and keep moving, we are likely to be caught by any one of the seventy-thousand men or more who are preparing for war somewhere beyond those trees.'

Rothgar flung out an arm towards the line of poplars just in case Buckingham hadn't noticed them.

'Now, you will only speak with your voice low. If you see a Frenchman, you will be quiet. Under both circumstances, you will continue to march unless I give the order otherwise.'

Rothgar turned back towards his place at the front, paused, then spoke to Buckingham again.

'Remember Buckingham, you do not need to survive this mission. You can still take the credit for it if you are dead.'

With that, Viscount Rothgar stalked off, making Buckingham's misery almost complete.

7 a.m.: Napoleon attends breakfast with his officers at a house named Le Caillou. To raise morale amongst the officers he tells them that Wellington is a bad general, with bad troops, and that the whole affair of the day's battle will be no harder than eating breakfast.

By the time Rothgar did finally call a halt, Buckingham all but collapsed onto a nearby tree stump.

'Are. . . Are we nearly there?' He asked no-one in particular.

No-one answered.

George Deed had returned, and he and Rothgar stood aside from the others to consult a map, which Rothgar had pulled from somewhere inside his coat.

Buckingham opened a water canteen and sipped from it as he took in his surroundings. They had been walking through farmland, shadowing two rows of poplar trees which he assumed lined a road. They had turned due south some way back. The Scott-Mansfield siblings took up lookout positions with rifle and musket close to a nearby hedge. The rest of them sat or crouched on their haunches, silent and warily watchful. On a brighter note, the clouds did not look like there was any more rain left in them, though the ground was soft and full of puddles.

'Can I interest you in a pinch of snuff?' The voice was gravelly and a welcome respite from Buckingham's own thoughts.

'Thank you, that would be wonderful,' Buckingham replied, turning to see Baron Black offering a tin which looked tiny in his fleshy fist.

Taking a pinch of snuff, Buckingham snorted it up his nostril, closed one eye, then sneezed violently. As seven pairs of eyes turned to glare, Baron Black sniffed his own pinch of snuff and put the tin back into his pocket.

'Not a snuff user, hmm?' He commented, not without sympathy.

'From time to time, but that is a particularly potent blend,' Buckingham replied.

'I know. Lord Ponsonby gave it to me. Apparently, he inherited a mountain of the stuff. Not the best, but it clears the airways though.'

'It certainly does that.' Buckingham continued to play with his nose to prevent a second sneeze.

Baron Black dropped to his haunches beside Buckingham and looked at him with interest.

'I visited your ancestral home once you know.'

'Really? Stowe? How so?'

'I was invited by your father to one of his parties. Wonderful gardens. I particularly enjoyed the Gothic Temple. Such an unusual building. I remember thinking it was a mausoleum, and how much I should like to be buried in such a wondrous place.'

'From what Wellington said, it sounds like that should have happened years ago. May I enquire into the story?'

The baron looked at Buckingham for a moment, perhaps weighing up whether he had an actual interest.

'My first injury was a sword through the guts during a duel over a girl. The doctors poked the insides back in, stitched me up and told the local priest to give me the last rites. A fever set in, and I remember very little after that.

Just snippets. I remember my mother and two other women standing over me, hands clasped, whispering a prayer under their breaths. I recall an altercation with the priest. When I awoke, I had a livid scar.

'The second came in the Dutch disaster of 1795. We were on the retreat, half-starved and facing freezing conditions. Some of us were ordered to go house to house to look for food. In one little cottage, the owner had died in their chair, but their dog was still ravenous. It flew at me. I raised my arm to defend myself, but it caught hold of my forearm and nicked the artery. I was saved by a hasty tourniquet and –'

'That's enough chitter-chatter. Gather round.' Rothgar's voice was low but cut through the air like a knife. The little band gathered in a circle.

The Viscount used a stick to make various marks in a flat patch of mud, then addressed the troop, pointing with the stick as he did so.

'We are here. The French army is about half a mile to the east, over here. Our goal, La Maison du Roi, is another two miles to the south, here. Now, the ground is still sodden and Deed believes it will be too wet for cavalry or artillery for a few hours yet, so if we are going to go in under the cover of battle, we will need to be patient.'

'The cover of battle? Surely we want to avoid that if we can. Don't we?' The idea alarmed Buckingham and he did not care who knew it.

Rothgar looked at him with pity.

'The sound of battle will disguise our presence. If we do not use the cover of battle, any use of firearms will be heard from a mile away and Boney will be sure to send a relief force to see what's happening to his book.

'Now, Deed has found a shepherd's hut here, a half a mile from the inn. We will wait here for the battle to begin. The inn is within sight of the hut, so it will also serve us well to observe and get a better idea of what we're up against. Any questions?'

Rothgar looked around the group as each shook their head, no. All except for Buckingham.

'Won't that be dangerous? If we can see the inn, the inn can see us, can it not?'

It was Rutherford who answered.

'We have the advantage in a number of ways. They will not be expecting any attempt as they are entirely unaware of our knowledge of the book. Also, we are dressed as French chasseurs. If we are seen, they are likely to consider us an added protection placed by Napoleon.'

'But –'

'In times of war, there is always risk. Marquess.' Rutherford's emphasis on Buckingham's title was not lost on him.

As Buckingham looked around the group, he could see a sense of expectancy. Waiting for him to ask more questions, to disagree with the plan. Edward Egret in particular had a stormy look about him, as though willing Buckingham to say more. As always, Buckingham looked away, sighed inwardly, and gave no further comment.

9 a.m.: Napoleon is forced to delay his attack due to the wet ground. His chief engineer reconnoitres Wellington's defences, while Wellington uses the time to tinker with his defence of Hougoumont. Knowing that Blücher is on the way, Wellington is happy to wait. Napoleon, by contrast, is eager to engage battle before Blücher arrives.

Buckingham felt very exposed in the little shepherd's hut. It was a single room stone building with a broken tiled roof.

The place had been ransacked. By the look of the footprints in the mud outside, it might have been the whole French army.

George Deed and Lady Jane Scott-Mansfield took the watch, though Rothgar, George the Third and Rutherford often joined them for short periods. They had taken bricks from a nearby dry-stone wall to sit on, just to keep out of the mud and puddles. Buckingham sat at the back of the hut, where the air was still and there was less water on the ground. He found that the water made his feet cold, even through his boots.

Most of the little band kept themselves to themselves. Only Egret and Drummington engaged in whispered conversation, boasting to each other about how many Frenchmen they were going to kill.

But even Buckingham could see why Deed had suggested waiting here. Although a half mile away, La Maison du Roi was visible behind the hedgerow which lined the road it sat upon. Its angle to the hut gave them as good a view as they could hope for of the layout. Two storeys, constructed from stone with a neatly tiled roof, it was not a hovel the likes of which they sat in now. A high stone wall surrounded the building with a courtyard to the rear and an angled thatch roof for the stables at the back of the courtyard. Other than the front door to the inn, the only other entrance appeared to be a double gate to the courtyard. There was no thatch to burn on the main building, the walls were too high to scale without assisting each other, and the windows were shuttered. Napoleon had chosen his hiding place wisely.

As the morning wore on, the clouds began to thin and the sun poked though. Before long, Buckingham had found a new spot on the south side of the little hut, out of sight of the inn. He knew there was a risk of being seen, but in his mind that was far outweighed by the chance to dry his clothes in the hazy sun's warmth.

The longer they waited, the more time seemed to drag. The occasional pop of a musket in the distance made Buckingham's heart jump more than once. Had the battle started? Were they going in? Each time, it was an isolated shot. "Hunting rabbits," or "some green idiot has dropped his weapon," Baron Black would mutter each time with a grin of amusement, "Either way, it's another round our boys won't have to face."

Buckingham was leaning back against the wall of the hut with his eyes closed when he heard a scurry of activity.

'Everyone, back inside. Now!' Rothgar's voice was a harsh whisper.

'What's happening?' Buckingham hissed to no-one in particular.

'Two men have exited through the gate,' George the Third replied, 'Taken the road north-east at a canter.'

'Surely that's a good thing? Two less guards,' Buckingham replied.

'Possibly,' came the uncertain reply.

'Were they carrying anything that could have been the book?' Rutherford asked.

'I don't think so,' George answered, his eyepiece whirring as it elongated slightly. There was no uncertainty in his tone.

'Then yes, Buckingham, it is probably a good thing,' Rutherford added.

'There is one fly in the ointment.' It was Lady Jane who spoke this time.

'Go on,' urged Rothgar.

'Did anyone else hear dogs just before those riders left?'

The group exchanged wary looks and Buckingham was quick to notice that while no-one else confirmed it, they all looked resigned to the revelation.

'Well, maybe it was boots on cobbles in the courtyard. Or maybe the sound carried from somewhere else. Yes, that's it. The breeze is up. It must have been from somewhere else.' Buckingham tried to be optimistic, but merely sounded desperate.

'Sir Geoffrey and Lady Jane used to keep dogs,' George the Third said to Buckingham with a smile, as though that explained why she had heard them when the rest of the band had not.

Looking from face to face, Rothgar felt the need to speak up. As he spoke, he used a short stick to draw a map in the mud of the little hut.

'Gentlemen. Dogs or no dogs, this does not change our mission. As far as we are aware, the Sabbatum is still inside. My guess would be first floor or cellar. If there are dogs, they are likely to be in the courtyard.

'We will use the road to approach. Rutherford, if you can get us in, we will sweep the ground floor first. That's when things might get difficult. The entrance to the cellar is likely to be in the courtyard, but that is where we are likely to encounter the dogs. Also, we can see that it is overlooked by possible firing positions on the first floor. However, if we try to clear the first floor without securing the courtyard, we risk allowing someone to slip out the back gate and fleeing with the book or for reinforcements.

'This is my suggestion: Jane, you will need to take up a firing position to the south where you can pick off any Frenchies who come out the gate. At the same time, keep an eye on those first floor windows for any shooters. The hedge-row along the road may be too close to see the first floor, so perhaps the copse of trees on that hillock over there.

'To avoid the first floor and courtyard from supporting each other, we will need to assault them both at the same time. Drummington, that steel will be far better off out there than in close quarters, so you will lead the charge alongside myself and Sir Geoffrey.

'Egret, you will attack the first floor, supported by Baron Black, Deed, Rutherford and George the Third. You will need to go room to room overlooking the courtyard as quickly as possible.'

'What about our fat Marquess here?' Egret asked. There was no malice in the insult.

'Buckingham will come with us, into the courtyard. I'll need him to locate the cellar door and secure it, to prevent any reinforcements from down there.'

'What? Me? But I'm not a soldier!' Buckingham sputtered.

'No, you're not,' Rothgar agreed with an icy glare. 'but you are going to be a door stop.'

10 a.m. to 11.20 a.m.: Napoleon commences his attack on the left, towards Hougoumont. His strategy is to force Wellington into committing his reserves to defend his right flank.

A sudden boom of cannon fire burst through the silence like a menacing roll of thunder. The noise of trumpets and horns were disturbingly close, and the *thrump, thrump, thrump* of marching feet which followed made the ground vibrate under Buckingham's feet. His look of alarm and confusion was more than enough to draw a smile and an answer from Baron Black.

'It seems the battle has finally begun,' he said sombrely, giving Buckingham's shoulder a comforting squeeze as he pulled himself to his feet with a grimace.

'Jane, take your position. We will give you five minutes to set yourself. Rutherford, are you ready?' Rothgar's jaw was set into an expression of stubborn determination.

'Whenever you are. Just get me to the door.'

Lady Jane had already slipped out of the hut, running fast and low towards her designated position on the hill.

'We're going now? Don't you want to give them more chance to march away so we won't be heard?' Buckingham asked. There was a tinge of desperation in his voice.

'We go now. While the French army is concentrating on its advance and before the injured start returning,' Baron Black explained.

Buckingham was unable to voice his fear. His head felt light and dizzy as the little hut erupted into activity. The men checked their muskets, while Drummington lifted his sabre, saluted, and whispered a few words. Presumably a prayer, Buckingham surmised. In what seemed far too little time, Rothgar checked his pocket watch and ordered the advance towards La Maison du Roi.

Buckingham was out of breath and struggling to keep up after the first fifty yards. Another rumble of cannon fire, louder this time, made him duck forward until he was almost bent double and struggling to keep the shako on his head. After a hundred yards, he wondered whether the weight of the musket he carried was going to pull his arms off. His relief was only short-lived when they finally reached the hedgerow beside the road.

One by one, the soldiers pushed through a gap in the hedge, then ran across the road to the cover of the inn's side wall. Buckingham looked up at the little copse of trees on the hillock. He saw no sign of Lady Jane. He seriously wondered whether they would miss him if he didn't follow through the hedge, but when another crack of thunderous artillery fire rolled sounded in the distance, he quickly decided he was better off with the little company than on his own.

Further along the wall, Rutherford was doing something. Although there were no windows on this side of the inn, Buckingham was still fearful of stepping out too far, but he was intrigued by Rutherford's actions. He was holding what appeared to be a long key, but the end which went into the locking mechanism was a plain square of iron. Rutherford placed a piece of cloth on the ground. Something circular was drawn upon it and he placed the key into the circle. Next, he cut his thumb on the edge of his bayonet and squeezed a few drops of blood onto the key while he whispered something to himself.

Another boom of artillery, and Rutherford snatched up the key, stuffed the cloth into a pocket and they were off, muskets and bayonets at the ready. Ruthford stood by the door while Egret, Rothgar and Drummington made ready beside him. The key slid into the lock, tuned, and the door swung inwards. The three comrades in arms entered quickly, followed by the rest of them in single file.

Buckingham had expected the sounds of fighting, the crack of gunfire and the screams of dying men. When he finally entered the inn behind George the Third, he was met by the sight of Rutherford trying to staunch the flow of blood from a nasty looking wound in Edward Egret's thigh and two dead French soldiers.

A reception area opened into a room which ran the length of the building. An area for seating at the far end showed the remains of the soldiers' breakfasts, while a door ahead of him was half open and George Deed knelt quietly at the foot of a curving set of narrow stairs to Buckingham's right, his musket ready.

Buckingham stared down at Egret, wide-eyed. Both his blood-stained hands were clamped around his upper thigh, while Rutherford applied pressure to a wound which was pumping dark blood through his fingers.

'A belt!', Rutherford hissed at Buckingham, 'From one of those soldiers, get me a belt.'

'Now!' He hissed when Buckingham failed to react.

Buckingham knelt by the first Frenchman and began to tug at his buckle, his fingers clumsy in his haste. He found himself looking up at the man's staring eyes every few seconds, as though making sure he was dead. After a short time, he pulled the man's belt free and returned triumphantly to Rutherford.

'Now tie it round his thigh. Tightly, man!'

Egret was beginning to look pale as Buckingham began his duty with distaste. He wrapped the belt round as high as he could, then pulled it tight, then, again, before Rutherford took over and pulled it tighter still.

'Hold this,' he said to Buckingham while he used his bayonet to make a new notch in the belt before fastening it off.

'Help me get him on his back and pull that chair over so we can prop his legs up on it.'

Again, Buckingham dutifully performed his task, then stood and stepped back as he absently wiped his bloodied hands down his coat.

The crack of a rifle from outside followed by a thump as something heavy hit the front door. Buckingham swung around in alarm.

Rothgar re-entered the room from the half-closed doorway opposite the front door, listening intently. He held a bloodied bayonet and a cocked pistol. Rutherford was on his feet like a cat, behind the door with his bayonet while motioning to Buckingham to do the same, but Buckingham was frozen in place between Viscount rothgar and the front door.

'Buckingham, get out of the way.' His voice remained low. A thud from upstairs, and Deed's rifle was at his shoulder, ready. The front door swung open to reveal a muddied French infantryman, pulling an injured man inside.

'Auguste! Laurent! Nous somme attaqués!' He shouted, without realising who was behind him.

'Buckingham! Get out of the way!' Rothgar shouted.

Buckingham turned to see Rothgar levelling a pistol at him. Dropping to the floor, a deafening bang rang his ears, making them whistle with the sound as he desperately tried to crawl away from under all the smoke. A second crack of gunfire and he tried to scurry away across the floor. He crawled directly into one of the dead Frenchmen, then gasped as he knelt on something hard. Pulling it away, he turned and gripped whatever it was to him as something heavy landed on top of him, sending a bolt of pain through his abdomen and pinning him to the floor.

Buckingham panicked. Struggling to push the weight from him, the smell of mud cut through the caustic gunpowder smoke. His belly and arm were wet, increasing his fear. Had he been stabbed? Or shot? It was only when he finally let go of whatever it was he was hanging onto that he finally pulled himself out. As the smoke cleared and he came to his senses, he realised that it was a dead Frenchman, a bayonet pushed through him to the hilt.

Buckingham's hands shook violently as he looked down at them, slick with the man's blood. Had he just killed a man?

Suddenly, Rutherford was beside him.

'Are you hurt?' His hands grasped Buckingham's wrists. 'Are you hurt, man?'

Buckingham absently shook his head and Ruthford was gone. Terrified and not wanting to be alone, Buckingham followed on hands and knees until he came across the foot of someone laying on the floor. Following it, he soon found Rutherford and Rothgar.

'Thank God!' He muttered to neither man in particular as he approached.

Rutherford knelt upright, staring down at Rothgar. His face was streaked with soot stains. As he looked down, he began to clean the barrel of a pistol.

'I thought he was going to shoot me,' Buckingham blathered, almost outraged.

'He was aiming at the man behind you,' Rutherford replied, 'But you were in the way.'

There was something in his voice, a catch which Buckingham noticed despite his terror. Why was Rothgar laying down? He moved up a little further to see whatever Rutherford was looking at.

Viscount Rothgar was dead, with a six-inch hole in face where a musket's bullet had hit him.

Suddenly they heard the sound of a rifle from outside followed by the clattering of hooves and men dismounting.

'Buckingham, bolt the door!' Rutherford yelled at him.

Something inside Buckingham sprang into action. Clumsily pushing himself to his feet, he heard Rutherford shouting through the door behind him: "Reinforcements!"

The door to the inn began to push open as another rifle shot rang out. Buckingham launched himself at the door, slamming it against whoever was on the other side. A shot from just outside sent splinters of wood bursting into the room just above his head. With a determination borne by sheer terror, Buckingham launched himself into the door again, satisfied by the grunt of pain he heard from outside. Several men shouted at one another in French, but he did not listen to the words. Instead, he snatched the first bolt across, then the second and the third before dropping to the floor and rolling away as another bullet punched the wood, causing sharp splinters to fly through the air above him.

Baron Black was suddenly by his side, speckled with blood. 'Through the door at the back!' he yelled as he grabbed Egret by the shoulders and pulled him through.

Buckingham did not need telling twice. As he passed George Deed, he was vaguely aware of the man's firing stance but still jumped as he pulled the trigger, shattering a window and splintering the shutter beyond. Buckingham threw himself through the door and into a rustic hovel of a kitchen with a fireplace and chimney at the centre. Rutherford and the baron followed, with Deed following up, pushing the door so it was open just a crack as he reloaded his musket.

Buckingham looked around at the others. Deed, Rutherford, Baron Black, Sir Geoffrey, Drummington, George the Third.

'George?' Rutherford asked.

George the Third's strange eye turned and whirred as it focussed on the occultist. He had a bloodied strip of cloth around his forearm.

This floor is clear. Two dogs left in the courtyard, perhaps four cavalrymen holed up in the stables,' he reported breathlessly.

'Rothgar?' asked the baron.

'Dead,' replied Deed.

'Has anyone seen my sister?' Sir Geoffrey this time as he reloaded a musket and two pistols.

'She was still shooting when we retreated in here,' Deed replied as he finished reloading his own weapon.

'So, we're trapped?' The baron again.

'We will need to push out as soon as we're ready. Can't give them any time to go find our sniper,' Deed added.

They readied their weapons in silence then, as Buckingham watched on, uncertain of what he could do to help. His mouth was dry, he felt cold and his hands would not stop shaking. Then, Rutherford was beside him. He pulled a pistol from

Buckingham's waistband and shoved it into his hand, then pushed a hatchet into the other.

'But, that is Egret's weapon,' Buckingham blustered, looking as though he was going to drop the hatchet.

'Egret's dead,' Rutherford mumbled angrily, 'So now it's yours.'

11.20 a.m. to 12.20 p.m.: The French infantry drive Wellington's forces from the woods at Hougoumont. Wellington orders a counterattack.

The plan was set. George Deed and George the Third would offer cover fire into the courtyard with their muskets, just in case any of the cavalrymen in the stables tried to escape on horseback. The others, led initially by Drummington in the close-quarters reception area, then by Baron Black as they exited the inn onto the road, would counterattack the reinforcements. Once on the road, Sir Geoffrey would take a horse in case Lady Jane's position had been compromised.

It was a risk. They were still uncertain whether anyone was upstairs or in the cellar, but with two men down, both experienced melee combatants, the volunteers could not allow any of the soldiers outside escape for reinforcements.

Drummington was through the door like a bull, then stopped dead. There was nobody in the reception area and the door was still bolted closed. Remaining quiet, the five men crept forward. An officer outside was giving commands and a peek through a gap in the shutters showed that he was just to the left of the door.

'What are they doing?' Buckingham whispered to Sir Geoffrey.

'It sounds like they're preparing to smoke us out,' Rutherford replied for him.

Rutherford tiptoed to the door. Using hand signals, he indicated that he would push the bolts, then Drummington and the others could charge out and go to work. Each man nodded his understanding in turn.

Rutherford held up three fingers, then folded down one, two, the last.

Swiping the bolts across as quickly and quietly as he was able, he swung the door open. Baron Black strode through and emptied his musket into the officer at point blank range. Just behind him, Drummington was through the door with the speed of a man half his age. Swiping left and right with his heavy sabre, he had felled two more cavalrymen before Sir Geoffrey managed to discharge a musket into the chest of a fourth. Snatching the reins of the officer's horse, Sir Geoffrey leapt into the saddle. Buckingham watched him grab the carbine from its holster beside the saddle as he kicked the horse into a gallop, off towards his sister.

'Damned Hussars,' Baron Black growled. He poked a foot at the dead officer as the man's blood poured into a muddy puddle.

'Do you see any more?' Drummington asked anyone who was listening. His grin was disturbing show of how much he had just enjoyed himself.

'Not that I can see. Buckingham, be a good fellow and tether those horses, would you?' Rutherford's tone was thoughtful.

Buckingham, relieved to be given a task he could actually do, went rounding up the remaining four horses and marched them to the hitching post outside the inn door.

'Perhaps this is as good a time as any to make our move on the stables,' Drummington said. His bloodlust was up, but the idea was not a poor one.

'Perhaps. They're cavalrymen in there and if they make off on a horse, we're done for.' Rutherford rubbed a hand over his chin in thought.

'Would it not be best to wait for Sir Geoffrey and Lady Jane before doing that?' Buckingham thought out loud.

The looks on the faces of his comrades were probably as surprised as he was.

'It is an excellent point,' Baron Black agreed. 'Is there any way we can secure the gates to the courtyard from out here?'

Drummington cleaned his sabre on a dead Hussar, then sheathed it with an air of resigned disappointment.

'We could block it with tables, but that would attract rather than deter if anyone should see,' the smaller man said.

'Hmm, indeed,' Rutherford pondered.

'If this book is so important, I assume old Boney will be sending people to check up on it every so often. Therefore, whatever we do to block the gate will look suspicious,' Buckingham interjected as he finished his task.

Rutherford, Baron Black and Drummington all stared at him.

'What? Did I say something wrong?' Buckingham's tone was that of a man resigned to being accused of stupidity, missing the point or both.

'I wonder. . .' Drummington began.

'If these Hussars were checking up on the Sabbatum?' Rutherford continued for him.

'And we just killed them,' the baron finished.

'You three stay here and wait for the Scott-Mansfields. I'll let Deed and Saunders know.' Rutherford disappeared back into the inn.

There was an awkward silence as Baron Black and Drummington looked at Buckingham. Unappreciative of the attention, Buckingham could feel himself beginning to blush.

'No need to stare, gentlemen. Makes me mighty uncomfortable,' he said, looking down at a dead Hussar.

'Well done, Buckingham. If this lot were here for that purpose, it means we're suddenly on a time limit.' There was a tinge of admiration in the baron's voice.

Buckingham, still uncomfortable under the continued scrutiny, was saved from replying by the arrival of Sir Geoffrey, with Lady Jane sat behind him.

'Jane! You missed all the fun!' Drummington greeted her, spreading his arms towards the dead soldiers littered around them.

'I killed two myself. Best you hide them behind the hedge, out of sight,' Jane grinned as she leapt from the horse, rifle in hand. She was suddenly vey sombre.

'Geoffrey told me about Edward and Viscount Rothgar. God rest their souls.'

'God rest their souls,' Drummington murmured in reply.

Sir Geoffrey had hitched the horse and they had cleared the bodies behind the hedge by the time Rutherford returned. Buckingham was hot, sweating and breathing hard at the chore. People were heavy enough, he knew, but how heavy must a Hussar uniform be? He wondered as he panted for breath.

'Reload your weapons, gentlemen. We attack the courtyard in ten minutes,' Rutherford said.

12.20 p.m. to 1.15 p.m.: The fighting intensifies around Hougoumont. French troops briefly gain entry to the farm, but they are repelled.

Buckingham lay in a ditch on the opposite side of the road from the inn. Wet through, muddy, and thoroughly miserable, he aimed Rothgar's musket at the courtyard gates. Beside him, Lady Jane aimed her rifle. Between them, raised up on stones to keep them from the damp, were Edward Egret's musket and three of the Hussars' carbines.

'Might I ask, whatever are you doing here?' Buckingham asked. He needed a distraction from his discomfort and his nerves.

'Fighting for King and country, just like you,' Jane replied.

'But you don't have to be here. They are the gentleman volunteers, after all.'

She spared herself a sideways look of disdain.

'Why should you have all the fun?' She asked, a coldness creeping into her tone.

'You call this fun?'

'Have you ever spent an afternoon sat at home in an uncomfortable dress doing embroidery?' She enquired.

'Absurd! Of course not,' Buckingham blustered.

'Then trust me. This is more fun.'

Jane's head lowered to the sight of the rifle.

'Time?' She demanded.

Buckingham huffed and puffed and pulled his pocket watch from his coat.

'12.30. Any moment.' He replaced the watch and took up position with his musket.

A series of explosions and the sound of drums and horns from far behind them made Buckingham shiver.

'How do you think the battle is going?' He asked casually.

'Shhh,' Jane replied, holding her aim.

A volley of musket fire from somewhere in the inn was followed by the unmistakeable growl of Drummington's war cry. A bead of sweat trickled down Buckingham's temple as he listened to shattering glass, the deeper boom of a carbine and the barking of dogs. Another shot was quickly followed by a whimper, then an order barked in French but lost somewhere amongst the tumult of battle.

Buckingham realised that his hands were shaking so violently that he would struggle to hit the inn itself, let alone a cavalryman galloping through the gate. Again, he glanced over at Jane. She was calmness personified. Statuesque in her stillness.

He suddenly jumped when something slammed against the courtyard doors, causing them to shudder loudly.

'Do you think we should go and help?' His voice was almost a whimper, as though dreading the idea that Jane might agree.

'We are helping. Keep your aim. Focus only on where the bullet will go, not what you can hear. Shut out everything except where the bullet will go.'

Buckingham tried to do as he was told. To begin with, he couldn't blot out the noise. The cry of a dying man was like a heavy weight on his bladder, but then, with a deep breath, he thought of home. The gilded halls of Stowe house, the grounds, the Temple of Ancient Virtue overlooking the Elysian Fields, sculpted in honour of the heroic paradise of ancient Greece, a stoic reminder of the paths one takes in life. This was certainly not a path he had imagined.

The courtyard doors burst open. Before he had time to think, Buckingham had pulled the trigger, sending the musket jarring into his shoulder, spattering his face with soot and leaving a high-pitched ringing in his right ear. Horse and rider stumbled across the road towards him and only by a feat of sheer luck did he manage roll out of the way in time before the creature fell dead in the ditch where he had been laying.

'Jane?' His first concern would surprise him when he reflected on it later.

Something moved amongst the leaves and broken twigs behind him, but Buckingham ignored it. He coughed as he inhaled the gun smoke, his eyes watering. Then, as he blinked away the moisture, there she was! On her back, rifle raised.

'Are you hurt?'

'Only my pride,' was her reply.

Looking back at the fallen horse, a sense of pride befell Buckingham.

'It worked! I hit it,' he said happily to nobody in particular.

'You missed,' Jane rebuked him. 'I hit it between the eyes. Your shot hit the wall.'

'What? How do you know?' Buckingham was crestfallen.

'Go see for yourself,' Jane shrugged, holding up a hand for him to pull her to her feet.

There was movement under the hedge as a bloodied cavalryman tried to pull himself from under the fallen horse.

'Are you going to finish him off?' Jane asked.

'What? Me? In cold blood? I can't!' Buckingham flustered, backing off as he spoke.

Jane took one of the carbines and stalked to the fallen soldier. There was a brief cry of "Non! Non!" before she shot him in the face.

'Thought we'd let you have some of the fun!'

Drummington slapped Buckingham on the shoulder hard enough that Buckingham's weakened knees gave way, dropping him to the floor in shock. Everything sounded hollow, distant. His ear rang, his head pounded. He could feel the dull pain of tiny burns on his cheek where the musket had fired. He had only wanted to get back home, with all the treasures he had purchased. What had he agreed to? Was this worth a dukedom? Was he even going to survive the day?

1.15 p.m. to 2.15 p.m.: Field Marshal Blücher approaches from the east, forcing Napoleon to send cavalry to head him off. Back on the battlefield, the French columns begin their advance, attacking Wellington's centre. The allied line is pushed back past La Haye Sainte. Napoleon is winning.

Following the battle for the courtyard there was good news and bad news. In terms of the good, there had been no-one trying to pick them off from the first floor. It went some way to allowing them to assume that Edward Egret had done his job properly when they had first entered the inn. Also, the volunteers had only picked up a minor injury between them, when Drummington had been bitten on the forearm by one of the dogs. Finally, they had located the entrance to the cellar: a trapdoor in the courtyard beside the back wall of the inn.

The bad news was that one of the courtyard doors had broken off its upper hinge when it had been forced outwards by the charging cavalryman. It had left the rear of the inn almost indefensible.

Rutherford ordered the horses they had hitched outside the inn to be brought into the courtyard. The gate was pulled closed as best they were able and barricaded from within, though a decent push would topple the broken one. There were four more dead Frenchmen to dispose of, including the one Lady Jane had despatched by the road. The dead horse was left in the ditch where it had died. The corpses, along with four dead dogs, were piled in a separate room in the stables away from the horses. The breed of the dogs perplexed them. Sir Geoffrey summed them up best when he declared them to have the muzzle and feet of a mastiff with eyes, hair and shoulders like a wolf.

Finally, while Jane and George the Third set themselves up with rifle and musket to cover any rearguard action from the cellar, the rest of them ventured upstairs. Other than two dead Frenchman, courtesy of the late Edward Egret, the advance upstairs was happily without incident. Rutherford order a search for the Sabbatum through the six rooms, but nothing was found.

When the tasks were finished, they gathered around a table in the reception area for Rutherford to give the next set of orders.

'Are we certain this book is even here?' Sir Geoffrey began. It was aimed at Rutherford, his voice full of accusation.

'This is where I divined it to be yesterday evening,' Rutherford replied calmly.

'That's wonderful, but what about today?' Sir Geoffrey barked back.

'Why would all these men be stationed here if it were for nought?' Baron Black pointed out.

'Excellent question. Misdirection?' Sir Geoffrey's reply had the bite of any good riposte.

'Then why send a troupe of Hussars?'

'To make any spies believe that there is something here.' Sir Geoffrey responded.

To Buckingham, both arguments carried weight.

'The book must be in the cellar,' Rutherford this time.

'Do you have your equipment with you? Perhaps you would good enough to check before we take any further casualties.'

'I do, but the Frenchman I used for the divination is recovering from his wounds back at headquarters.'

'We have several dead Frenchmen in the stables. Take your pick.' Sir Geoffrey would not let it go.

'Gentlemen, please.' Rutherford held up his hands in frustration. 'I do not wish to begin a lecture about how there are things in the world you know nothing about, but you force my hand. This book, the Sabbatum, is incredibly dangerous. I doubt there is any one person still living who knows it's true power. Stories from the witch trials in Germany in the 17th century and hearsay from survivors after the Battle of Austerlitz in 1805, when we believe Napoleon last had his hands on the damnable thing, liken it to a holy relic. There are those who say that the book is intertwined with fate. It manipulates the world around us for the benefit of its user. I say user because no-one ever truly owns the Sabbatum. The book will not allow it. It is a vehicle created solely for the dreams of ambitious men. Fleeting power in life given at the cost of their immortal souls.'

'Who would have written such a thing? And how did Napoleon come by it?' Buckingham asked, horrified.

'I do not know the answer to either question, I'm afraid. I have always wondered whether his acquisition of the book was the real reason for his campaign in Egypt. Rumours persist that Napoleon wanted to use the book to make himself Emperor of Europe but was thwarted when Francis II, the Holy Roman Emperor, abdicated and dissolved the position following his defeat at Austerlitz. Although Napoleon held power in France, I can only surmise it was not the power that the pact had promised. Perhaps he lost faith in the book, or which whichever foul being he made his pact with. Napoleon did not fall for another nine years, until 1814, so I would surmise that the Sabbatum was pushed aside or found a way to remove itself from the French court. A few months ago, when he rose again and left Elba, perhaps it allowed itself to be found again, to give him a second chance at the title of Emperor of Europe. Perhaps it never left his side. Who's to say that this was not the grand plan all along. The Devil's unique way of teaching the French Emperor how to be more humble in His presence.'

The group were silent for a time, each man and woman reflecting on what they had just heard.

'And after all that, you believe we have a chance?' Despite only being a whisper, Buckingham's voice carried clearly over the dull pounding of faraway artillery.

'Of course. The Devil cannot account for the actions of any man, woman or child who has rejected him. Wellington knows that, and I wonder whether you, Buckingham, are his insurance amongst this little troop of ungodly volunteers.'

'What? Surely not. That's ridiculous! There's nothing wrong with any of you,' Buckingham's cheeks burned bright red at the suggestion.

'Not wrong, ungodly. We have all been touched by the Devil at some point in our lives. The baron has cheated death more times than he ought. Edward Egret was a murderer. I have done things in my pursuit for occult knowledge that I would not tell any of you. We are all here through choice. We have all been touched by His shadow. You are the only man who is here under duress, who is, even with the promise of favour, reluctant to be part of the gentleman volunteers.'

'Hokum!' Sir Geoffrey interjected.

The group looked at him for explanation, which he promptly gave.

'Buckingham is a selfish, gluttonous coward. His greed for a duchy is the only reason why we he is here. That and being too lily-livered to say no. Other than his obvious lack of ability to fight, he is as good a match for the gentleman volunteers as any one of us.'

With that, there was a clattering of hooves from outside.

2.15 p.m. to 3 p.m.: Nearly 15,000 troops continue to battle over Hougoumont. Wellington's heavy cavalry relieve the allied infantry in the centre by dispersing Napoleon's troops, but they suffer heavy losses when counter-charged by Napoleon's own cavalry. To the east, Blücher's army is making slow progress. Wellington's situation is now critical.

Lady Jane was out of her seat so fast that it turned over. Rifle in one hand, Viscount Rothgar's musket in the other, she headed straight for the first floor with George the Third in hot pursuit.

'To the door, gentlemen. Fire at will, don't let any of them escape. Buckingham, you take those two carbines and head through there to the corridor. Anyone enters the building at the rear, you shoot them, do you hear? Be careful. If anyone is in the cellar, they might have the bright idea of offering support.'

Buckingham simply nodded to disguise the fear he knew would be in his voice. He could feel the colour drain from his face. His heart raced, his hands trembled, and his belly felt like it was going to hit the floor.

Rutherford, Sir Geoffrey, Baron Black, and George Deed fixed their bayonets as they headed for the front door of the inn. Before he turned away, Buckingham noticed Drummington kiss his sabre and mouth a few words before following his comrades in arms. The door was opened, and they were all suddenly gone, out onto the road amidst the crackle of musket fire.

Although Buckingham knew he should be watching the courtyard at the back, he found it an almost impossible task with all the sounds of fighting coming from behind him at the front of the building. A fleeting glance over his shoulder through the reception door saw a lazy cloud of gun smoke shroud the front of the little reception area. A shout in French carried above all else, the words lost amongst the din. The screams of men and horses alike would haunt his sleep in the years to come. Something heavy hit a shutter on the left-hand window, knocking it off its hinge. Glaring daylight suddenly filled the reception. Through the window, Buckingham could see the shadow of a rearing horse. A gunshot from upstairs was followed by a thud, the piteous cry of "Non, non, non!" then nothing.

Buckingham licked his dry lips. The carbines shook in his hands, partly through fear, but partly from their sheer weight. He turned back towards the courtyard. A part of him did so to please Rutherford when he returned. If he returned. But he also knew that there was a part of him that did not want to see the bullet coming, just in case it was a Frenchman who walked through the door and found him instead.

He tried to blot out the sounds of fighting. Instead, he concentrated on the ticking of the old clock nearby, finding a wisp of comfort on the monotony of its tone. When he finally heard footsteps coming down the stairs, he found himself breathing a tremulous sigh of relief. His eyes welled up and his body relaxed to the point of exhaustion. He laid the two carbines on a nearby chair and rose to greet his colleagues.

'Did we win?' It was a ridiculous question, he knew, but even the act of talking made him feel better.

'We did,' George the Third replied, his mechanical eye twisting towards Buckingham, before he and Jane headed to the door.

There was a gravity about the blind man which sent a chill through Buckingham. Following them, he exited the inn onto the road outside.

Six horses lay dead. One, further away and presumably trying to escape, still had the rider beneath it. Sir Geoffrey was ambling towards the flailing man with his musket in hand, the bayonet already bloodied.

Buckingham dragged his gaze away. As he absently walked forward, he kicked something heavy. Looking down, Buckingham gasped as he saw George Deed's head laying in the mud. His body was slumped against the wall of the inn, his blood leaving ruddy trails over the stone walls and filling the puddle in which he sat.

Lady Jane, realising they were all outside, shouted at Buckingham, but her words were distant and unrecognisable. As he walked away, he was aware of her re-entering the inn behind him.

A little further away, Rutherford and George the Third were busying themselves around someone. Buckingham stumbled over to seen them silently and efficiently tying a tourniquet around Drummington's upper arm. The lower part of his arm lay in the mud a few feet away.

'Where,' Buckingham took a moment to swallow a mouthful of bile, 'Where is Baron Black?' He managed to ask.

'Over there,' was George's curt reply.

Buckingham followed the nod of his head and walked around a fallen horse to find the baron sitting against the beast's belly.

'Just a flesh wound,' he said, smiling up at Buckingham.

One arm clutched at his midriff. Blood bubbled through his fingers and had saturated the top part of his trousers. A dead hussar was crumpled in a ball near the baron's feet with his own sabre driven through his chest.

'Let me help you inside,' Buckingham began, but the baron raised a weak hand and stopped him.

'No. Give me a musket. Any more French come and I'll take one of them with me. It'll warn the rest of you as well. The book is what we came for, go find it.'

Buckingham paused, uncertain. Helplessness washed over him in a wave of rage which was almost as paralysing as the fear he had felt listening to the battle from inside the inn. Unsure what else to say, or what more he could do, Buckingham found a musket, loaded it with shot and left it beside Baron Black.

'Good luck. We will see you again when we have the book,' he said quickly, his voice husky with bitterness.

He stood and turned just as Rutherford and George the Third were pulling Drummington to his feet.

'The baron?' Rutherford asked.

'On watch with a musket,' Buckingham replied evenly.

Rutherford merely nodded and turned away as they helped Drummington back inside. Buckingham picked up the big man's sabre as he followed them in and sat him down.

'Thank you, Buckingham,' came the strained growl as he leaned the sword against the wall beside its owner. There was an appreciation in Drummington's voice which shone through his pain and made Buckingham nod back.

'Right, gather round,' Rutherford ordered sternly.

Sir Geoffrey had already returned and stood alongside his sister. Rutherford and George the Third began reloading their muskets, a task which Buckingham helped with on two of the used carbines.

'With all that mess outside, we need to get down there before more reinforcements or scouts or whatever they might be arrive. Someone must be noticing troops of hussars riding off and not coming back, so sooner or later they are going to send a larger force. I will set a grenade to blow the doors in. Geoffrey, George and I will go in. Buckingham, Jane, you're cover.

'I can go in.' They all turned to look at Drummington.

'You might have noticed you only have one arm,' Sir Geoffrey stated.

'I only need one to wield this,' Drummington replied, standing to pick up his sabre.

'Alright. Drummington goes in first,' Rutherford corrected himself. 'Any questions?'

3 p.m. to 4 p.m.: Hougoumont is ablaze. Marshal Ney mistakes the movement of allied casualties for a withdrawal and orders his cavalry to charge, but they are frustrated by allied infantry in square formation behind the ridge. Napoleon reorganises his army and orders his artillery to open fire. To the east, Blücher engages Napoleon's cavalry.

The grenade exploded, destroying the cellar door completely. Drummington was quick onto the steps, sabre raised as he disappeared into a roiling cloud of gunpowder smoke. Sir Geoffrey was close behind him, sword in one hand, bayonet in the other.

Rutherford was about to follow when a noise from the cellar made him pause. A brief cry, the sound of steel on stone, then nothing. George the Third moved towards the steps, but Rutherford held out a hand to stop him.

Buckingham's coat was tight and uncomfortable, drenched in sweat. He found himself holding his breath as Rutherford backed away and motioned to George to do the same. He could hear the creak of wooden steps as someone heavy footed scaled them. He peered into the lazy swirls of smoke, then saw a shadow emerge.

Buckingham swallowed hard when Drummington's lifeless corpse was thrown into the courtyard. As the smoke began to disperse, a man in French uniform trousers and black boots emerged from the cellar. He still wore a red cummerbund, but above that he was naked. His torso was old and wiry, covered in raised white scars. On his hands he wore gloves made of blackened steel, the fingers shaped into sharp, dagger like points. In his left hand, fingers pushed through the throat and clenched into a fist, he dragged the lifeless body of Sir Geoffrey.

But what made Buckingham whimper was that most of the man's head was missing. His neck was there, his jaw too, albeit missing some teeth, but the skull itself was absent.

'God in heaven, what witchcraft is this?' He murmured.

Buckingham jumped and almost pissed himself when a shot rang out from beside him. The bullet slammed into the centre of the creature's chest and burst from its back.

Lady Jane was already reloading her rifle, her teeth gritted together in anguish at the sight of her dead brother.

'Stand still!' Rutherford hissed, 'It's an Akephaloi, and its only senses are touch and taste. It can't sense you if you stand still!'

Everyone froze except for Jane, still loading her rifle. The creature paused, dropped Sir Geoffrey's body, then fell to its hands and feet. Buckingham covered his mouth in horror when he saw the creature's tongue darting around within its jaw, flicking this way and that as it tasted the air. The steel tip of one finger tapped against the ground rhythmically as the head moved from left to right, then back again.

Jane had almost finished her reload. Dropping the powder horn in her haste, the Akephaloi's jaw swung round towards it as it hit the ground beside her. Its tongue undulated in her direction as she hurriedly put the rifle into full cock, then the creature launched itself as she brought the weapon to bear. The rifle fired, shrouding both combatants in a cloud of smoke.

Rutherford took the opportunity to run inside the inn. Buckingham, forlorn at the abandonment, took a step to follow, but George the Third closed the distance and stopped him.

'Don't move. Look!' He whispered.

The lens of his eye was close enough that Buckingham could hear the faint clicking of cogs as the lenses adjusted. Jane lay dead on the ground, great holes torn from her chest and abdomen by the Akephaloi's dripping metal fingers. Buckingham's knees weakened as it reached into its own jaw to lick the grue from its hands with a tongue that resembled an undulating worm of livid red flesh.

As the two men held their breath, the only sounds in the courtyard were the distant rumble of artillery and musket fire and a sticky, slurping grunt from the creature before them. Its throat pulsed open and closed like an horrific sphincter as the rolling muscle of its tongue lapped at the back of its teeth, rising from the jaw occasionally to taste the air like a thick red slug. Buckingham could see now that the scars on its torso were old and new alike, some white raised lines, others red where they were still in the process of healing. How could it be alive? He wondered, at the same time happy not to know the answer.

The creature lowered itself onto hands and feet again. The tongue tasted the air this way and that, while metal clad fingers tapped an occasional rhythm on the flagstones. Slowly, it advanced across the courtyard, zig-zagging towards the two men. Once it was within eight feet, Buckingham found it difficult to remain still. George's hand was still on his arm; a minor thing, but quite possibly the only thing preventing him from bolting after the cowardly Rutherford.

By the time it had closed to five feet, Buckingham was certain it knew they were there. His body swayed as every part of his being told him to run. The inn door was what? Five paces away? Six? Could he make it and slam the door before it closed the gap? What would happen to George if he did?

The grip on his arm tightened. Did George sense what he was thinking?

Suddenly, something hit the Akephaloi's back and burst into flame. A shrill haunting screech rose from the creature's throat as it rolled to one side and rose to its feet.

'Run!' shouted George the Third, pulling at Buckingham's arm as he ran for the inn, pulling the larger man behind him.

Its back aflame, the Akephaloi gave chase. A crash sounded just behind Buckingham and he felt a whoosh of heat singe his legs as flame sprang to life between him and the creature. At the doorway, he turned to look as a burning headless nightmare sprang from the flames towards him. All he could do was vainly raise an arm to defend himself when something moved beside his head. Opening one eye, Buckingham saw the Akephaloi squirming and wriggling on the end of a bayonet where George the Third had thrust the musket over his shoulder.

'Get behind me!' George shouted. Buckingham did not need telling twice.

George advanced into the courtyard, the monster still skewered through the shoulder and trying to wriggle itself free. The stench of burning flesh was acridly pungent, some-how brought more vividly to Buckingham's senses by the creature's shrill screams.

Once in the courtyard, George looked up. He yelled something, but Buckingham could not hear what. Then, as he pushed the creature, musket and all away from himself, a bottle of liquid with a flaming rag in it fell from the first floor to land beside the monster, instantly engulfing it in flame. It staggered for a moment or two, its piteous noises no longer audible over the roar of the flames. Black smoke billowed into the sky as it fell to the ground and finally lay still.

Buckingham stared. His heart pounded against his chest in a way he never knew it could. He jumped as a hand hit his shoulder, then turned to see Rutherford.

'What?' He asked, dazed.

'I said, are you hurt?'

Buckingham shook his head slowly, unable to form the words to respond further. He could only watch on as his two remaining comrades warily checked the burning monster. As the flames began to die, Rutherford picked up Drummington's sabre and severed its jaw from the neck.

4 p.m. to 6 p.m.: Napoleon's cavalry run rampant. Wellington's troops are forced to remain in square leaving them vulnerable to artillery. Napoleon's infantry capture La Haye Sainte, allowing them to move skirmishers and artillery forward to inflict heavy losses on Wellington's squares. Wellington's situation is now so dire that his command is ambushed. He is forced to take the unprecedented step of moving his colours to the rear.

Buckingham, Rutherford and George the Third watched in silence as the creature burned amidst the corpses of their three dead comrades. The air was heavy with smoke. The courtyard door was ajar, and the muffled sound of whinnying horses could be heard from the stables.

'Let's search the cellar,' Rutherford muttered eventually, 'We need to be away from here before more reinforcements are sent.'

He turned and led the way down a flight of creaking wooden steps into a cold, dark cellar which reeked of stale alcohol and straw.

While Rutherford fumbled around to light some well-worn candles on the wall, George the Third disappeared into the darkness. Buckingham watched after him, fearful of what might be there. Some banging noises, the scratching of wood against iron and the occasional cough caused by the dust were amplified in the underground space.

'How on earth can he see back there?' Buckingham asked.

'The eyepiece allows him to see in the dark,' Rutherford replied as the candles finally took hold and filled the area where they were standing in a warm, if faint yellow glow.

Sensing something sticky underfoot, Buckingham looked down to see a patch of dark wetness. Realising it must be a puddle of Sir Geoffrey's or Drummington's blood, he stepped away to leave bloody footprints nearby.

'I think this might be what we're looking for,' George said excitedly as he rolled a barrel towards them from out of the darkness.

''It's lighter than anything with liquid in, and the little fellow in here is getting very excitable,' he smiled as he tapped the side of his eye piece.

'Alright. Let's take a look.'

As Rutherford lifted the candles from the wall mount and held them close to the barrel, Buckingham could see lines and symbols branded into the wood. The lines formed a five-pointed star on the end of the barrel. Around the widest part at the centre of the barrel was a circle of strange looking glyphs, each about six inches in height.

'It is protected,' Rutherford stated grimly, pulling a pair of spectacles from his pocket. 'You're right, George, I think this is what we're looking for.'

'Protected? How so?' Interjected Buckingham.

'These glyphs are from the Key of Solomon. There's a pentangle on the top here and I suspect there will be a similar one on the bottom. I need to read the enchantment to be able to open it.'

'Can we not just throw it down the stairs?'

'Not unless you wish to unleash whatever trap may have been set into it.'

George manhandled the barrel into the patch of light from the cellar entrance. Rutherford began to examine the glyphs, his lips moving silently as he deciphered their meaning. As he worked, Buckingham began to look around the parts of the cellar he could see. Dusty bottles filled shelves along each wall. As his eyes adjusted to the light, he could make out the shapes of stacked barrels to the rear. Finding a lantern, he lit it from a candle and ventured over. Ale filled most of the barrels, but then, sitting precariously on a rotting wooden shelf, he found a smaller cask with a tap. He placed down the candle, wiped his finger round a nearby glass to clean it, then ran some liquid from the cask. Brandy! He took a sip and smiled for what felt like the first time all day as the warm liquid burned its way down to his stomach. He hurriedly poured a little more and excitedly headed back to the others.

'Gentlemen, we have brandy!' He announced, holding the glass aloft.

George looked up at him, then up at the steps as the crack of a musket sounded from the road outside.

'The baron!' There was a worried edge to George's voice as he grabbed his musket and headed up the steps and into the courtyard.

'What are you doing, man?' Rutherford enquired, peering over his spectacles at Buckingham.

Buckingham stared at him, uncomprehending.

'Go help him!'

The urgency in Rutherford's command spurred Buckingham into action. He glugged the brandy, dropped the glass and hurried as best his frame could manage up the steps and into the courtyard. Upon arrival, he realised he had left his carbine in the cellar, so quickly drew the pair of pistols from his belt.

More musket fire from outside, then shouting in French, something he couldn't quite catch. Buckingham hurried over to the broken gate and cautiously peered out onto the road. George the Third was laying down near the baron, behind the dead horse where they had left him. George was trying to reload a musket while the baron aimed a carbine, tracking something behind the hedgerow. He disappeared into a cloud of smoke as the gun fired and a scream rattled agonisingly from somewhere unseen.

George noticed Buckingham as he exchanged his loaded weapon for the one Baron Black had just discharged.

'Voltigeurs! Find anything that fires and protect the gate,' he shouted as he fumbled for a cartridge.

Buckingham was unusually quick off the mark. Tucking the two pistols back into his belt, he rounded up a carbine, a musket and Lady Jane's rifle before bringing them back to the courtyard gate. A glance outside and he could see a skirmisher's plume behind a dead horse further down the road. Even with his limited knowledge of warfare, Buckingham knew the dangers of voltigeurs; veteran light infantry who were trained to fight in loose skirmish formations rather than the lines and columns of regular infantry. Where the hussars had to stick to the road to avoid the treacherous mud, these seasoned soldiers would use it to their advantage.

His hands shook as he tried to push the ramrod into the barrel of the rifle to press down the cartridge. Another shot made him flinch, but Buckingham knew he needed to load the weapon if he had any hope of survival. He wondered how many voltigeurs there might be. Five? Ten? Twenty? Was it even worth him trying? He clumsily poured the powder, spilling it on himself and the ground in his nervousness.

A bang was quickly followed by the splintering of wood above his head. Buckingham jumped with fright, then rolled to the floor. The rifle shook in his hands as he tried to aim it at an aggressor he could not yet see. A plume of smoke rose from behind part of the hedgerow, a sure sign of the shooter's presence. Aiming as best he could, he fired back then rolled behind the gate to reload.

More shots from where George and the baron lay along the road drove him on. He knew he was the only chance the two men had of not being surrounded, but he tried to push the pressure of that responsibility from his mind as he willed his fingers to do what they needed to do.

The noise of snapping undergrowth made him freeze. A quick glance around the gate told him he had missed his target as the soldier was kneeling in the ditch, reloading his musket.

Buckingham thought back to how Viscount Rothgar was killed, because he, the Marquess of Buckingham, had not reacted in time. He exhaled slowly, deliberately. His hands squeezed the rifle, twisting backwards and forwards as though trying to ring its neck. Rising to his feet, he took a second look. The voltigeur was preparing to fire. He looked at the bayonet, mounted on the barrel of the rifle in front of him. Blowing out his cheeks once, twice, a third time, he stepped around the gate and charged the few paces across the road, bayonet levelled.

The voltigeur glanced up at him and fired the musket. Buckingham ran headlong into the smoke, thrusting at where he believed the Frenchman to be. The rifle hit something, then he toppled forward as he lost his balance. Suddenly he was tumbling. He hit the edge of the ditch, grass and mud filling his mouth as he struggled to twist away. Someone strong was on top of him, forcing the rifle to one side and punching him so hard that his breath almost left him. The smoke cleared enough for Buckingham to see the man, his shako missing from his head. It took a few more heartbeats for Buckingham to realise he had skewered it on his bayonet, the yellow feather and chevrons waving raucously as the two men fought over the weapon.

Another punch to the gut and Buckingham could feel himself weakening. The Frenchman was trying to wrench the rifle from him, so Buckingham thrust it forwards, causing the soldier to fall backwards with the momentum of his own pull. Buckingham, without thought, pulled one of the pistols from his belt, aimed and fired.

The report left his ears ringing. He wafted away the smoke to see the man lying dead in the road, a blackened hole in his chest. Another musket shot brought Buckingham back to his senses. He pried the rifle from the dead man's hands and looked along the road.

George the Third and Baron Black were still working as a firing team, though now it was the baron reloading while George fired into the thick smoke which blotted any view beyond five yards past where they were positioned. As Buckingham watched, a voltigeur emerged like a shadow from the smoke, only to be shot down by a flash of fire from George's musket.

Ignoring his aches and pains, Buckingham pulled himself to his feet. He grabbed the rifle and headed back towards the relative safety of the courtyard gates to reload. As he plunged the ramrod to pack the round, he noticed his hands were no longer shaking. Once loaded, he picked up the pouch with the remaining cartridges then waited for the smoke to be as dense as possible before he hurried along the wall of the inn to where the baron and George were fighting their defence. As he dropped down beside them, George fired a round from a musket, handed it to Baron Black, then snatched the rifle away.

'About damned time, Buckingham,' George admonished as his lenses whirred, shortened, elongated then clicked. He fired the rifle which sent a smattering of burning powder shooting into Buckingham's face, burning his cheek.

'One was trying to get behind you,' Buckingham sputtered.

'Well, don't just stand there, man, go kill him! We're rather busy.'

Buckingham, slightly wounded by the reprimand, rose to leave.

'Where are you going? Give me a hand to load these, would you?' Baron Black grimaced as he passed a pair of carbines to Buckingham which he reloaded dutifully along with his pistol.

By the time he had finished, everything was suspensefully quiet. The smoke from the guns hung low on the road, blocking any view beyond a few yards. Buckingham was about to return to the gate, when George shushed him and held a finger to his lips. Everything was silent except the continuing thunder of distant artillery. It was only a minute or so before Buckingham's patience wore thin.

'Perhaps you killed them all,' he whispered.

'Six by my count. I wouldn't mind betting there are another four out there somewhere,' George muttered back.

'Well, I killed one,' Buckingham replied.

The two men looked at him for a moment.

'I did! Over there, the one that was trying to circumvent you,' Buckingham pointed back to where the dead voltigeur lay.

'Baron, I think it may be time to get you back to the

courtyard,' George said. There was a wariness in his voice which spoke of his mistrust of the whole situation.

With the weapons in their free hands, George and Buckingham helped Baron Black to his feet. He was pale and grimaced as he moved, but the bleeding from earlier seemed to have stopped. Slowly, patiently, they placed one of the baron's arms over each of their shoulders so he could drag his feet one in front of the other. Several minutes later they placed him down in the courtyard against the side of the inn with a musket, just in case.

George put Buckingham on watch while he went to see how Rutherford was getting on. Waiting by the broken gate with a musket across his lap, Buckingham was the picture of misery.

'Chin up, Buckingham. We're still alive,' Baron Black smiled through a grimace of pain as he tried to adjust his position.

'All this. So many dead. And just for a book?' Buckingham held up a hand to study a painful hangnail on one of his muddied, smoke-smeared fingers. He noticed it had begun to shake again.

'The shaking is shock,' the baron said. 'It will go soon. Eating something often helps.'

'A stiff drink sounds more appetising at the moment,' Buckingham replied.

He looked over at the baron. The older man's skin was pale and waxen. Sweat beaded his face, but his eyes were clear blue, unclouded by the injury which could prove to be his undoing.

'How long have you been a member of Wellington's volunteers?' He asked, suddenly curious.

'A solider, not a member.'

The baron took out his snuff tin, picked out a generous

pinch and snorted it up his nostril. He offered the tin to Buckingham who declined with a shake of his head.

'Six years ago, during the Peninsular War. Back then we would terrorise the French with hit and run tactics. Ambush them, draw a few of them out if we could, then melt back into the mountains. That changed when Rutherford joined, just before the Battle of Salamanca in Portugal. Suddenly we were retrieving artefacts, holy relics stolen by the French to be taken back to France. To this day, I'm still unsure whether Wellington enlisted Rutherford for the task, or whether Rutherford convinced the duke. The marquess, as he was back then.'

For the last sentence, he looked at Buckingham with a wry smile, keen to make his point about the duke's rank.

'Why? What good did it do? Retrieving artefacts?'

'You've seen what religion can do to a man. Back then, when the French captured a piece of bone from Saint Sebastian, or the skull of some old pope, it gave them righteous belief in their cause. It offered them an invincibility that no commanding officer could match. But when they lost such an item? Well, then God had deserted them, and they became fearful enough that their morale deserted them with it. It was an extremely clever strategy, whichever one of them thought of it.'

Buckingham's forehead furrowed in confusion.

'But those were relics of holy people. This Sabbatum was described as a devilish thing, not to be tampered with.'

Baron Black smiled slyly as he took a second pinch of snuff before snapping the tin shut and tucking it back into his jacket.

'Religion is all about belief, my friend. Whichever one it is. Ten thousand men without belief will be defeated by an opponent half their number if they believe they are doing God's work. If they are safe in their conviction of an afterlife.

If they know their wife and children will cross over and come to find them one day. What has a man with such faith got to lose?'

'His life?'

'Replaced by the paradise of Heaven, my friend.'

The crack of a musket was quickly followed by a puff of shingle as a ball landed near Buckingham's feet before deflecting up into the courtyard gate, shuddering the wood.

Standing abruptly, Buckingham twisted round to see a voltigeur sitting atop the wall on the other side of the courtyard. Baron Black had already aimed and fired by the time Buckingham had even shouldered his weapon, though the shot scuffed the wall some way below the Frenchman's feet.

A second voltigeur climbed onto the wall as the first dropped into the courtyard, charging across the open area with bayonet lowered. Buckingham fumbled the musket with renewed urgency. He lifted the butt to his shoulder, pulled it to full cock and tried to aim but his nerves caused the muzzle to move wildly. A sudden flash of blue light from the opening of the cellar distracted the voltigeur just enough to give Buckingham time to drop to one knee and rest his elbow against his thigh. He tried to steady the sight, but the enemy was almost upon him, so he pulled the trigger, closing his eyes against the blast as he did so. As the powder ignited in the pan he felt the sudden burst of heat against his cheek, then the jarring recoil against his shoulder which pushed the muzzle upwards. A sudden force threw him backwards to the ground, jarring the air from his lungs. His ears rang. In a panic, he opened his eyes to see a swirl of smoke. Amidst the smoke was the French soldier, a hole in his stomach and impaled through chest on the end of his bayonet.

Buckingham dropped the musket and the voltigeur fell to the ground with it. He was briefly distracted by another flash of blue light flickering through the smoke when he noticed the second soldier had dropped into the courtyard. He could see Baron Black racing to reload his musket, while the Frenchman began to sprint towards him, yelling a ferocious battle cry as he lowered his bayonet towards the big man. The baron's gritted teeth told Buckingham that Black knew he wouldn't be able to reload in time. Without thinking, Buckingham rolled to his feet and charged towards the Frenchman, catching him in the side and throwing him to the ground just yards short of his target. A tussle erupted as both men grasped the voltigeur's shorter musket, grappling to push the point of the bayonet towards the other man. Buckingham was turned almost immediately so he lay on the floor with his aggressor above him. The soldier changed tactic and pressed the musket down towards his throat with the hope of cutting off the Englishman's air supply. Buckingham tried to push upwards, but the weight of the man was too heavy. Stars erupted into his vision and he tried to gasp for breath when a gunshot rang out and the Frenchman went limp.

Blood dribbled onto Buckingham. Gasping a great lungful of air, he pushed the man off and looked over to where Baron Black sat with a smoking musket. There was a third flash of crackling blue light before someone shouted something unintelligible.

Just before he passed out, Buckingham saw the stable roof go up in flames.

6 p.m. to 7 p.m.: Blücher's Prussians take the village of Plancenoit to the rear of the French right flank, forcing Napoleon to send more troops. Meanwhile Marshall Ney is on the verge of breaking Wellington's centre.

'Is he alive? I'd be dead if it weren't for him.'

The words were distant, hollow, as though listening through a long tunnel.

'He's alive.'

Something slapped his face and Buckingham lifted an arm to fend it off. When he opened his eyes, Rutherford was kneeling over him.

'Ah! There you are. Been killing Frenchmen, I hear. Up you get. It's time we got going unless you want to be killing more of them.'

Buckingham swallowed, coughed at the pain, then touched his throat tenderly.

'A bruise, nothing more. Come on, we have work to do.' Rutherford stood and stalked off towards the stables.

As Buckingham lifted himself onto his elbows, he could see the stable roof ablaze. The fire sent great plumes of grey-white smoke billowing into the sky, the flames hot enough that he could feel the heat from where he sat.

Despite the heat, he felt a cold sense of dread as he pulled himself to his feet. All that smoke would be seen for miles. An easy tip off to Napoleon that something was amiss with his book.

George the Third came trotting out of the stable door with four horses. He shouted something which Buckingham did not quite catch above the roar of the flames, but his gesticulations indicated something in the other side of the stable building.

Buckingham shuffled forward on shaky legs when Rutherford turned and beckoned him on. He raised an arm to protect his face from the heat as he caught up to Rutherford by the open entrance to the left of the stables.

'Help me get this cart out,' Rutherford yelled above the conflagration.

Buckingham paused only as long as it took Rutherford to dart inside. Following him in, he was surprised how much cooler it was inside, though the smoke was thickening by the moment.

Each man took hold of one side of the pulling bar, then leaned into it. Slowly, steadily, the cart's four wheels began to move. Pieces of burning straw began to fall from above, but Buckingham tried to pay it no mind as he strained aching muscle and sinew to force the cart from the building. Rutherford shouted something, but he was no longer listening. As the wheels began to turn, the momentum made it easier to push. Within moments they were at walking pace as part of the roof to their left collapsed into a bale of hay and roared to life. It served to spur the two men on to push harder still as they dragged their prize from the building and into the courtyard beyond.

'Stop! Stop!' Rutherford shouted.

Buckingham leaned backwards as he gripped the pulling bar, fighting against the weight behind him until they finally managed to bring it to a halt.

'George, harness two of the horses to the cart, I'll get the book,' Rutherford ordered, then was off into the cellar again.

When Buckingham noticed Baron Black trying to get to his feet, he hurried over to lend a hand. Removing the bayonet from his musket, Black leaned on it heavily on one side while Buckingham supported him on the other. They headed for the back of the cart where the baron sat on the edge before Buckingham helped swing his feet up and shuffle safely inside.

Moments later, Rutherford was back holding something large wrapped in a piece of greying cheese cloth. He passed it to Baron Black before placing a carbine beside him. With a haste that was infectious, he snatched up a couple of muskets then turned to Buckingham as George finished with the horses.

'Can you drive this thing?'

Buckingham nodded.

'Good. George, you're with me on horseback.'

George finished his work then mounted one of the two remaining horses as Buckingham climbed up to the driver's seat. He pulled a carbine from the saddle holster, checked it was loaded, then replaced it before trotting to the courtyard gates.

'Clear!' he shouted as Rutherford mounted his own horse equipped with Drummington's sabre.

Buckingham flicked the reins to guide the horses through the gates, turning left where the road was still clear. When he passed the stables, he flinched as the roof collapsed, then pushed the horses into a trot to put as much distance between the inn and the cart as possible.

It was not long before they turned off the road northward, past the little shepherd's hut they had waited in at the beginning of the day. The going was slow. The ground was still wet and despite Buckingham wanting to get back to safety as quickly as possible, he was acutely conscious of the injured Baron Black being jostled around in the back of the cart. Rutherford and George the Third took turns to scout ahead or occasionally to the left or right of the cart. As they reached the crest of a hill, they all paused briefly to look out to the east where plumes of smoke rose intermittently from the countryside and the sounds of war drifted towards them on the light summer's breeze.

'Is that what I think it is down at the inn?' It was Baron Black's baritone.

They all turned to look at the plume of smoke, seemingly small now about a mile away below their position.

George's eyepiece whirred and clicked as it elongated.

'Lancers!' There was a hint of despair in his voice as he tried to keep his mount still to be able to see better.

'How many?' Rutherford sounded no less concerned.

'Six. But fanning out in different directions. They're hunting us.'

'How many this way?'

'One, two at worst.'

Buckingham had heard several tales on his travels lauding the of bravery of Napoleon's Polish Lancers. They were elite light cavalry attached to the veteran Imperial Guard and were believed to have saved the emperor's life on more than one occasion.

'Stay together. Make sure all your weapons are loaded. And let's get off this damned hill.' For the first time since he had met the man, Buckingham heard fear in Rutherford's voice.

7 p.m. to 8.30 p.m.: Running out of time, Napoleon commits his last reserves to the attack. The previously undefeated Imperial Guard advance in three columns to break Wellington's line, but they are themselves broken by Wellington's gun line and artillery. At the sight of the Imperial Guard in retreat, Napoleon's army collapses. Wellington signals the advance.

The cart was frustratingly slow, but Baron Black was in no fit state to ride a horse. He offered to be left behind, but the others, to a man, would hear no more of it.

'Then at least one of you take the damned book and race it back to Waterloo!' He had pleaded.

Rutherford had wavered for a moment before Buckingham told the big man in no uncertain terms to save his breath.

They were another half mile further on when the lancer caught up with them. They had been forced onto a road to avoid boggy ground and a line of sycamore trees now made it impossible to manoeuvre the cart into a more defensive position.

'George, you go right. I'll go left. See if we can catch him in a pincer,' Rutherford shouted as he pulled Drummington's sabre free.

George the Third spurred his horse off the road and through the line of trees, carbine in hand.

The lancer came on, hooves thundering on the road as he closed the gap with alarming speed. The sight of Baron Black levelling a musket from the back of the cart caused him to swerve right through the trees towards where George had gone. Buckingham, still driving the horses as fast as the cart would allow, kept turning his head, listening intently. The deep boom of a carbine was followed by the whinny of a horse. Rutherford suddenly dashed onto the road behind the cart, and then he was off, cantering back up the road from where they had come.

'Rutherford!' Buckingham yelled after him, 'Where's he going?'

'Don't worry about him, worry about us,' Baron Black replied. The baron was propped up in the back of the cart using the wooden side as a support for his musket.

'Stop the cart,' The baron said.

'What? We need to keep going!'

'Pull up the horses, damn you! We need to try and hear where he is.'

Understanding the reasoning, Buckingham brought the horses to a standstill and pulled one of the pistols from his belt. Over the ever-present rumble of distant gunfire, he could hear birds nearby. One of the horses snuffled. Then, from their right, the plod of hooves. Buckingham held his breath, hoping to see George the Third emerge from the treeline, but his disappointment embodied itself in a whimper as the lancer took to the road and faced them. The man was close enough that they could see the weatherworn skin of his face beneath thick, greying moustaches, but not so close that Black had an easy shot. The cavalryman's horse, a grey, sweated and stamped its feet, eager to finish the job of killing.

The rumble of hooves from somewhere further up the road made Buckingham's stomach lurch. Had they been found by a second lancer? The first lancer turned his horse just enough that Buckingham could see past him, and the sight brought a quivering breath.

Charging along the road towards the lancer, sabre held aloft, was Rutherford.

'He'll be killed! Shoot him!' Buckingham shouted.

The lancer's horse reared up. The baron pulled the trigger and both men held their breath, peering through the smoke to see if the bullet had hit its target. It had missed! The Frenchman lowered his lance and kicked his horse into a charge at Rutherford. Buckingham and Baron Black held their breaths as the two men raced at each other like knights of old until everything happened in the blink of an eye.

As the lancer braced for the killing blow, Rutherford dropped to the side of the saddle and swept his sabre through the horse's legs. The grey screamed and went down, taking the lancer with it. Rutherford pulled up and swung his horse around, swinging the sabre down once, twice at something behind the fallen grey. The second blow produced a spray of blood that spattered his trousers. Looking off through the trees to their right, Rutherford rode past the sycamores and out of sight.

'George!' Buckingham yelled, moving to the edge of the seat and climbing down from the cart as quickly as he could manage.

Jogging over to where Rutherford was dismounting, he could see George's horse standing nearby. As he approached them, already out of breath, he saw Rutherford kneeling over his comrade.

George's shirt and tunic had torn outwards. A dark red stain had spread across his chest, and he was quite dead.

'I'm sorry,' Buckingham whispered, not knowing what else to say or do.

Rutherford lifted his head, then took the eyepiece from George's head and placed it in his knapsack.

'Help me get him to the cart,' he said.

The look on Baron Black's face as they approached said what they all felt when they returned to the road. Placing the body carefully on the back of the cart, Buckingham wordlessly took up his driving position again while Rutherford stayed close on his own horse. The three men were quiet for the remainder of the journey back to Waterloo.

8.30 p.m. to 10.30 p.m.: Wellington advances and meets Blücher at La Belle Alliance. Blücher's fresher troops pursue the remains of Napoleon's army.

Once they had made certain that they could be identified as allies by waving a white flag, entry into Waterloo was simple. The town was awash with news that Napoleon's army had been defeated and all were eagerly awaiting the triumphant return of the Duke of Wellington.

Rutherford sent runners to find the surgeon who had Baron Black helped from the cart and taken inside the inn for treatment. George the Third was taken to a field mortuary. Both Buckingham and Rutherford stood to attention as he was carried away on a stretcher. Finally, Buckingham left the cart and horses with a stable boy before entering the inn to find Rutherford in the same room where the baron was being stitched up.

'Will he live?'

'Apparently so,' Rutherford replied. 'It appears he has a sixth life to live.'

Buckingham noticed the book laying on a nearby table still covered in the cheesecloth. He stood beside it, eyeing it with mistrust and intrigue in equal measure.

'Fascinating, isn't it?' Rutherford was suddenly beside him.

Buckingham needed to see it, to see what all his dead comrades had sacrificed their lives for. He watched as Rutherford carefully unfolded the cloth to reveal the book within, running his fingers lightly over the surface of its cover. There was a sense of wonder about the older man, like a child with a new toy.

'Didn't you say that was human skin?' Buckingham whispered.

Rutherford, his thoughts broken, flicked his head up.

'It is. Though it feels like the softest leather. The workmanship is exemplary.'

Buckingham frowned at the admiration in the other man's tone.

'You seem to be appreciating the horrible thing just a little too much,' Buckingham scolded as he approached.

The book was a little over twelve inches long. It was thick, but he could see that the pages themselves were thick. Vellum perhaps? The cover was creamy pale in colour. Buckingham was horrified to see what looked like a raised brown mole near the spine. The title was scorched into the cover, bumpy and taut in contrast to the smoothness of the rest of the binding, like a reddened burn scar.

'Sabbatum: Foedus per Rituale, Rituale per Dominium, Dominium per Foedus,' Buckingham murmured.

'Covenant Through Ritual, Ritual Through Dominion, Dominion Through Covenant.' Rutherford translated.

He gently opened the book to pages somewhere near the middle. The pages were stiff and heavy, crackling in protest as they were turned. The left page showed a beautifully illuminated picture of a ghastly scene. A man clutched a book to himself with one hand while he thrust his other arm into a raging fire. The tongues of flame above the man's arm formed a face of sorts, with two diagonal yellow eyes, long jagged teeth and a crown of horns. The right-hand page showed the diagram of a circle with various lines and smaller circles within it. Strange glyphs decorated points within the circle and around its circumference, not unlike the barrel in the cellar, Buckingham recalled.

'What does it mean?' He asked, his brows knitted into a tight frown.

'Without research, I do not know. And I do not want to know,' Rutherford muttered.

He turned a few more pages to another illumination, this time of a young woman, standing in front of a pine forest with arms spread high and wide. She was naked but for a yellow ram's fleece which hung from her shoulders, the curled horns of its hood decorated in gold leaf. There was a small fire at her feet.

'The trees. . .' Buckingham whispered.

'I see it.' Rutherford's reply had an unsettling tone.

Within the drawing of the treeline there were three faces: a child, a woman and an old toothless crone.

'What does the writing say?' The characters were different from the other page, the ink darker and in a bolder hand.

'It's Enochian. A warning about someone it refers to as Satan.'

'The Devil?' Buckingham was quick to spit the word.

'No, more a reference to the name's true meaning. An accuser or adversary.'

'I don't understand,' Buckingham began, but Rutherford slammed the book shut.

'Good. We should never try to understand a book such as this. It will suck you into its depths like Charybdis herself. It will tempt you, taint you and corrupt your very soul!'

Buckingham was taken aback by the venom of Rutherford's outburst, though he thought he detected the slightest hint of disappointment in his tone.

'Then let's destroy it!'

'It cannot be done. It was enchanted during its creation.'

'We don't know that.'

'Then throw it on the fire. But when it turns up some-where else, you can be the one who explains himself to His Grace, the duke.'

Buckingham baulked at that idea. He stared at the other man warily, weighing up what had been said. He quickly decided that even if it was all just a fairytale, Rutherford firmly believed that the book would not be destroyed.

'You at least realise that winning the battle today was a happy coincidence, despite us retrieving this book, don't you?'

Rutherford looked at Buckingham, then removed his spectacles to clean them.

'At this stage, I am happy for you to believe whatever you wish,' Rutherford replied with a weary smile.

The surgeon had just about finished stitching the baron when there was a knock at the door. A woman entered carrying a tray of hot stew and a jug of ale which she set at the table once Rutherford had hastily wrapped and cleared away the Sabbatum.

Buckingham took a bowl over to Baron Black. The man was tired and weak, but in better shape than he had any right to be.

'It will take more than a few Frenchmen to kill me,' he said with a chuckle before wincing at the pain.

As soon as Buckingham took his first mouthful, he realised he was famished. He ate his share with gusto, then finished the remainder of the pot plus a spare dumpling. It was not long before the baron was fast asleep, and Rutherford was dozing with his head resting on his fingers. Buckingham thought he had managed to stay awake but jumped from his seat and wiped drool from the corner of his mouth when the door slowly creaked open.

It was dark outside and the only light in the room was a lamp beside the bed.

'There you are, Buckingham. I am delighted to see you made it back in one piece. Who else have we got here?'

The Duke of Wellington entered the room with a candelabra, which he placed on the table. Rutherford stirred, straightened his spectacles and rose slowly from his seat.

'Are you alright, Rutherford?' Wellington enquired.

'Too much horse riding for my liking, Your Grace,' he grimaced, rubbing at his lower back.

'I see Black made it again. The others?'

Rutherford shook his head almost imperceptibly.

'A damned shame,' Wellington stated matter-of-factly.

Buckingham was so tired that he struggled to keep up with the conversation. How on earth was Wellington still so full of vigour?

'The battle went well, Your Grace?' Rutherford asked as he lifted the Sabbatum onto the table.

'It was touch and go, Rutherford, touch and go. But that book there probably turned the tide.'

Wellington smiled with admiration as he watched his volunteer unwrap the ghastly binding of the Sabbatum. He stalked over to it, hovered a hand above its surface as though about to touch it, then balled his fingers into a fist and pulled away.

'So, this is what it has all been about,' he murmured before turning towards Buckingham.

'Now it's up to you Buckingham.'

'Hmm?'

'It's up to you to take that infernal thing and hide it somewhere where no-one can ever find it. You do that, you finish your part of our little deal, and I will keep my word. I will make certain you become a duke. There's only one stipulation.'

'Yes, Your Grace?'

'Make sure it is on English soil. These continental wars are tedious, draining and have become too much for me.'

'I will do that, Your Grace.'

Buckingham walked to the table and reverently picked up the Sabbatum. He felt a sudden weight of responsibility, of sadness for the gentleman volunteers he had known for less than a day, but who had spent their lives so that he could stand there holding the book now. He glanced at Rutherford who was looking back at him with a curious expression.

'You saw the horror of an akephaloi today. And you have touched the Sabbatum, one of the infernal tomes of the Septem Voluminibus Diabolica. Very often, when one is exposed to these mystical things, the soul becomes attached to that world.'

'What are you trying to tell me, Rutherford?'

There was a dread to Buckingham's tone which said he did not really want to know the answer. As Rutherford spoke, the candles flickered and the room seemed to darken and a red spot of light gleamed from behind Rutherford's spectacles.

'I suppose I'm telling you to be careful. Very often, once one encounters the esoteric world, one continues to see glimpses of it. More dangerous still, it sees you. Be careful, Buckingham. Do not tell the tale of what happened today to anyone. Lose that book and forget about it as best you can. If you're lucky, other worlds will forget you exist.'

A chill ran through Buckingham then as he watched the red lights in Rutherford's eyes fade as the shadows retreated.

'Of course, if you need anything, you can always contact me,' Rutherford finished with a smile.

Buckingham shook the man's hand and looked over at the sleeping figure of Baron Black.

'Say goodbye for me, would you?'

'I will, but aren't you going to find a bed for the night?'

'No. With His Grace's permission, if I travel through the night, I can be on a boat to England tomorrow. Like you, Your Grace, my time in Europe has become something of a chore.'

'I will have a troop of reserves accompany you and your belongings, Buckingham.'

'Thank you, Your Grace.'

The two men shook hands. With that, and shrouded in a solemn air of reflective sorrow, Buckingham clasped the book to him and walked out into the night.

Afterword

When I write Victorian Gothic, I try to pay tribute to the events of history. Each of these three novellas is set in a different historical period, but each setting has its roots in a truth of some kind.

A Spurned Woman

A Spurned Woman (originally entitled A Woman Scorned) could be set in almost any country in western medieval Europe. Witch trials, sporadic outbreaks of bubonic plague and the mention of potatoes (a vegetable brought to Europe from the Americas) date the story to the 100 years between the late 16th century and late 17th century.

In some parts of Europe the witch trials became a frenzy. Despite being condemned by the Inquisition, Heinrich Kramer's infamous witch hunting manual the Malleus Maleficarum, Hammer of Witches, was often used as a guide to find and condemn witches. Kramer's work recommended torture to obtain confessions. An accusation led to torture, then torture would result in more accusations as the poor victim named anyone they could think of in the hope that their suffering would end. It was the very definition of a vicious circle. Finally, after torture and trial, there came the bonfires. It is estimated that 40,000 to 60,000 men, women and children were executed throughout the course of the witch trials in Europe.

Medea is an important figure in Greek mythology. She was a sorceress and the princess of Colchis whose magic helped Jason steal the golden fleece. Knowing her father would execute her for her treachery, she fled Colchis with Jason on the Argo. Her father, King Aeëtes, pursued the lovers, so Medea dismembered her brother and threw the pieces into the sea. Aeëtes gave up his pursuit to retrieve the pieces of his dead son. 10 years later, Jason decided to abandon Medea and their two sons to wed the daughter of King Creon. In her revenge, Medea not only murdered the hero's bride to be, but also her own two sons by Jason before fleeing once again. Arriving in Athens, she married King Aegeus. When the king's long lost son Theseus returned to the city, Medea almost managed to poison him with a cup of wine, but Aegeus recognised his son and accidentally knocked the cup from Theseus's hand. Depending on the account, she either fled Athens or was driven from the city by Theseus. It is unknown what became of her.

The myth portrays a haunting story of sorcerous love and scheming vengeance. Medea is a woman who will do anything to help and protect the ones she loves but once scorned, offers up her own justice in the most shocking and devious of ways.

Bedlam

The story for Bedlam was a labour of love, the events of which happen between Victorian Gothic Volume 2: A Most Perilous Name and Volume 3: The Acceptable Face Of

Insanity. The story fills in several gaps and events which are alluded to in Volume 3.

Bethlem Royal Hospital was first founded in 1247. It is believed that it was first used to house the insane from around 1377 and began to be referred to as Bedlam around the same time. It was not until the early 17th century that the word bedlam became the everyday word for chaos and madness.

By the early 19th century, the old hospital at Moorfields fell into disrepair and was barely habitable. It was embroiled in controversy for the conditions the inmates had to live in. A competition was held to design a new hospital at St George's Fields. There were three different winners, and the final design was based on different elements from each of the winning entries. The building was built between 1812 and 1815 and was used until the hospital moved to Croydon in 1930.

The story mentions various crimes, misdemeanours and misunderstandings which resulted in imprisonment in the wing for the criminally insane. Sadly, these stories have all been based on real-life Victorian accounts.

The Gentleman Volunteers

The Gentleman Volunteers is unique in that it features none of the characters from any of the 3 volumes of Victorian gothic. Set decades in the past in 1815, it was originally going to be called Fall Of An Empire, but the title felt too grand. I wanted something more personal, and, to me, The Gentleman Volunteers was more intriguing. It was a completely different style of story to write and I describe it as Waterloo meets The Dirty Dozen.

The protagonist, Richard Temple-Nugent-Grenville, was born 20th March 1776. He became Earl Temple in 1784 and was elected as the member of parliament for Buckinghamshire in 1797, before being appointed to a host of roles due to his family connections. He left parliament in 1813 following the death of his father, when he became the 2nd Marquess of Buckingham.

In 1796 he married Lady Anne Brydges, the daughter of the 3rd Duke of Chandos. The family name became quintuple-barrelled: Temple-Nugent-Brydges-Chandos-Grenville. The match was a good one for Richard, because Lady Anne was the sole heir to her father's wealth, a much-needed resource in the upkeep of the lavish house and gardens at Stowe.

The marquess was given the title of 1st Duke of Buckingham and Chandos in 1822. He died 17 years later in 1839. The property at Stowe is now a private school and a National Trust property which is open to the public. I thoroughly recommend it.

If you have enjoyed this book,
you can follow the author at:

www.drmillerauthor.co.uk

with links to Facebook and Instagram

Also by the author:

Victorian Gothic Volume 1:
The Uncanny Death Of Katherine Kramer

Victorian Gothic Volume 2:
A Most Perilous Name

Victorian Gothic Volume 3:
The Acceptable Face of Insanity

Chilling Shorts

www.ingramcontent.com/pod-product-compliance
Lightning Source LLC
Chambersburg PA
CBHW060710190726
48289CB00002B/628